An EARTHLY KNIGHT

An EARTHLY KNIGHT

JANET McNAUGHTON

HarperCollins*Publishers*

Library of Congress Cataloging-in-Publication Data
McNaughton, Janet Elizabeth, 1953–
An earthly knight / Janet McNaughton.—1st U.S. ed.
    p. cm.
Summary: In medieval Scotland, sixteen-year-old Jenny Avenel is chosen as a
potential bride for the king's brother and must navigate the tides of tradition
and the power of ancient magic to define her own destiny.
    ISBN 0-06-008992-X—ISBN 0-06-008993-8 (lib.bdg.)
    [1. Fantasy.] I. Title.
PZ7.M23257Ear 2004
[Fic]—dc21

                                                              2003009561

Typography by Larissa Lawrynenko
1 2 3 4 5 6 7 8 9 10
❖
First U.S. edition, HarperCollins Publishers, Inc., 2004
Originally published in Canada by
HarperCollins Publishers Ltd., 2003

For Pam because she is my sister,
and for Barbara Rieti,
intrepid charter of the
fairy realms

O I forbid you, maidens a'
That wear gowd on your hair
To come or gae by Carterhaugh
For young Tam Lin is there.

—FROM THE BALLAD "TAM LIN"

There was an elf knight come from the north land,
And he came a-courting me;
He said he would take me unto the north land,
And there he would marry me.

—FROM THE BALLAD "LADY ISABEL
AND THE ELF KNIGHT"

An EARTHLY KNIGHT

Chapter One

"ISABEL, LOOK TO YOUR KING. You left him exposed to my bishop again." Jenny drew her sister's attention back to the chessboard, careful to keep any hint of frustration from her voice. She had spent most of the morning coaxing Isabel out here into the sunlight. The slightest misstep would send her sister back to her endless, useless prayers in the family chapel.

Isabel sighed. "My heart is not in this, Jenny. One of the stable lads would have given you a better game."

"I care nothing for the game, Isabel. Your company was all I wanted." But Jenny kept her eyes on the chessmen as she spoke. It was painful to look at Isabel now. Her long dark hair was uncombed. Purple smudges marred the skin under her gentle brown eyes. Her feet were dirty and bare. Worst of all, she wore the clothing of a penitent, a shapeless garment of coarse brown sackcloth, tied at the waist with a piece of rope. The sister who had delighted in beautiful clothes seemed gone forever. Again, Jenny silently cursed the man who had left Isabel in such a state. After two months, her store of curses was running dry.

Isabel finally made her move, blocking the white bishop. When Jenny looked up to praise her, she saw a stranger behind Isabel, coming toward them. That he was a stranger was no surprise. Certain types of men were freely admitted to her father's bailey. Young knights with no land of their own found a place in her father's great hall for as long as they chose to stay, bedding down on pallets on the floor each night among the servants. Every such knight added to the prestige of the household. Also welcome were peddlers and traveling entertainers of every kind—the acrobats, jugglers, and musicians who earned their keep by enlivening the dull days of noble families. Jenny guessed this man fell into the last group. His clothing marked him as someone without rank, but the linen-wrapped bundle on his back was too small for a peddler's poke.

He would have to be a stranger to approach Isabel now. Most men avoided her. Jenny knew they blamed her sister for everything that had happened, as men will blame women, always. The stranger looked more and more bewildered as he tried to make sense of what he saw. Everyone had their place on this earth: the lord of a bailey, the neyfs who belonged to the land, the brothers in their abbeys. It should be possible to tell who and what anyone was at a glance, to read them, as Jenny herself had just read this stranger. That was no longer true of Isabel. She had become something without a name.

Jenny could see the man struggling to understand what someone like Isabel might be doing at a chessboard with a lass of noble birth, as Jenny plainly was. She had worn one of her best robes today to cheer herself, made of fine red cloth from the Low Countries. This, the soft leather belt at her waist, even the yellow silk ribbon Galiene had braided into her fair hair that morning, all declared her rank.

From his gait and the dust on his clothes, Jenny could also tell that this man had traveled many days before reaching her father's bailey. His brown eyes betrayed a sharp wit, a desire to understand everything he saw, which Jenny and her sister had thwarted. The man responded, as most men did, by simply pretending Isabel was not there.

"Would you be a daughter of this house, my lady?" he asked Jenny. He spoke the Scots English of the common folk, but with a lilt. This was not the harsh, guttural accent of the Low Countries, or the round inflections of Norman French. Jenny guessed his native tongue was Gaelic, the language spoken in the lands to the north and west, a language she did not understand, for it was rarely heard in Teviotdale.

"Aye, I am the lord's daughter. My sister also," Jenny said, nodding toward Isabel. She had fallen into the habit of trying to make Isabel visible to those who pretended she did not exist.

The man looked shocked. "This is not the noble lass who—" He caught himself. "Forgive me. I spoke out of turn."

So news of Isabel's disgrace had spread far enough to reach this traveler's ears. The story must be told all over Teviotdale by now. Jenny made no reply.

"Can you tell me where your lord father would be?" the man said.

Jenny looked around. From the shade of the family bower, she had a good view of this side of the bailey, with its wooden palisade and buildings. Her father often spent time in the stables, kennels, and mews she could see from here, but she had not noticed him today. "He might be out hunting."

"No, my lady. The man at the gate said he is within."

"Seek him in the great hall, then, on the other side of the bailey. I have not seen him this afternoon. But first, please, tell us who you are. We have not had a visitor these many weeks."

"My name is Cospatric. I come from Girvan on the western sea."

Jenny drew back before she could stop herself. He was from Galloway. In all the stories she heard, Galwegians were murderous savages. But this man seemed peaceable enough. If he noticed her reaction, he only shifted the bundle on his shoulder gently. "I am a harper."

"Oh, Isabel, a harper! How delightful. My sister . . ." Jenny would have told the harper of her sister's beautiful voice, but Isabel would not raise her eyes from the chessboard. Jenny sighed. It would be best to let the man go now, but her curiosity got the better of her. "What news do you bring?"

"Very little. I spent the last five days walking through that endless forest across the glen." He gestured past the wooden palisade that enclosed the bailey toward the land beyond the small village of Langknowes that lay in the valley beneath them.

Jenny stared at the man. "You came through that forest

alone? And you still have your wits?"

He laughed. "I hope so, my lady. Why do you ask?"

"Those woods belong to the fairies. Folk say—" Jenny stopped herself. Her father's men always laughed at her for speaking of the fairies. She waited for this man to mock her now, but he did not.

Instead, he let out his breath slowly, as if he had just discovered he had escaped great harm. "I could believe that place to be haunted by the wee folk, or any unearthly spirit," he said. "At first, I feared wolves or robbers, but the forest was as empty as a tomb, and as quiet, too. By this morning, I thought myself lost. I was fair glad to be out of there."

"Most travelers follow the river path. It adds a few days to the journey, but there are fermtouns all along the way. The folk in those towns would gladly have fed and sheltered you for your music." Jenny knew her father's farmers in those small settlements would have welcomed him like royalty. Their lives were filled with hard labor, and they could not travel without their lord's permission.

"I wished to come here directly. When I asked the townsfolk on the other side for the quickest route, they sent me through the forest. No one warned me of the wee folk. It must have seemed a fine joke to them." He shook his head and gave her a rueful smile.

"You do not disbelieve me? My father's people, the Normans, laugh, and our priest, Brother Turgis, scolds me for speaking of the fairies. They say it is wrong for me to hold such un-Christian beliefs. But the folk about here have always believed."

5

"I disbelieve nothing, my lady. Galloway was one of the first lands in Scotland to embrace the Christian faith, but my people have always told stories of the wee folk, too." He looked puzzled. "But you are not Norman?" This was, after all, the household of a Norman lord.

"My father is as Norman as any of the Conqueror's men were. Our brother, Eudo, is a knight in the household of Comte Robert de Burneville at Lilliesleaf. My sister, also, is a true Norman lady." Jenny knew it might seem strange to call someone dressed in sackcloth a lady, but she hurried on without pausing to consider. "Eudo and Isabel lost their mother when they were but small, and my father took a wife, my mother, from a highborn family near here. But she also died. I am half Norman, but it is said that I am the child of my mother's folk. I can speak the Norman French, but I have not been raised to make a fine marriage with some Norman lord, as Isabel—" Jenny stopped in confusion. The pleasure of speaking with someone who did not scorn her beliefs had caused her to forget the sadness of the past few weeks. Her face burned with shame, for Isabel more than herself. She lowered her head. "My tongue, I am told, is always two steps ahead of my brain. Forgive me."

The harper gave her a look of sympathy that was not marred by pity. "You need never ask forgiveness of me, my lady," he said. "Now, I will find your lord father." And he was gone.

Jenny was profoundly grateful for the man's tact. It was true that she need not excuse herself to someone of his rank, but, in fact, few freemen could bear to admit that any woman might be above them. Most swaggered to show they were better than Jenny, regardless of her rank. A few fawned over her until she felt sick. The man who could give proper respect without seeming to lower himself was rare. She felt herself warm to Cospatric. Perhaps he had also meant to say he did not dislike her for her clumsy tongue. That eased Jenny's feeling of shame.

Until she looked at Isabel. To hide her discomfort, Jenny began to babble, saying whatever entered her head. "I do hope that man is clever with his harp. Isabel, do you not think you would sing with him? Your voice is a gift from the angels."

Isabel said nothing. Jenny saw that the harper's arrival had driven her sister back into complete silence. Or rather, the thoughtless words from her own mouth had. The little ground she had gained with Isabel this day was lost. Tears stung Jenny's eyes.

"My move," Jenny said. She picked up a rook without thinking and set it down again.

Jenny knew she spoke too often and too soon. In happier times, her father often joked that she could do more damage with her tongue than a man could do with a broadsword. She knew this made her seem clumsy, even stupid. But she was not stupid. She could look at anyone and see past the rank, into the heart, and know its worth. Her one skill, Galiene called it. And Jenny felt sure that this man, Cospatric, was more worthy than most. In spite of everything, his arrival had lifted a little of the weight from her heart. Isabel loved music. If Jenny could somehow find a way to persuade her father to let the harper join their household, it might be possible to coax Isabel out of the shadows of the chapel, back into the land of the living.

Jenny sighed. Her skill had failed her only once, with Bleddri, the knight who had brought Isabel to disgrace. For he had kept his heart hidden while he won Isabel's trust and then her love. Jenny's misgivings had come far too late.

Jenny looked up to see her father coming from the stables. So she had misguided the harper. Her father must have passed earlier, without notice. He looked angry, but that was no surprise. Isabel raised a pawn to make her move, unaware that he was bearing down on them like a warship. Jenny saw him take a deep breath to launch into a rant, but it was too late to whisper a warning.

"I forbid you both to come or go by Carter Hall!" he said, his voice a roar. Jenny ducked her head. Isabel's graceful white hand hovered over the chessboard for an instant, then plummeted like a dove caught in midflight by a falcon, knocking half the chessmen onto the grass. The game was ruined.

Before, Isabel had always been the one to calm their father. Now, she sat unmoving, and the job fell to Jenny. She took a deep breath to calm herself and decided to speak French. She preferred English, but knew it would please her father to hear her speak the language of his people.

"Why, Papa, what do you mean? Carter Hall is promised to me as my—my—*tocher*." Her French failed, forcing her to use the Scots word, but Jenny met her father's eyes steadily. She knew he valued her boldness, her ability to challenge him.

He almost smiled and answered in her own language. Although born in Britain, French was his first language—as it was for all Normans—and it flavored his English heavily. "Jeanette, the word is *dowry*. I ask you not to cross me, little one. This is no small matter, since I value your virtue . . . and what might remain of your sister's."

Isabel flinched as if struck in the face. Their father had not spoken directly to her since her disgrace.

"But please, Papa, tell us why," Jenny said. She was more upset than she liked to show. Carter Hall was a ruin, but the old house was the only thing of value she had to take into a marriage. She stole away to visit it whenever she could.

Their father sighed heavily. The strain of the past few weeks showed in his face. His eyes were red-rimmed and bleary from sitting too close to the fire and drinking too much ale. "They say young Tam Lin is back from Roxburg. He has been seen at Carter Hall," he said.

Jenny's chin went up. "No one can live there. The roof is fallen in." Ruin or not, the place was hers.

"This land was his father's once. But that was twenty years ago. The king himself granted me this fief. No one can challenge that." His voice rose in outrage. "If he be fool enough to lay claim to my land, my men will hunt him down like a beast of prey." He paused to let the anger drain from his voice. "So be good, little one, and keep clear of that place until this is settled. And your sister, too." He began to walk away, then turned. "Jeanette, you know Brother Bertrand, the almoner from Rowanwald Abbey, is bringing that cripple today. I expect you at my table tonight, dressed to suit your rank. No brooding about with your sister."

As soon as he was gone, Isabel rose. "Isabel," Jenny cried, but her sister's eyes never left the ground as she walked away. Jenny did not follow. She had been no help to her sister at all today. It would be best to let Isabel shed her tears alone.

Chapter Two

A S SOON AS ISABEL WAS GONE, Galiene came bustling through the door of the family bower. Jenny knew there was no need to tell the old nurse anything. Eavesdropping was one of the chief joys of Galiene's life.

"Your lord father still has no good word for your sister, my honey," Galiene said, gathering the fallen chessmen. "Once, he thought the moon and stars shone in her eyes."

"Not so long ago, either," Jenny said, "though it seems like years. Every day of my life, I curse Bleddri's grave."

Galiene crossed herself. "That one has no grave," she said with satisfaction, and Jenny noticed her making another sign that had no place in a Christian church, the sign to ward off evil.

Jenny sighed. "Isabel's marriage was always meant to bring my father power. I was never raised to have her graces. My father cannot overcome his disappointment."

Galiene straightened her stiff back with difficulty and slammed a handful of recovered chessmen down on the board. "Your father should be pleased to find a Scottish husband for either of his daughters. The Normans may be conquerors, but we are not the folk they conquered, hen. Old King David only invited them here out of fondness for the English court where he spent his childhood."

Jenny sighed. "I fear no man will marry Isabel now, Norman or Scot."

A gleam came into the old nurse's eyes. "Will her tocher not come to you then, my honey?"

"Of course not! Isabel's tocher will go to the Church when she takes the veil. My sister's money is not for me."

"Well, no harm in hoping, is there, hen? You could catch a fine husband with the rich tocher set aside for your sister."

Jenny knew there was no point in scolding Galiene. She had come into the household with Jenny's mother when Isabel was a small child. Galiene was fond of Isabel, but the old woman's loyalty was to Jenny alone, and she made no effort to hide this.

"Isabel's tocher is bound for the Church," Jenny repeated firmly. "Brother Turgis says the sisters at Coldstream are waiting to receive her." Jenny tried to ignore the pain she felt in her heart when she said this. She could not imagine her sister spending the rest of her life in an austere priory as a Cistercian nun.

Galiene scowled. "Brother Turgis! It may be a sin, but I cannot like that priest. These new clerics come here from across the sea, and suddenly everyone is supposed to abide by their rules. I liked the old ways better. When I was a girl, the priests and brothers took wives if it suited them. It goes against nature for a man to live without the warmth of a woman and children."

"Well, that is the way of the world now, Galiene. King David invited the new orders here to make Scotland more like other Christian countries. They will not be leaving," Jenny said, but secretly she agreed. Brother Turgis seemed to have no love for any earthly thing. Surely a man who could love a woman would have a kinder heart.

"Leave?" Galiene cried. "No, and why should they? The old king gave them so much, you can hardly find a scrap of land that pays no tribute to them now. That fine forest across the glen, haunted by the wee folk it may be, but it now belongs to Broomfield Abbey." Galiene never used the word *fairies* if she could help it. She told Jenny it might make them angry.

"Well, none of our folk will set foot in that wood, so what should it matter to us?"

Galiene snorted but fell silent. It was true. The forest just across the glen stood unused while everyone went to more distant woodlands on this side of the river for firewood and timber.

"Come into the bower now, honey," Galiene said after a moment. "We have work to do."

Jenny followed Galiene into the family's private quarters. Even in a noble household, every woman with time to spare helped make cloth. As Jenny's eyes adjusted to the dim light, the loom came into focus. Taller than Jenny herself, it was braced against a stout roof beam near a window to catch the daylight. She sighed as she took up the shuttle. Jenny's cloth was never as even as Isabel's, but Isabel had not touched the loom for weeks.

Galiene's eyes were no longer fit for weaving, but she

was so skilled at spinning that she could work with scarcely a glance. She picked up her spindle and a tuft of clean, carded wool. Jenny paused to watch the spindle twirl as the wool spun into a long, even thread of yarn in Galiene's capable hands. The old nurse walked back and forth, plucking new wool from the basket without pause, without looking, while the spindle twirled. This was one of Jenny's earliest memories: watching Galiene expertly tease raw wool into yarn. Jenny's own yarn was full of lumps when it didn't break. She turned to the loom and shot the shuttle between the warp threads, then lifted the heddle bar to change the warp. As she did, the round, gray river stones that weighted the warp threads clacked softly together near her feet, a comforting sound.

"When can we expect Isabel to go to the sisters, then?" Galiene asked after they had worked some time in silence. Jenny had expected this question for weeks. Although the knights who wintered with them had spread Isabel's story everywhere, it was seldom talked about within the household. It was not like Galiene to curb her curiosity for so long. This showed, as much as anything, how very serious Isabel's troubles were.

"Brother Turgis says she must first confess her sins."

Galiene was so shocked she sputtered. "What would she have to confess? Poor lamb. What she did to Bleddri was surely no sin."

"It was not. But she left my father's hall, taking all her tocher they could carry and two of his best horses. That was theft of my father's property. Even Isabel was his to give. She must confess to taking what was not her own."

"That seems a small enough thing for her to do."

"Aye, Galiene. But she will not confess. I think there must be more."

The old nurse clucked. "At least enough time has passed now that we know she does not carry that monster's child."

Jenny winced but said nothing. The same thought had troubled her for weeks. Even now that it was no longer a worry, it was too painful to consider. She quickly changed the subject.

"Galiene, what do you know of the Lin family?"

Galiene sounded happy to be asked. "All this land belonged to Lins since the beginning of time." Jenny smiled into the loom. Galiene could leave no truth unadorned. "I first saw Andrew Lin when your mother was a wee lass. A group of young, highborn lads chased a stag over your grandsire's land. The hounds lost the scent, so they stopped for a few days to pass the time. As fine a lad as ever carried a falcon on his wrist was Andrew Lin. He married the earl of Roxburg's only daughter. They had just one son, and they died not a year later."

"How did they die?" Jenny asked. She was not surprised. More died young than lived to see old age.

"Bad beef," Galiene said. "Or bad ale. Whatever it was, it killed everyone at Carter Hall, excepting the bairn in his cradle and one stable lad who was being punished for stealing food and had only bread and water for his supper. He rode for help, but by the time help came, death had taken everyone. Only Tam Lin was alive. His grandsire, the earl of Roxburg, took him soon after."

Jenny pictured an entire household lying dead around one screaming baby. She shuddered. "What became of the stable lad?"

"Oh, he is still about somewhere," Galiene said in a tone of voice that Jenny knew well. It meant she should ask no further questions.

But Jenny could not let the story go. "Galiene, why did you never tell me this before?"

"Carter Hall will be yours one day, and what a picture is that for a bride to carry into her home? I never would have told you, but now Tam Lin is here. If he thinks of the place as his, you should know why."

"But it is my father's to give me, is it not?"

Galiene nodded. "The land is certainly your father's, Jenny. But in Tam Lin's eyes? That would be another matter." She paused. "Strange stories are told about the lad by travelers who have passed through Roxburg."

Jenny stopped working and turned to Galiene. "How do you mean?"

"Something happened when he was a boy. Tam Lin went out hunting alone. His horse came back with no rider. They found his hawk, but not the lad. Not for days."

"What happened to him?"

"Well, the folk in Roxburg tell one tale, his household quite another," Galiene said, and she fell into a satisfied silence.

Jenny almost stamped her foot with impatience. "Then tell me both stories, for you know you have me hanging on your words now, Galiene."

Galiene chuckled. She loved to play out a story, like a

cat with a mouse. "At Marchmont, the earl of Roxburg's hall, they say Tam Lin fell from his horse and had the sense knocked out of him. He wandered the woods for days. When he was found, he knew no one, not even his own kin."

"How horrible." Jenny felt an unexpected stab of sympathy for this young man who had somehow lost his entire family twice, forgetting for a moment that he might want Carter Hall.

"Oh, the other story is worse," Galiene said, her voice full of cheer. Jenny knew the old nurse was waiting to be begged. Instead, she gave Galiene a dark look that brought the story forward quickly. "Folk say the lad was taken. By them, you know."

"The wee folk?"

"Aye, the very same. They say he stayed with them years, for time passes differently in their world. The folk say Tam Lin has never been the same, that he is with the wee folk still, even when he walks the world of men. They say other things too, things not fit for a maiden's ears." Galiene plucked another tuft of wool from the basket and clamped her mouth shut.

Jenny turned back to her work. If she could feign complete lack of interest, Galiene might tell her more than she ought to hear. But Galiene's silence held until Jenny knew the ploy would not work this time. The rumors about Tam Lin must be dark indeed. She made one last attempt to draw Galiene out.

"How is it that you know so much about Tam Lin?"

"I asked anyone who came from Roxburg way, my

honey, ever since Carter Hall became your tocher. I always hoped to hear the lad was betrothed to someone far from here, to a lass with land. But then the strange stories started. Somehow I feared he might come this way."

Jenny shivered in spite of herself. Galiene's unexplained "somehow"s were not to be ignored. "But how could he even feed himself here? Do you think he might fall in with the freebooters?" Jenny had only heard stories of the men who refused to accept the Normans as their lords and lived in the woods as outlaws.

Galiene lowered her voice. "The freebooters would take him, if need be. Everyone remembers the Lin family. But you must say nothing of that to the others within this household, Jenny. Not even your sister."

Jenny nodded. She knew folk helped the freebooters when they could, even though they pretended to be outraged by the young bandits. The men of Langknowes would come to her father begging recompense for the loss of a sheep—which Jenny suspected had been freely given. Some of the freebooters were, after all, their own sons.

Jenny was a good weaver only when she kept her mind to the task. Galiene's stories had distracted her, and now she realized she had shot the weft too tightly, pulling the cloth in on either side. "Oh, look, Galiene, the selvages are spoiled. Should I undo it?"

Galiene came over to examine her work. "What are you making?"

"A blanket for the new bondsman, the cripple from Rowanwald Abbey."

Galiene peered at the imperfect cloth on the loom.

"Why are you wasting your time? There are plenty old blankets about, mended and clean, that will do for a beggar."

Jenny took up her shuttle again and sighed. "My father says, if the queen of England could wash and kiss the feet of lepers, I can weave a blanket for a cripple."

"Eleanor of Aquitaine wash and kiss the feet of lepers!"

Jenny laughed. "Of course not. He was speaking of good Queen Maud, sister to our old King David, who was queen of England when my father was a boy. He told me she would care for lepers with her own hands as an act of charity. But he forgets that I know the end to the story, which he sometimes tells when he is in his cups." She turned and gave Galiene a mischievous grin. "Queen Maud summoned her younger brother, David, so that he might learn by her example how to treat the poor, but he said, 'Be careful, sister, where you put your lips, or the king may hesitate to kiss them.'"

Both women laughed.

"Weaving a blanket is certainly nicer than kissing the feet of lepers." Jenny dropped her voice in case anyone was passing outside. "But the almoner is too important a man to be bringing us a beggar. Brother Bertrand may hold Isabel's fate in his hands, so we must be sure to please him. Did you not notice how much fuss went into the food for tonight's meal?"

Galiene nodded. "Aye, but I thought you were having trouble filling your sister's shoes. You never had to act the lady of the house before."

"I do find it hard to take Isabel's place, but I fear for her fate as well." After a pause, Jenny smiled. "Besides, if

19

the almoner is pleased, perhaps he will take pity on us and say the daily mass tomorrow morning. Brother Turgis puts me to sleep."

Galiene shared her smile, then asked, "Has this lad always been a cripple?"

"No. He was a stonemason's apprentice. He worked at the abbey until a stone block crushed his foot last winter. The canons nursed him, but the foot did not heal."

"And he has no family?"

Jenny shook her head. "They say he came from Tewkesbury with the master mason's men when work on the chapter house began. He would not be able to travel so far now, crippled. I hear he has no family, in any case."

"Well, he could do worse than to find himself here. Your father's table is generous and his hand is light. I heard a stranger earlier. Have they already arrived from the abbey?" Galiene asked.

Jenny smiled. She had almost forgotten this one bit of good fortune. "No, that was a harper. From Galloway."

"Galloway? One of those baby-eating savages?"

Jenny made a pass with her shuttle and tamped the cloth firmly with the wooden weaving sword. She smiled at the selvage ends, which now looked even. The blanket would be flawed, but only a little.

"Galiene, that man had better manners than most of my father's men. Have you never noticed how folk always say the same bad things about anyone they fear?" Jenny burst out laughing as Galiene frowned.

"How you will ever find a husband with that sharp tongue is beyond my ken," the old nurse grumbled.

Chapter Three

W HILE SHE FINISHED THE blanket and took it from the loom, Carter Hall stayed in the back of Jenny's mind. Falling asleep at night, Jenny often thought about restoring the old stone ruin. She saw the men so vividly she could hear them grunt as they pulled the massive oak roof trusses into place. She could even smell the fresh heather thatch that would be tied over wattle frames to make her roof snug against the weather. Sometimes, she decorated the walls with hangings and joined her unknown husband by the fire.

Did she want the place now, knowing what tragedy had befallen the Lin family there? Jenny asked herself as she supervised the setting up of the trestle tables in the great hall. She did. Plenty of halls had seen bloodshed. Enemies invited to a banquet in the name of peace might suddenly prove murderous. Brothers had been known to turn against one another. What had happened to the Lins was different. Many had died, but no one had raised a hand against them. Now that she feared Tam Lin might lay claim to Carter Hall, Jenny wanted it more than ever.

It was almost dark, late for the evening meal, when the party from Rowanwald finally arrived. Unlike the harper, they did not slip into the bailey unnoticed. The commotion they caused was enough to alert Jenny in the great hall even though it was far from the bailey gate. She slipped from the hall and followed the crowd, curious to see the important visitor.

Jenny approached just in time to see Brother Bertrand dismount from a magnificent black stallion. Even those in holy orders could not resist the Norman passion for horses. The priest was a tall, strongly built man with graying hair, who looked as if he might have been a warrior as easily as a priest. He went directly to Brother Turgis, embracing his fellow canon in greeting. Although he tried to hide it, Brother Turgis shrank from this display of affection. Jenny smiled in spite of herself. Galiene was right. Brother Turgis had no love for anyone.

Brother Bertrand had never been to Langknowes before. As almoner, he supervised all the charity dispensed to the poor within the abbey and in the town of Rowanwald as well, a huge responsibility. He looked around with undisguised curiosity and an open, generous smile. He stepped past Brother Turgis to greet Jenny's father, clasping his arm with both hands.

"Vicomte Avenel, you will be blessed for your charity."

Jenny could not hear her father's reply—his back was to her—but Brother Bertrand said, "Thanks be to heaven, the trip was without event. We did have to stop a few times. Brother Jean kindly gave us one of the abbey's ponies for the boy, but the journey was painful for him nevertheless. Armand, help the boy down." Brother Bertrand issued commands with the air of someone who had been giving them all his life. Jenny guessed that he was, like her father, a younger son of an aristocratic household. Such men brought money and ambition to their offices, and the Church welcomed them.

Jenny slipped quietly back into the hall just as the steward at the door sounded the *assemblée* on a hunting horn: three short blasts, one long, that echoed wildly over the glen. From their kennel on the other side of the bailey, the hounds responded with excited baying, for the same call was used to assemble hunters and their hounds before a hunt. Now, even those in the most remote buildings of the bailey would know the meal was ready, and Jenny's father would bring the important guests to the great hall.

Jenny was pleased to see the harper seated near the high table and ready to play. Her father must have arranged this. The timing of Cospatric's arrival was excellent. The music would make her household seem elegant and well prepared. She smiled but only nodded as she passed him. For the next few hours, she must play the lady of the house, speaking to those of lower rank only to give commands.

As her father brought Brother Bertrand into the hall, servants arrived with ewers of warm water, basins, and towels. Since much of the food would be eaten with the fingers, washing was no small detail.

Jenny sat at the high table with her father and Brother Bertrand. Brother Turgis took his place awkwardly beside the almoner. As the first dishes were brought into the hall,

Jenny felt a flutter of anxiety. She was responsible for the quality of everything on the table, and feeding Brother Bertrand was a delicate business. Someone of his rank would normally be served the best meats: venison, a pie filled with songbirds, at the very least some roasted chicken if the hunt had failed. These Augustinian canons were ordained priests, but like monks, they did not eat meat unless they were ill. Instead, they ate grains, pulses, and greens, food that was cooked every day without care. At least cheese and eggs were allowed, so there was hope for a few fine dishes. Jenny had saved eggs for a week and had agonized in the kitchen, trying to draw a suitable menu out of Hawise's limited repertoire.

She tried to calm herself by taking a quick sip from the horn cup at her place and had to suppress a grimace. The cup contained a sour red wine, heavy with sediment. Of course, it would. Wine was the drink of France, the only suitable drink for such an occasion. But wine did not keep. Both money and luck were needed to find good wine this far from France, and her father rarely had enough of either.

It was a joke among the Scots. Jenny had heard it all her life. The Normans favored bad wine over good ale. Luckily, the folk said, they kept it all for themselves. Jenny, true to her mother's people, favored the good barley ale made in her father's brew house for daily use. She silently wished for it now.

After Brother Bertrand blessed the food, he turned to Jenny's father. "Sir Philippe, I bring you greetings from your son. He sends his love and respect."

Both Jenny and her father leaned forward to hear the

news. "How is my lad? I have had no word of him for months."

"He came to Rowanwald some weeks ago with a party from Lilliesleaf. He seems a great favorite in Sir Robert's household."

The vicomte smiled. "Everyone is fond of Eudo. He was home last Christmastide. I hear he has earned his knight's spurs now." He sighed. "I wish we had news of him more often."

Jenny knew it pained her father to be separated from Eudo, but sons of nobility were always raised in the households of other noble families. Eudo had not lived at home since he was ten.

It might be easier on her father if another family would send them a son to raise, but Jenny knew no one would. A household headed by a widower was simply too odd to be entrusted with a son. Only the wandering knights who were free of family control stopped here.

When news of Eudo was exhausted, the vicomte said, "Tell us, Father, how does building proceed at the abbey?"

Abbey dwellers were always happy to talk about the endless construction that surrounded them. Brother Bertrand smiled. "Work on the new chapter house is progressing nicely. It should be finished in ten years, perhaps eight if God favors us. And that will be good, because the huts that have housed the brothers were not made to last as long as they have. One blew over in a storm last winter. You may have heard." Jenny's father nodded, and Brother Bertrand continued. "So this summer there must be new huts, which takes time away from the building of the chapter house. Of course the huts are quickly built, and our masons are not distracted by such insignificant work. They continue their carving all the same. But the hauling of stone from the quarry will suffer. We are delighted with the church, though. Earthly comforts pale in comparison. Twenty-two years it took to complete, but it has proven worth the wait."

"Twenty-two years, or a thousand, are but a day in the eyes of Our Lord." Brother Turgis spoke for the first time. "The abbey may take centuries to complete."

"Yes, certainly, Brother Turgis," Brother Bertrand said, but somewhat impatiently.

Jenny looked down quickly to hide a smile. Brother Turgis had a habit of saying things everyone already knew as if he were revealing profound truths. Jenny was pleased to see she was not the only one who found this annoying.

When the first course came, most were served from huge bowls of pease pottage with bacon, but the two canons were given a pottage of fresh spinach and almond milk. Jenny watched anxiously. Brother Turgis would likely eat hay without noticing, but Brother Bertrand would know good food. His bowl went untouched, though. Brother Bertrand had other matters on his mind.

"Sir Philippe," he said, "I also bring you greetings from the earl of Roxburg."

The vicomte's spoon paused midway to his mouth. The earl of Roxburg was one of the most important men in Scotland. His hall was one of a few that regularly housed the royal court. Brother Bertrand continued. "As you may know, the earl has a grandson, a young man called

Tam Lin. I believe he was born not far from here."

Brother Bertrand must have heard the whole story. He is giving my father a chance to tell his side, Jenny thought.

"Indeed, Father," Vicomte Avenel replied, putting down his spoon. "My land once belonged to Andrew Lin, the earl's son-in-law. When he died, the earl took the orphaned lad. The Battle of the Standard came not a year later. I was a young knight in the household of King David in those days and fought in the cavalry, beside Earl Henry, God rest his soul." He paused for a moment to show his sorrow—heartfelt, Jenny knew—for Earl Henry, King David's only son, who had died not a year before he would have been crowned. "Not to speak ill of our young ruler, Father, but the grave robbed us of a great king when Earl Henry was taken."

Brother Bertrand did not contradict him. King Malcolm, Earl Henry's son, was only twelve when he came to the throne eight years ago. He was known as Malcolm the Maiden for his vow to remain unmarried. Earl Henry had been raised all his life to be king. He would have been a good and wise ruler, like his father, King David. But an untried lad had been crowned in his place.

Jenny's father took up his story again. "It was felt that I had distinguished myself in the Battle of the Standard." Jenny smiled at her father's unaccustomed modesty. In other company, the story of the battle could last for hours. "And these lands, being without a lord, were bestowed by the king upon me." He puffed himself up a little. "I have no overlord, you see, but the king himself." It was a point of pride for him not to be enfeoffed, as most small landowners were, to a greater earl or baron, although an overlord might have provided him with more social connections.

Jenny noticed the music had stopped. When she glanced over, she was surprised to see the harper listening intently to their conversation. She frowned at him. With a small nod of apology, he began to play again. Such rudeness seemed out of character with the man she had met earlier.

"Perhaps you know Tam Lin may now be on your land, Sir Philippe," Brother Bertrand said. "The earl of Roxburg dearly loves his grandson, who is perhaps not sound of mind." He did not elaborate, trusting that the gossip would be known. "The earl knows this land belongs to you. There is no question of claiming the Lin birthright. Roxburg hopes his grandson will soon tire of living in the forest and return home. He begs you to show the lad kindness."

The vicomte sat straighter in his chair. "Please tell the earl that his grandson will come to no harm by my men. I swear."

Jenny saw how flattered her father was to be begged a favor by a great man. She knew the promise would be honored. She was glad to know no one would support Tam Lin if he tried to claim Carter Hall, but this promise would surely prolong his stay on her father's land. Carter Hall was hers. She wished Tam Lin away.

Brother Bertrand finally tasted his pottage. "This is excellent fare, my lady."

"Thank you, Father," she said. Her relief must have shown in her smile.

"Your daughter takes care with your table, Vicomte,"

Brother Bertrand said. Only Jenny noticed him wince a little as he tasted the wine.

"My daughter just lately assumed these responsibilities, but she has taken pains to see that you are well cared for this evening." Her father smiled at her.

"And what age have you now, my child?" Brother Bertrand asked, slipping out of the formal style of a courtier into the more comfortable manner of a priest.

"I am sixteen, Father."

"A grown woman, and so pretty."

Jenny blushed. The frank compliments of the Normans always unsettled her. The same words would sound blunt in the mouth of a Scot, but Brother Bertrand was the soul of decorum. "I am amazed she still graces your table, sir," he continued. "Has no one spoken for her hand?"

The vicomte looked uncomfortable. "I thought to make a match for her sister, Lady Isabel, first, and then . . ." He paused awkwardly.

"And then this unfortunate matter of the dangerous suitor." Brother Bertrand had introduced the topic no one else dared mention. His tact left Jenny amazed.

Her father looked unhappy, but relieved rather than upset.

"Yes," he said, his voice low.

Jenny glanced around quickly. Brother Turgis appeared to be the only listener, and the harper's music provided cover.

Brother Bertrand lowered his voice as well. "This matter concerns us greatly, Sir Philippe. I bring you words from the abbot himself. But let us say nothing of this now.

Tomorrow morning after mass will be time enough." He raised his voice again, including everyone. "Tonight, we must savor your good daughter's efforts to make us happy." He raised his cup to Jenny with a smile, but, she noticed, barely sipped the wine.

So the crippled boy was not the only reason for the almoner's visit, as she had suspected. Jenny could understand why the abbot and the earl of Roxburg had trusted Brother Bertrand. In just a few minutes, he had raised two very difficult problems, settling one while flattering her father. Brother Bertrand would certainly rise within the Church. Such a man might even be abbot one day.

"Have you heard of the healings at the holy well of Broomfield Abbey?" Brother Bertrand steered the conversation to safer ground. "I find it difficult to learn of these local saints. The land seems full of them, but they come to us from the Irish church, not Rome, so we learn nothing of them in our teachings. Do you know anything about the saint of this well?"

Her father shook his head, so Jenny spoke. "The well belongs to Saint Coninia, Father. She was one of the first heathens in this land to be converted to Christianity. She was a noblewoman and led many to the faith by her example." Jenny smiled. Galiene's endless storytelling was sometimes useful.

"So she is a saint for her good example?"

"There's more to her story, Father. The folk say that the well at Broomfield belonged to the devil until Saint Coninia cast him out."

"Then the land around Broomfield has been holy for

centuries. That would explain why the Cistercian brothers chose Broomfield for their abbey. Holy ground is always auspicious."

"That," Brother Turgis said, "and the fact that Broomfield is without settlement. The Cistercians like a wooded glade by a river, where they can withdraw from the world." He sighed, and Jenny wondered why he had not joined the Cistercians himself. Their cloistered life seemed more suited to his nature than the ways of the outgoing Augustinians.

"The place is not so quiet of late," Brother Bertrand said, "for the well is now said to have miraculous healing powers, and pilgrims come clamoring to Broomfield Abbey. The brothers must provide food and shelter for charity, no matter how many come to disturb their peace." For an almoner, Brother Bertrand's smile seemed almost uncharitable. Jenny remembered hearing of a rivalry between the two abbeys.

At the end of the meal, after dried fruit and wafers and cheese, the crippled boy was brought to the hall. Jenny had made sure that the servants' portions were especially generous tonight so that none of the abbey servants could carry tales of stinginess back to Rowanwald, but the boy looked so thin and pale, she wondered if Hawise or Galiene had taken care to see that he ate.

"Tell the lord your name, child," Brother Bertrand gently prompted.

"I am Alric, called the Reed, my lord," the boy said. His accent was strange, but his voice was surprisingly clear and bold. He looked to be about twelve.

The vicomte smiled. Jenny knew that spirit pleased her father better than servility. "Well, Alric the Reed, are you here to pledge your oath to me?"

"Yes, my lord," the boy said, and he plunged on without hesitation. "Food and clothing both for my back and for my bed, and shoes, thou shalt procure me, and all that I possess shall remain in thy power." Someone at the abbey had taken trouble to prepare him.

Jenny's father laughed and slapped his knee. "Well spoken, Alric the Reed. What possessions you have, I cannot guess, but I accept you as my bondsman. Come, place your hand in mine." The boy limped forward. "From this day forth," the vicomte said, "you are mine. Take, as a token of our bond, these possessions." A servant placed a bundle in his hands. Jenny knew it contained a wool jerkin, the blanket she had finished that afternoon, a small knife, and a few other trifles. The boy ran his fingers over the blanket, plainly pleased to see it was new.

The vicomte noticed. "Mind you care for that blanket, boy. My daughter, the Lady Jeanette, wove it with her own hands."

Jenny was not surprised that her father would make her gift a matter of public record. The Normans loved to boast of any charity, however small. She smiled at the boy, who seemed awed for the first time.

"Thank you, my lady," he stammered before a servant led him from the hall.

"So you wove the boy a blanket," Brother Bertrand said. "That was generous, my lady."

Jenny could not lie. "My weaving is nothing to be

proud of, Father. The boy may wish for better come winter."

"Modest as well as beautiful." Again, that Norman flattery confounded Jenny. If any other man had spoken to her in that way, she would have blushed with shame. Yet she could see Brother Bertrand only meant to be kind.

Jenny felt sure her father was about to launch into a story. Afraid he might tell Brother Bertrand about Queen Maud and the lepers, she quickly jumped in. "How is it that the boy comes to us, Father? He is welcome, as you have seen, and perhaps I am too bold. . . ."

"Not at all, my child. Curiosity is a virtue."

"In its place." Brother Turgis sounded scandalized.

"Yes, of course, Brother Turgis," Brother Bertrand said, with barely concealed annoyance. "We thought it best to remove the boy from the abbey. His master is most bitter about the injury. He feels he lost what money he spent on the boy's apprenticeship. He is a bitter man by nature, and violent when in his cups, which is often. A most profane man. We would dismiss him if masons were plenty, but they are not. Indeed, we feel the boy's loss ourselves. He held great promise.

"Now, it is late for both Brother Turgis and myself to be abroad, and we still have many matters to discuss," Brother Bertrand said. "We will see you in the family chapel in the morning, and after breakfast, meet in your private chamber. Come, Brother."

"May the Lord keep you from the terrors of the night," Brother Turgis said, his customary blessing. Jenny wondered how these two men could call themselves brothers.

Everyone rose as a sign of respect until the canons left the hall. Jenny could see that the mention of tomorrow's discussion troubled her father. It unsettled her as well.

"Harper," she said quickly, "pray, give us a song."

Cospatric smiled. "I will sing you a song of the Battle of the Standard, my lord." The lines of worry vanished from Vicomte Avenel's face, and Jenny silently forgave the man for eavesdropping earlier.

Cospatric's voice was more than pleasant, low and true. His song was so long and detailed, it could only have been made by someone who had witnessed the battle himself. The bravery and skill of the Scots was stressed; the fact that the English had won the battle was delicately glossed over. Everyone seemed transported to the battlefield. When Cospatric sang of the cry that went up from the Scots saying King David was dead, and how the old king had torn off his helmet to show his face, regardless of the danger, cheers went up from the listeners. There was even a verse about Earl Henry's cavalry, how they were surrounded by the English and, at the earl's command, threw down their colors and mingled with the enemy, so that most made their way back to safety. This was Vicomte Avenel's own moment of glory. When Cospatric's harp finally fell silent, her father looked happier than Jenny could remember him being for weeks.

"Well sung, harper!" he cried. "I have never heard that song. Where did you learn it?"

"Indeed, my lord, it is my own. For I was at the Battle of the Standard, as you were that day."

"This cannot be. You are too young."

"I was, my lord, no older than that crippled lad who pledged his oath to you this night, but I was there. Do you not remember how the Galwegians brought poets and musicians into battle with them? It is the Irish custom, and our own as well."

"I do. And I recall the strange garb they wore, so like the dress of women that we were told one poor old chronicler mistook the lads for dancing girls."

Cospatric allowed the laughter to die away before he answered. "The kilt is honored in most of the kingdoms of Scotland, my lord, even if it seems strange here in the borderlands. We were proud to wear it that day."

"And many of your men gave their lives on Cowton Moor. They fought bravely on foot against the mounted Norman knights of England, with spears of wood against good Norman steel, and they did not falter even as they fell. Though we came from different lands and spoke different tongues, we were all Scots together on that day.

"The hour is late and we should take our rest, but you are welcome in my hall, harper. Most welcome. Stay as long as you choose." He left the hall smiling, and Jenny, behind him, smiled as well. The harper had won his way into her father's household without her help. The battle he had shared with her father, those many years ago, might help her in her battle to win her sister back again.

Chapter Four

T HE NEXT MORNING, GRAY RIVER mist shrouded the bailey as Jenny entered the small chapel with her father to hear the daily mass. Most of the household followed, but Isabel had refused. Their father's roaring still echoed in Jenny's ears, but her sister would not be moved. She seemed determined to make things as difficult for herself as possible.

Jenny tried not to think ahead to what might happen after breakfast. Instead, she wondered what Brother Bertrand would think of the chapel. It was almost a shed, small and dark, made of woven wooden wattle coated with peat and clay, the poorest kind of structure. Even the stable was a better building. Jenny's father always said he would build a stone chapel if the abbeys would only let their masons work for others. There was no danger of this, of course. Jenny knew it was only a ploy to save her father's pride, for he could never afford to house and feed the masons and the larger crew of workers needed to quarry and transport the stone.

Jenny was happy to see Brother Bertrand before the

altar. He brought a gracious touch to the humble chapel that was unknown in Brother Turgis's blunt services. Brother Bertrand's voice was soft and musical, and, although Jenny could not understand it, every word of the Latin service was clearly audible. Her father noticed too, and he complimented the priest after breakfast as they walked to the family bower.

Brother Bertrand's smile was almost mischievous as he replied. "When I was a novice, we were taught to say our services with care. The novice master told us that the father of evil commissioned a special little devil, Tittivillus by name, with the task of gathering all the holy syllables carelessly dropped in our services. He then carried them back to hell. Indeed, some novices even saw this fiend lurking about the abbey with a great poke around his neck for the gathering of our carelessly mumbled words."

"Brother Bertrand, why do you you smile?" Brother Turgis said. "The world is thick with angels and devils. I saw that evil fiend myself when I was a novice."

"Just so, Brother Turgis. The thought of such a harmless devil is amusing, but of course he is real. The world is full of things unseen."

Then why not fairies? Jenny thought, but, for once, she held her tongue. This was not the time for such talk. Brother Bertrand carried a roll of parchment in his hand that must have held the abbot's judgment for Isabel. Before they entered the bower, he had stopped smiling.

Isabel sat on a stool, her head bent as if she had already heard the harsh words that must certainly fall on her now. When Brother Bertrand saw her, he frowned. "Bring me a table and a stool," he said to Galiene. "Then leave us, woman. The abbot's words are for the family alone."

Galiene obeyed without a peep. The stern officer of the Church who unrolled the parchment seemed a different man from the gracious courtier Jenny had met the night before.

"I will first read the words our good abbot sends you, then translate so you will understand what he has said."

He began to read the Latin on the scroll. The tension in the room grew with every incomprehensible word. Jenny tried to escape by imagining what it would be like to read. She would probably have to learn Latin first. She had been told of stories that were written in French, but she had never seen or heard of anyone who could write in English. The written word allowed the Church to move thoughts and knowledge through time and space in ways Jenny could hardly comprehend. It was said that the brothers at Broomfield were making a chronicle so that others, even those yet unborn, might know of important events long into the future.

An abrupt silence brought her back to the room. Brother Bertrand had finished reading. He allowed the silence to hang heavy in the air before speaking, deliberately increasing the tension, it seemed to Jenny.

"My lord abbot says that many wrongs were committed to make this sad situation. Chiefly, Vicomte Avenel, you brought the wrath of God upon your house by remaining these many years unmarried, leaving your daughters without the guidance of a mother. This fiend who made his home in your hall could not have captured your daughter's heart under a mother's watchful eye. The primary sin, therefore, is yours."

Jenny gasped. Even Isabel raised her eyes in amazement. The failing at the center of their father's life had been dragged into the light of day. If anyone else had spoken in this way, he would have shaken the bower with rage, but he bowed his head before the priest like a meek child.

"I took two wives, Father. They gave me three children. I loved each wife with all my heart, and both were taken from me in the very flower of youth. When Jeanette's mother died, I had not the heart to take another." He sighed. "Men speak well of Eudo. Perhaps I have served the girls less well."

When Brother Bertrand spoke again, he was more kindly. "You take the judgment of our abbot with humility, Sir Philippe. That is good. The abbot further says that the matter of your eldest daughter's conduct must be resolved as quickly as possible. He charges you to accept my judgment as his own."

The vicomte nodded. Jenny held her breath, wondering what would come next.

"It seems to me the damage of your failure to remarry has been done. Your daughters are grown women and would profit nothing by the introduction of a new mother. The next bride who comes into this household should rightly be that of your son." Jenny heard her father's sigh of relief. He must have feared that the Church would order him to marry.

Brother Bertrand continued. "Let us begin with the

easiest problem. Your youngest daughter is capable of managing a household. She is too pretty and charming by far to be left unmarried. Brother Turgis tells me she is even more willful than her sister, which seems difficult to believe. A match should be made for her as soon as possible so that she does not prove too great a temptation for some poor young man. If you permit, I will see to this matter myself. I am well acquainted with some noble families who might find favor with such a maiden."

"Yes, certainly, Father."

The vicomte was so relieved to be excused from remarrying, Jenny knew, that he would willingly give her away. But she would think of herself later. Her problems were small compared to Isabel's.

"Now, in the matter of your older daughter." Brother Bertrand rose and looked at Isabel. Without raising her eyes, she flinched as if his gaze burned her. "This situation is serious indeed. Of course, the woman is always to blame for leading a man astray. Women are the root of all evil in such matters, just as Eve betrayed our forefather, Adam. We do not know to what degree your daughter played the role of seductress." He sighed, as though the complexity of the situation defeated him. "But her case is hardly typical. Knowing what we do about this man now, if man indeed he was, the role she played in causing his death could hardly be considered a sin. All that is required of the girl is a simple confession. Her refusal to confess places her soul in danger. The idea that a mere girl might defy the rule of the Church is troubling and offensive. This behavior cannot be allowed to continue."

40

Brother Bertrand's voice rose. "Look at the girl. Even her dress is an act of contempt. She dares to assume the clothing of a penitent, yet remains unrepentant and unforgiven. Vicomte, what action have you taken to bring her to her senses?"

"Father, she spends her days in prayer and meditation. She eats bread and water."

"Yet she did not attend mass this morning. Have you beaten her?"

Jenny had to clamp her mouth shut to keep from crying out in protest.

The vicomte hung his head. "Forgive me, Father. I cannot raise a hand to either of my girls. It seems too cruel."

"Brother Turgis tells me you are entirely too lax in the punishment of your servants as well. This is another grave weakness, Vicomte. Just as God shows his love by punishing us for our sins, though it pains him to do so, you must show your daughter your love by beating her to submission. Indeed, the abbot does us this kindness within the abbey. Brothers who have sinned gravely are whipped."

They waited for Jenny's father to reply, but he hung his head and said nothing. For all his bluster, Jenny knew her father could never hit his girls. This might be a weakness, but she loved him for it.

"Vicomte, if you cannot bring your daughter to heel, I have the abbot's authorization to bring her to Rowanwald, where she will answer to the ecclesiastical court. I will take her this day."

"Oh, Father, please, I beg you, do not take my sister!" Jenny burst into tears. She had no idea what the Church court might do to Isabel, but Brother Bertrand's description of discipline in the abbey left her shaken.

Brother Bertrand seemed moved by Jenny's tears. "Come now, my child," he said. "Do not be distressed. I have no wish to take your sister to Rowanwald." He turned to her father. "Vicomte, if I am to leave your daughter in your care, you must agree to certain conditions."

"Certainly, Father," the vicomte said. He sounded almost as terrified as Jenny.

"The girl must leave off this mockery of penance immediately. She must bathe and comb her hair and don proper clothing again. She is forbidden to brood about. She must join you at your table, see to her household duties, and attend mass daily." He turned and spoke directly to Isabel for the first time. "Isabel Avenel, do you swear before your Maker to do these things?"

For a long moment, Jenny was afraid her sister might defy the priest, but finally, without raising her eyes, Isabel whispered, "I do."

Brother Bertrand's shoulders relaxed. "Very good, my child. I am pleased to see you are not without sense." He turned to Jenny's father. "Vicomte, I would take no pleasure in bringing this young woman to justice before the Church court. It will be much better if she simply makes her confession."

He crouched in front of Isabel so that he could look into her eyes. "Isabel, Isabel, the sisters at Coldstream are waiting to welcome you. The Heavenly Father is ready to pour the cleansing waters of forgiveness on your head. You have only to ask."

This kindness undid Isabel in a way that threats and anger could not. She buried her face in her hands and burst into tears.

Brother Bertrand let her cry for a while, then said, "Come now, Isabel. Your sins are not so great. Are you ready to confess? I will hear you myself before I go." He was gentle now.

Isabel's voice was muffled through her hands. "Father, please, I am not ready. I beg you for a little more time."

Jenny could have cried in frustration. They had seemed so close to putting this terrible episode behind them. For the first time, she understood the anger her father felt toward Isabel. Why could she not release everyone from this suffering?

Instead of losing his temper, Brother Bertrand said, "Isabel, why do you deny yourself the comfort of confession?" At first, it had seemed to Jenny that he wished to punish Isabel, but now that she was yielding, his manner had changed. Perhaps he was only trying to accomplish the abbot's goals.

Isabel lowered her hands and raised her tearstained face. "Please, Father," she whispered, "I do not feel worthy of forgiveness."

This answer seemed to soften Brother Bertrand's heart completely. Jenny thought she even saw some small approval in Brother Turgis's eyes.

"Isabel, the decision is not yours to make." He sighed and rose. "But now, at least, I understand. Vicomte, the abbot will not be pleased when I return without your daughter's confession, but, now that I know her heart, I am willing to bear his disapproval. I cannot say how long he will wait, however." He paused, it seemed to Jenny, to calculate how much time he could buy. "Because Isabel is not defiant, I am not so worried about her soul. Perhaps we can give her a season. I will return again at the end of the summer. By that time, if Isabel has not confessed to Brother Turgis, I will hear her confession myself. Otherwise, I will have no choice but to take her to Rowanwald. Do you understand?"

"Yes, Father. This is most generous. I feel certain we will find a way to bend her heart to receive the mercy of the Church before autumn," the vicomte said. Jenny was relieved to notice that beating was not mentioned again.

"Sir Philippe, I asked my entourage to be ready to travel as soon as I finished here. Let us go to the stables now, to tell the men your daughter's horse will not be needed for the journey."

Jenny would have gone to Isabel, but Brother Bertrand stopped her. "Come bid us adieu, Lady Jeanette. Leave your sister alone to examine her soul."

Jenny left Isabel reluctantly. But before they were halfway to the stable, she glanced back to see what she had hoped for—Galiene slipping into the bower. Jenny smiled. If she knew Galiene, water for Isabel's bath was already warming in the kitchen shed. Galiene would happily spend the rest of the day restoring Isabel's appearance. She might be inclined to eavesdrop, but Jenny knew the old nurse could soothe a troubled soul as no one else.

When the entourage was mounted and ready to leave, Brother Bertrand said, "I almost forgot. A small favor,

Vicomte. I noticed while riding here that your land is blessed with many great oaks. We are always fearful of running out of ink at the abbey. Oaks make galls on their twigs, small, round boils. You may have seen this. From these galls, we make an extract for our inks. The old ones are useful, but the newest crop is always best. If your men could collect some galls this summer, I will take them in the fall. It sounds like a small thing, but in truth, we cannot manufacture ink without them. You would be doing us a great favor."

"It would be my pleasure."

Brother Bertrand turned to Jenny. "For you, my child, I hope the best of suitors will come." With a flick of the reins, he set out for Rowanwald.

In less than a day, he had done so much to change their lives.

Chapter Five

"WILL YOU SEE TO YOUR sister, Jeanette?" her father asked as the last rider disappeared through the bailey gate. It was only midmorning, but he sounded exhausted.

"Galiene already has, Papa." Jenny pointed to the servants carrying buckets into the bower. "She will care for Isabel better than I could. This is a new beginning for my sister. Let Isabel come to your table tonight as if reborn."

"I hope she may, little one." Jenny could see her father struggling to put his feelings into words. "You . . . you have been a comfort to me in all of this."

She kissed her father's cheek. "Everything will be better now, Papa. You will see."

"Have I been a bad father to you, little one?"

"You have given me freedom, Papa. Even if others think me willful, I will always love you for that."

He said nothing, but Jenny knew, for once, she had said the right thing. Perhaps the worst was over now. She sighed and looked around. The sun had burned off every wisp of mist, leaving a cloudless spring day behind. In weather like this, Jenny could hardly bear to be indoors. She thought of La Rose, her little chestnut mare, trapped in the dark stable. She decided to test her luck.

"La Rose has been inside all spring. She will sicken if no one rides her. Perhaps I could take her out." She held her breath.

"You must not go alone. One of my men will come with you."

Jenny's heart sank. "Oh, Papa, please. I have always gone into the forest alone."

"Not today, Jeanette. What if you overtake the party from the abbey? Brother Bertrand would not approve."

"But Papa, if I am to have a husband, I must find him a falcon."

As she had hoped, her father laughed. It was an old joke between them. Jenny had been no more than seven when she first declared she would find a falcon to give her husband before she would marry.

"Very well. If you seek a falcon, take Ranulf. I keep the man for that very purpose."

"Yes, Papa," Jenny said, hoping he would not hear the disappointment in her voice. Of course, the falconer could be expected to help capture falcons. She cursed herself for not thinking of that.

"He will meet you in the stable," her father said, turning toward the mews where the falcons were kept.

Jenny ran to the kitchen shed, dodging serving girls who were still fetching water for Isabel's bath. "Hawise, give me some oatcakes and cheese and something to drink."

The red-faced cook looked up from the fire. "Away to the forest, are you?"

Jenny laughed. "How did you know?"

Hawise took a leather flagon from the wall and filled it with ale. "To keep you in the bailey on a day like this, we would need to tie you down. Be careful not to lose yourself in the woods."

Jenny made a face at her joke. "My father insists on an escort today. Ranulf will come with me."

"Only because the priests upset everything, pet," Hawise said, reaching for a second flagon. Jenny was not surprised that she knew what had happened. Galiene told her everything. "Just do as he wishes for now," the cook continued. "Your lord father will be back to his old ways soon enough, and you will have your freedom again." She winked at Jenny. "As for Ranulf, half the fish that come to your father's table are caught by him. Give him the chance to spend an afternoon tending his weirs. He should be gone before the words are out of your mouth. I packed food enough for him, too." And Hawise handed her the leather sack that was kept in the kitchen for Jenny's rambles.

"Oh, Hawise, thank you," Jenny said. They both knew she was not talking about the food.

The sweet fragrance of hay and the sharp smell of manure hit Jenny together as she entered the stable. Ranulf stood beside a big gray gelding named Bravura, holding the reins of Jenny's own mare. The falconer had come into the household only a year ago. He was a tall, thin man with a hawkish face that Jenny thought entirely appropriate for one in his trade. Her father valued his skills, but Jenny had never spoken to him because he was so repulsive. Smallpox had disfigured his skin with so many pockmarks and bumps, it was impossible to guess what he might have looked like before. He seemed to know how a girl like Jenny would feel about him, for he averted his face as he handed her the reins. "Your horse, my lady," he mumbled. Jenny felt a stab of sympathy for this man who knew that no woman would look on him with favor.

La Rose whinnied with pleasure to see her. "*Bonjour,* La Rose," Jenny whispered, rubbing her neck, for the little horse understood French best. The mare buried her soft pink muzzle in Jenny's hand. Jenny was up on her back in a flash, to spare Ranulf the embarrassment of having to help her. His look of astonishment made her laugh.

"Now, man, up on that horse and see if you can keep pace with me," Jenny said. Ranulf smiled, for Bravura stood head and shoulders above La Rose. But as soon as they were out of the stable, Jenny and La Rose left the big horse in a cloud of dust.

La Rose raced down the broad main road as if she, too, could not wait to be in the forest again. Past plowed riggs and pastures filled with new lambs they cantered until a canopy of branches covered them. Here, Jenny slowed La Rose to a safer trot, for the roots of the great trees made dangerous traps for a horse on the forest roads. Jenny caught her breath as she looked up. Huge oak and ash trees towered so high, Jenny often felt as if she were at the bottom of a great, green sea. But now, these giant trees were just beginning to show their leaves. Bluebells flooded the forest floor, and the smaller trees that would go unnoticed in the summer were having their moment of glory. Hawthorn and cherry flowers blazed white in the sunlight that streamed through the mostly bare boughs of the larger trees.

Jenny looked over her shoulder as Ranulf and Bravura caught up. The falconer kept a respectful distance as they rode on.

"You ride like a knight, my lady." Many men would have said this with a sneer, but the falconer's admiration was honest.

"Most women ride only because they must," Jenny said. "When I was a child, I rode beside my brother. We used to spend long days in this forest. Now, I must beg for permission to come here."

"Most women fear the forest," Ranulf said.

"Most Normans fear the forest. Have you never noticed? They prefer the open fields, where the land has been plowed into submission. But I love the wild heart of the woods. Comfort and peace are here for anyone who cares to seek it." Jenny stopped, a bit embarrassed by her passion. She rarely spoke this way to anyone, but when she looked at Ranulf, his ugly face was softened by a smile.

"Your lord father tells me we are to look for falcons. Do you know where they nest in these woods? I trained on a great fiefdom in England where the land is flat. The falcons build their aeries in trees there, though it is more in their nature to nest at the top of rocky hills." As soon as he began to talk of the birds, Jenny noticed, his awkwardness was gone.

"Then they are true to their nature here. When I was a child, falcons nested in the crags at the top of the knowes."

The falconer nodded. "I would expect so. How did you come upon them?"

"Eudo and I were playing at battle near the top of a knowe early one summer. I was seven. I remember well because it was the summer before Eudo went to live at Sir Robert's. We came close to a nest without knowing. One of the adults, the mother I think, came at us, screaming. I thought she would tear us to pieces. Eudo waved his wooden play sword to keep her off while we backed away.

"She was a canny creature. After she had chased us, she sat on a dead tree, just watching. We had to pass her on a lower ridge to climb down, and I was afraid she would come at us again, but she seemed to know we could not reach her nest from there. Eudo spoke politely to her. He said, 'Madame, if we had known where your aerie was, we would never have passed that way.' And at that, she flew back to her nest as if she understood him."

Ranulf laughed. "Well then, you have seen the best and worst of these birds. They can be fierce when defending their young, but, even then, I doubt the falcon would have harmed you. Most of the time, they are more docile than most horses. But they are wise beyond telling and know an angry word from a kind one." Jenny could see this man loved his work. "Can you still find where that aerie was?" he continued. "The birds use the same sites faithfully, year after year if left undisturbed."

"Oh yes, at the top of the nearest knowe. The track that leads that way is just ahead." Jenny led the way. As the track to the knowe began to climb, the soft earth turned stony. The open forest gave way to stunted trees and heavy undergrowth until the woods thinned to nothing at the foot of a steep slope covered in broken bits of shale. "We can tether the horses here," Jenny said, pointing to a stout little birch. "La Rose would wait for me, but Bravura might decide to make his own way home."

The falconer gazed up. "It looks like a hard climb, my lady. You could wait here."

"Nothing could keep me from going with you."

"As you wish."

Soon, Jenny was panting too hard to talk. She pointed out the path where the falconer might have missed it. He took direction wordlessly but without resentment. Sometimes they set off small rock slides that clattered down the slope like broken crockery, but neither lost their footing.

Near the crest of the knowe, he put out his arm to stop her. "Wait," he whispered.

She followed his gaze to see a pair of falcons wing to the ridge above them. "We can go now," Ranulf said. "That was all I needed to see."

"But I thought we would find the nest," Jenny said. The depth of her disappointment surprised her.

"The capture of a falcon takes patience, my lady. If we bother the birds so early in the spring, we might drive them to nest elsewhere. Even after the eyases hatch, the parents must raise them. The males, the tiercels, leave their nest first. They are of no account to us. The females, the falcons proper, remain a few days more, so we may know then if there is one worth taking. But the eggs are a month or more in hatching, and the eyases grow another month before they fledge. We have until midsummer."

Jenny sighed. "Patience has never been one of my virtues."

"Patience may be the only virtue I possess, my lady. Perhaps I can teach it to you." Behind the mask of his disfigurement, Ranulf's blue eyes twinkled. Jenny was surprised to find his looks no longer mattered to her. She liked this man.

When they returned to the horses, Jenny opened her leather sack. "Hawise gave me a lunch for you," she said, handing him one of the flagons and a napkin filled with food.

He looked around, puzzled. "You intend to eat here?"

"No, I was hoping to spend some hours alone in the woods." She saw a look of protest forming, so she hurried on. "I will come to no harm. These woods are like a home to me. La Rose knows them as well as I do, and you have seen how well I ride. I was told you might appreciate an afternoon with your fishing weirs."

She could see he was swayed, just as Hawise had predicted. "But I promised your father you would not go to Carter Hall," he said.

Jenny sighed. "Then I shall not. I swear. We can meet on the main road, return together, and pretend you trailed about after me all day. We will both be much happier."

"A maiden should not traipse around in the woods alone," Ranulf said, but without conviction. Jenny knew she had won.

"Thank you, Ranulf. Meet me where this track joins the main road when the shadows are longer than your height." She was off before he had a chance to reconsider.

Jenny quickly returned to the main road and guided La Rose onto a nearby track, away from the knowes and into the heart of the forest. This path did indeed lead to Carter Hall, but to keep her promise, Jenny would stay on this side of the river. The air was still and smelled of healthy decay. Jenny remembered the oak galls. Perhaps she could find some for Brother Bertrand now. Tree climbing was hardly a lady's sport, but Jenny had always loved to be up in these old giants.

She spotted a likely oak and guided La Rose toward it. The main boughs were as big as the trunks of lesser trees and ran level with the ground like outstretched arms. Jenny brought her mare up to a bough not far above her head. "Steady now, La Rose. Steady, little one," she coaxed as she slowly swung her legs around and tried to stand on the saddle. La Rose shied and Jenny almost fell. "Come now, *joli coeur*. Remember how I taught you."

This time, the mare held still and Jenny stood. Leaning toward the tree, she threw herself over the bough, legs pumping as La Rose trotted away. Grunting with effort, she swung a leg over to straddle the bough. There was nothing graceful about this trick. Jenny giggled to think what Brother Bertrand would say if he could see her. She brushed the front of her dress, happy she had chosen an everyday tunic of coarse, undyed wool. The rough oak bark had snagged it, but the cloth was easily repaired.

La Rose was already away, searching for greens to graze

on. The little mare would not wander far and always came when Jenny whistled. Jenny stood, grabbing a branch above to steady herself. The bough was as level as a road. Her flimsy leather shoes were more trouble than help. She slipped out of them and her stockings, leaning on the main trunk, which stood at her back like a solid wall. The tree was so unmoved by her weight, she might have been a butterfly on a branch.

Jenny looked up. The leaves were just tight little clusters emerging from newly opened buds. Each pale green, translucent bunch was decorated with tassels. These were catkins, the flowers of the oak. She brushed a bunch with her hand, and golden pollen dusted her fingers. Then she found what she was looking for, a cluster of galls hanging down from the tip of a branch. The small, hard galls were almost perfectly round. They seemed to have no purpose at all, and Jenny wondered why the tree would make them. She found more galls on a slightly higher bough. They were plentiful. She took a small knife from her sack and cut the galls cleanly from the twigs. Others might think it silly to be so careful, but she felt these ancient trees deserved her respect.

Satisfied, Jenny returned to the lowest bough and put on her stockings and shoes. Then she sat cross-legged and spread Hawise's napkin on her lap. The oatcakes were fresh, but the cheese was salty and somehow tasted of the sheep. Still, Jenny found she was ravenous. She washed the food down with the ale, licking her fingers and wishing for more. Then she lay down and stretched out full on the bough, pressing her back into the bark with her hands behind her head. She gazed up at the sky through a deep tangle of boughs and branches, feeling as if she were cradled. The profound peace of the forest washed over her, taking her troubles away.

A sudden gust of wind blew her hair across her face, causing her to brace both arms flat on the bough beneath her. Then she realized nothing could shake her from this solid perch. It was as if the wind had played a joke on her. Her laughter rang across the open woodland. She closed her eyes, still smiling. The song of distant birds, the hum of bees in the catkins around her, the wind high above in the trees all lulled her into a doze.

"Lady, are you the spirit of this tree?"

The voice was so soft, Jenny thought it must have come from somewhere inside a dream. "If I were such a spirit," she murmured to herself, "an oak like this would be my home." Then her eyes flew open. She had not dreamed that voice. It was real. She raised herself on her elbow and looked down. A man was sitting on a white horse, smiling up at her. A young man on a fine horse, with a smile that matched his gentle voice. Jenny should have been afraid, but nothing about him inspired fear. He had spoken in English, so she answered the same way.

"How did you come upon me so silently?" she asked, trying to make her voice stern. It might be unwise to be too friendly under these circumstances.

The man patted his horse's neck. "Snowdrop is silent by nature, but we were not so quiet as that. You seemed to be asleep. I heard laughter a moment ago and wondered what sort of creature might be afoot. Are you a wood sprite?"

Jenny sat up and smoothed her dress. He must be teasing, yet he seemed to expect an answer. "Of course not. I am an ordinary lass."

His smile widened. "Not so ordinary as those who live on the ground. I can assure you I feel no disappointment."

Jenny laughed. "You sound like a Scot, but you must be a Norman, to flatter me so without blushing."

To her surprise, her blunt words did make him blush. "In truth, I am both. My father was a Scot, but my mother's people are Norman."

"Just like me!" Jenny said. "My mother was a Scot, but my father is Norman. We are the same."

"Hardly. I live on the ground."

"As I do. My father's hall is just beyond the forest. My name is Jeanette Avenel, but I am mostly called Jenny." She waited for him to tell her his name. He smiled but did not speak. To hide her disappointment, she turned and gave a shrill whistle. "La Rose, *viens ici*."

La Rose appeared from behind some nearby trees.

"Now I see how you got up there. And how do you propose to get down?"

"I will jump onto my horse's back."

"Does that work?"

Jenny shrugged. "Only about half the time, but the ground is soft."

He shook his head. "You could break your neck. I will help you down." He sidled his horse beneath the bough and held his arms up to catch her.

Jenny hesitated. Should she trust this man? His clothes were worn and dusty but finely made. The horse obviously belonged to him in the way La Rose belonged to her. He was a man of rank, not some horse thief who might be tempted to hold her for ransom. Still, the stories and songs she heard around the fire were filled with maidens who were carried away by strange men.

He frowned. "You do not trust me."

"I do not know you."

She expected he would finally introduce himself, but he did not. "Look at me," he said instead. "Ask yourself if I am someone you can trust."

She did. His eyes were hazel, almost gold. He had a high brow, the kind the harpers would call noble. His fine, fair hair was worn long and he was clean-shaven. He carried himself like a knight, but in his voice, his eyes, and his manner, Jenny saw a gentleness that made him unlike any young man she had ever met. He seemed incapable of harming anyone.

"Good," he said, as if he had somehow read her thoughts. "La Rose, come here." The mare obeyed as if he were an old friend. "You see? Your horse awaits. I will not run away with you, my lady." Once more, he opened his arms.

Jenny pushed off the bough and fell about a yard, landing squarely in his lap. His horse bolted in alarm. The man held Jenny tightly. For one awful moment, she thought he was going to ride off with her, but he calmed the horse and brought him back to La Rose, who had watched all this with a look of mild astonishment.

He was taller than he had seemed from the tree. Jenny fitted under his chin, against his chest, as if she belonged there. A long moment passed. Finally, he eased his arms open and cleared his throat. "Your mare awaits, *demoiselle*." He held Jenny's arm with both hands to slow her fall while she slid from his tall horse. She took La Rose by the reins.

"I must go," he said abruptly, and wheeled his horse away.

The thought that she might never see him again filled Jenny with panic. "Wait," she cried. "Who are you? Where do you live?" He was retreating rapidly. "Will I see you again?" The question was out before Jenny realized how bold she sounded.

He must have thought so too, because he turned and grinned. "To see me, my lady, you need only come to Carter Hall." He kicked his heels, and his horse took flight.

Jenny stood frozen beside La Rose, her mouth open in astonishment.

Chapter Six

"SO THAT WAS TAM LIN. Why did I not stop to think he might be?"

Jenny walked toward the main road, leading La Rose as if she had forgotten how to ride, talking to the little horse as though she were human.

"He is not what I expected, La Rose. Not at all. Galiene spoke as if he were some madman. Even Brother Bertrand said he might not be of sound mind. But he was as sane as you or I. He could have harmed me, but he did not. You saw that, did you not?" She looked at La Rose as if she expected an answer. Jenny reached the main road before she noticed the light had changed. It was growing darker. She thought the sun must have gone behind a cloud, but the sky through the branches was still pure blue. Pure blue, but growing darker. How could that be?

Up the road, she saw Ranulf waiting by the track to the knowes. The moment she appeared, he spurred Bravura toward her. At the sight of them, Jenny remembered what La Rose was for and mounted her horse.

As he approached, she could see worry in Ranulf's

60

eyes, even anger. "This is not what we agreed upon, my lady. The day is almost over. Your father will have words for me. Perhaps even the back of his hand." He was struggling to control his temper.

"Forgive me," she said. "I . . . I must have fallen asleep." Jenny rubbed her eyes as if to chase the sleep from them, but she was really trying to bring the world back into focus. It seemed impossible that so much time had passed.

Her sincerity seemed to calm him. "I could not think what to do. I could hardly return to you father's hall without you. I feared you had come to some harm. I was almost sick with worry."

"Please forgive me," she said again. "I was not late through willfulness." At least that was the truth. "As for my father, I have never seen him raise a hand in anger."

"Neither have I, but the care of his daughter must matter to him more than most things."

"His anger will not fall on you. I will find a way to take the blame. Did you find fish in your weirs?"

Ranulf almost smiled. He patted his saddlebag. "More than enough."

"That may curb his temper," Jenny said. She was beginning to come back to herself now, trying to think of an excuse. "Could we not say that a wild animal ruined your weirs, a bear perhaps, and we stopped to mend them and forgot about time?"

Ranulf shook his head. "Your father's huntsmen would be off at dawn tomorrow, seeking a quarry that does not exist. A bear leaves signs, and they would find none. Try not to think of lies. Ride as quickly as you can to lessen the damage."

The April sun went down quickly. It was almost dark when they approached the bailey. In the stable, Jenny found the crippled boy who had come into the household yesterday, waiting by La Rose's stall. "May I take your horse, my lady?" he asked.

"Aye, if you can. Are you able to handle the saddle by yourself? Do you know how to care for her? I have ridden hard, and she must be kept from a chill."

"Yes, my lady. She is small enough for me. At the abbey, they let me help with the horses. I will brush her down and cover her. You will see."

"Very well. What a good lad you are. Has anyone been looking for me?"

The boy blushed. "I was, but no one else seemed to be."

Jenny laughed. She liked this forthright boy. "And why were you waiting for me, Alric the Reed?"

The boy blushed again, his fair skin turning so red that it glowed in the fading light. "You made my blanket," he said. "No one ever made me anything. Not as I remember, leastways."

She smiled. "And you found a way to repay me. I will not forget."

Jenny rushed to the bower. Everyone had already gone to supper. Her absence would certainly have been noticed by now, but this snagged and moss-stained dress would not do for her father's table. She pulled it off, then the sweaty linen kirtle beneath. Diving into the trunk where her clothes were kept, she shook out a fresh kirtle and slipped into it. The cool, soft linen calmed her as it fell the length of her body. She snatched up the red tunic she had worn the day before and quickly pulled a comb through her hair, stopping to untangle a twig. She hoped there were no others. There was no time to check. She braced herself for the confrontation ahead.

The great hall was brightly lit, everyone seated and eating. When Jenny saw Isabel at the high table, her breath caught in her throat. Her sister was dressed in a fine yellow tunic, her hair elaborately braided. From this distance, Jenny could imagine that nothing bad had ever happened, that Isabel would be as cheerful as she had always been. Jenny moved to her place on the bench beside Isabel with what Galiene would call "seemly haste," quickly but in a ladylike manner.

"So there you are," her father said. "Did you find your falcon?" There was no anger whatsoever in his voice.

"We found a pair, Papa. Ranulf said it is too early to disturb them, but he marked the nesting place. We also visited his fishing weirs, and I found some oak galls." Jenny hoped all this would excuse her lateness, but her father ignored her words.

"See, Jeanette, your sister is returned to her rightful place. All our troubles are behind us now. Everything will be good again." He raised his cup unsteadily to his lips. Jenny could see it was not the first time he had drained it. She sighed to herself. It was plain that Isabel was transformed in appearance only. She picked at her food without speaking or smiling and kept her eyes on the table. My father sees only what he wishes to see, Jenny thought.

With Isabel beside her again, Jenny found it impossible to keep her eyes from the empty place at the second table, reserved for the young knights who attached themselves to her father's house. This space, directly opposite Isabel's, was always empty now. No one would sit there. It had been Bleddri's. Again and again, Jenny looked up expecting to see Bleddri as he was all last winter, his handsome blue eyes fixed on Isabel. His attentions were so blatant, Jenny was amazed no one else had seemed to notice.

Bleddri was unlike the other knights. Isabel had been drawn to his courtly manners, and he captivated her with his stories, for he had traveled the world. He told her of his childhood at the court of the duke of Aquitaine, the father of Eleanor, who was now queen of England. When Eleanor became queen of France, he had gone with her retinue to Paris and later journeyed to the Holy Land on a Crusade to Jerusalem.

Every night, after supper, sitting around the fire, Bleddri found a place by Isabel's side and beguiled her with his tales. Jenny listened too, but silently. From the beginning, she had known his words were for Isabel alone. "Let me tell you, my lady, about the Hall of Lost Footsteps in Poitiers," he would begin. While the rest of the household sang songs, told stories, and played riddling games, Isabel and Bleddri made a little world of their own. He told her of his own lands in Languedoc, "where grapes grow on every vine." But he had used his land to fund his journey to the Holy Land. He was quite young, but his father had died when he was no more than a lad, leaving him in charge of his own fortunes. The crusaders had been promised riches beyond telling, but the Crusade failed and Bleddri's lands were forfeit, so he became nothing more than a wandering knight.

Jenny had held her breath all winter, wondering if Bleddri would seek her sister's hand. Isabel might want him, but their father would not. Seeing the past in the light of Brother Bertrand's words, Jenny now realized her father should have protected Isabel from Bleddri. Instead, it seemed to Jenny that their father had used Isabel as a lure to keep the promising young knight in his household.

That February, the weather was too wet for hunting, and everyone was sick of being trapped inside. One day, Bleddri found Jenny alone in the stable, grooming La Rose out of sheer boredom.

"Will you ride with me, Lady Jeanette?" he asked.

"I do not ride in wet weather." This was a lie, and she was fairly sure he knew it, but it was out before she could stop to think. Something about his manner bothered her. Was he standing too close? Was his smile too familiar? She only remembered her discomfort now.

She thought she saw a spark of anger flare in his eyes, but he recovered himself so quickly it was hard to be sure. He glanced around to make sure they were alone. "Then we shall speak here. Your sister has no suitors?"

Jenny knew why Bleddri was asking. She also knew her father would never consider this landless knight a suitable match for Isabel, even if she loved Bleddri. Jenny wished she could lie again, but the truth could not be hidden. She echoed his words with reluctance. "My sister has no suitors."

He smiled. "I mean to ask your father for her hand. He seems to like me well enough. How do you think my suit will go?"

Jenny spoke the truth, hoping to discourage him. "My father means to make a good marriage for my sister, and you have no land."

Her blunt words brought such a dark look that Jenny's heart began to pound. Now, she realized that she had seen him for himself in that one instant. But he quickly became the polite courtier he had always been with Isabel.

"Alas, my rank is the only wealth I possess. But it was so for your father once. He may smile on me yet." And he left her.

A burst of laughter wrenched Jenny back to the present. Her father was joking with the men more urgently now. Neither she nor Isabel had spoken during the meal. Her father was growing desperate to maintain the pretense of happiness. If he failed, Jenny was afraid his anger would turn on Isabel again. She saw Cospatric, the harper, slip in through the doorway of the hall. "Oh, Papa, is the harper going to play by the fire tonight?" Jenny said. She rushed on without thinking. "Perhaps Isabel will sing." She immediately knew she had said the wrong thing. Isabel looked shocked. But the knights took up the cry, "A song from the lady!" Jenny was appalled.

Galiene often said the knights were more trouble than a pack of dogs, and it was true. They came and went too often to keep track of. There might be eight or ten one day, as few as two or three the next. They were dirty and lazy, did no work beyond hunting, had terrible manners, and few could be trusted alone with a woman. Yet her father loved them, for in their eyes, he was a great lord.

The trestle tables were quickly put away, and everyone

went to the fire, which was set on the stone floor behind the high table. The fire was placed here to make the high table the warmest in the hall. In fact, the smoke hole in the roof let the wind in as often as it let the smoke out. Tonight, though, the spring air was mild and still, so for once the fire did indeed give off a pleasant heat.

Everyone sat on benches moved from the dining area, on stools, or on the floor, except Jenny's father, who sat in the only chair, a mark of honor. Without waiting to be asked, Cospatric struck up a lively tune that set everyone's toes to tapping. His playing seemed to spare Isabel, but when he finished, the knights began to chant "A song from the lady" again and would not stop.

Jenny half expected Isabel to run from the room. Instead she turned to the harper. "Do you know *'L'Anneau d'Or'*?" she asked.

The harper shook his head. "I have much to learn about the Norman songs, my lady. But I will follow your lead."

So Isabel began. Her voice was breathtaking, clear, agile, each note true. After the first verse, the harper came in quietly, hitting chords so original they surprised Jenny, though they suited the music perfectly. The song, "The Gold Ring," was about a young man who drowns while diving for a ring lost by a young woman. Like most of the old songs, the story was sketchy. As children, Isabel, Jenny, and Eudo had spent hours discussing the meanings of these songs, so Jenny knew that Isabel thought the girl in the song had thrown her betrothal ring into the sea to rid herself of an unwanted fiancé.

This was the first time Isabel had sung since the night she disappeared with Bleddri. Jenny could not shake the feeling he was in the room, standing just behind her.

She remembered sitting at the fire that last night. Because of the conversation in the stable, Jenny had watched Bleddri and her sister more closely. Isabel had not sung "*L'Anneau d'Or*" then. All her songs had told of love. Her eyes had shone. Even to Jenny, her voice and face had never looked more beautiful. All the men seemed intoxicated by her, and Jenny's father had boasted, "See what a jewel my daughter is."

When Isabel had finished singing, Bleddri said, "Let me tell you a story, my lady." As the winter wore on, his tales had changed. He no longer spoke of himself. Now, his stories were all about knights who faithfully loved ladies they could never have, stories he claimed were popular in the courts of France. This evening, he told of a knight who stayed faithful to his lady even after she married a man of greater rank and wealth. Later, the faithful knight threw himself in front of a charging boar to save the lady's life, dying in her arms. Jenny thought it a poor story, but Isabel was deeply affected, wiping tears from her eyes when Bleddri finished.

After weeks of wet and cloudy weather, the sky had suddenly cleared that very night. Someone suggested a moonlight ride. It was really too early for such an outing, but the bored men seized on the plan eagerly. "Off you go, then," the vicomte said. "I am too old for such frivolity." Jenny was tired, but was afraid to leave Isabel alone with Bleddri.

When she remembered it now, that night had the quality of a nightmare in which something terrible is about to happen, and the dreamer knows it but can only watch helplessly. She had tried to keep close to Isabel, but the other knights surrounded Jenny, demanding attention. It was as if Isabel had made them all hungry for the company of women. It was innocent enough, but Jenny could not escape them. Soon after they reached the forest, Isabel and Bleddri disappeared. Patches of white snow shone under the dark trees, almost glowing in the moonlight, but Jenny could see no couple in the woods.

Now Jenny knew that their father should never have left his daughters unchaperoned, but at the time, it had seemed to Jenny to be her fault somehow. She had vowed she would warn Isabel about Bleddri as soon as they were in bed. If Isabel would not listen, Jenny told herself, she would speak to their father. She never had the chance.

When Jenny returned to the family bower, Isabel was still missing. Jenny could not bring herself to raise the alarm. Isabel's virtue would suffer if the household were alerted to search for her with Bleddri. So Jenny went to bed alone, her fitful sleep punctuated by bad dreams.

Sometime in the night, she drifted out of sleep thinking she heard Isabel return, but when dawn came she was still alone. By the time Isabel and Bleddri were discovered missing the next morning, the late winter rains had returned, making it impossible for the hounds to track the couple. Six days later, just when Jenny was sure her sister was gone for good, Isabel returned alone, leading two horses.

Silence brought Jenny back to the present. Isabel's

song was finished. As usual, her voice had cast a spell over the listeners. No one moved or spoke for a long moment.

"Sing us another," a knight said. "Sing *'Blanche comme la Neige.'*"

But Isabel shook her head. A poor choice, Jenny thought. A cruel choice if the man had thought, for how could Isabel sing a song about a girl who pretended to be dead and was placed in a tomb for three days rather than lose her honor to the knights who had carried her away?

The harper turned to her father. "Your daughter sings like an angel, my lord."

The vicomte sighed. "As did her mother before her. Sing another, Isabel."

Isabel thought for a moment. "*La Triste Noce,*" she said at last.

"The Tragic Wedding." By the end of this song, Jenny recalled, the bride, the groom, and the groom's beloved were all dead. The bride kills the beloved in a fit of jealousy, then the groom slays his bride and falls on his own sword. Jenny knew the servants sang the same song in English. "Lord Thomas and the Fair Annette," they called it, and the tune was different, but the story was just the same. No happy songs for Isabel tonight. But at least she seemed more like herself.

When it was time for bed, the harper caught Jenny's eye. No one in the family had thought to thank him for his skillful playing. She could at least do that.

"A voice like that would make any harp sound sweet, my lady," he said in reply to her praise. "Your sister sings just as they said she would."

Jenny looked at him, puzzled. "Who said she would?"

He blushed. "The folk on the other side of the forest. When I heard the stories, I thought your household might welcome some music now."

Jenny winced. She wished she were strong enough to walk away without asking, but she had to know. "What else do they say about my sister?" she asked. "Do they speak of her disgrace?"

He looked startled. "My lady, do you not know? To the common folk, she is a heroine. They even sing a song about her."

Chapter Seven

꧁

"**N**OW, YOU SEE HOW MANY barrels of oats are left, and how many of wheat and barley flour. This year's crops will not be reaped until after Lammastide. You know who gets wheaten bread, and who does not. How can you divide this much to feed everyone without running out?"

Jenny groaned. "Oh, Isabel, how do you manage this?"

"It comes with practice, Jenny." Isabel almost smiled.

The distant oaks had greened with May, but Jenny resisted their call. Instead, she stayed close to Isabel, helping to ease her into this world again. Had Brother Bertrand known that forcing Isabel back into her life would restore her like this? Jenny wondered. She was still a pale shadow of the sister Jenny loved, but she was more like herself in many ways. It had been Isabel's idea to teach Jenny how to manage the household. They both knew these responsibilities would soon fall to Jenny, for Isabel seemed fated for the priory in Coldstream.

As they worked together, Jenny wished Isabel would speak of what had happened after she had left with Bleddri. Jenny knew no more of this part of the story than any stranger might. If Isabel could tell her, she might finally understand what her sister had been through. Then, perhaps, Jenny would find a way to tell Isabel what Cospatric had said. The thought that some might think Isabel a heroine had been hard to understand at first, but Jenny was gradually coming to see how that might be. The freebooters and the folk who secretly helped them had a very different way of looking at things. But Isabel's new-found peace of mind seemed too fragile to disturb just yet, so Jenny kept these thoughts to herself. The unaccustomed secrets reminded her that she now had a secret of her own.

Setting up the loom or supervising the washing of linens, Jenny would suddenly remember the scent of the woods, the flight of the falcons, and Tam Lin. She had told no one of this meeting, which now seemed almost like a dream. The sensible knight she had encountered in the forest was nothing like the madman everyone gossiped about, but Jenny had to admit the memory was touched with something like magic. Not only because of the way time had scrambled when she was with him, but in the tingle she felt even now as she remembered his arms around her.

"She must be away with the wee folk," Galiene joked to Isabel. Jenny realized that Galiene had asked a question she had not heard. She pulled herself back to the task of taking inventory.

"Do you suppose they would want me?" Jenny joked back. But after that, she put her secret thoughts aside and tried to focus on her work.

That afternoon, Jenny and Isabel oversaw the weeding

of the kitchen garden while Isabel made sure Jenny knew the uses of the herbs. As the shadows grew long, Jenny looked up to see the boy Alric hobbling toward them. "Your lord father says come greet the noble family," he said.

When Jenny rounded the corner of the stable, she found a couple wearing the broad-brimmed hats and plain garb of pilgrims. But the humble clothing did nothing to disguise the man's noble bearing. The couple looked unaccustomed to traveling by foot, especially the wife, who was stout and red-faced. Before Jenny could greet them, four strong servants arrived, bearing an open litter. The wife rushed over to tend the child they carried.

Isabel hung back.

"Come meet Thane Ethenan mac Askil," their father said to Jenny in English. She gave the man her hand, wondering if she dared to ask what would bring a thane to their hall. The Scottish nobles who were loyal to King Malcolm were not unfriendly, but they held themselves apart from the Normans.

Thane Ethenan seemed to expect her curiosity. "You must wonder what brings us to your gate." He gestured to the litter. "Avece, my youngest, has been taken with a wasting illness. When the king kept court at our household during Lent, his chaplain told us of Saint Coninia's well. My lady, Bethoc, pledged then we would make this pilgrimage south to Broomfield Abbey as soon as the weather was mild enough. We sailed to Berwick to spare the child and made our way from there. When we stayed at the hospital at Rowanwald, the almoner, Brother Bertrand, told us we might seek your charity for a night."

The child was about four, lying pale and listless on the cushions of the litter. Her blond hair was plastered to her head with sweat. Her eyes were glassy and unseeing. Lady Bethoc was urging her to take a little water.

"You shall stay in our family bower," Jenny said, without stopping to consider what anyone else might think. This was unheard of. Travelers, even nobility, always bedded down on the floor of the great hall with the rest of the household.

Lady Bethoc took her daughter in her arms and came to her husband's side. "You must be Lady Jeanette," she said. "Brother Bertrand speaks well of you indeed, and I see he is not mistaken. You are generous and kind." She exchanged a look with her husband that made Jenny blush to the roots of her hair.

Jenny's father looked pleased. "You are welcome in our bower. Come to the hall for refreshment while the servants prepare beds." He glanced over his shoulder as they left. "Isabel, see to the servants." It was the first time anyone had spoken to her.

Jenny realized her father was acting out of embarrassment. Gossip of Isabel had probably reached the thane's ears at Rowanwald, or even before. But this abruptness seemed too cruel. She stayed behind while he left with the visitors.

"Isabel, I wish he would treat you more kindly."

Isabel gave her a sad smile. "The thane is a powerful man, and our father has his pride. In any case, you are the one who caught their fancy. I would not be surprised if they have an older son in need of a wife."

Jenny flushed. "Can I help with the servants?"

"No. Go be lady of the house for the thane and his wife. The child seems gravely ill, and you are the one they wish to see. And Jenny," Isabel said as she turned to go, "I hope the son has his father's graces."

In the great hall, panic swirled around the visitors as the servants struggled to produce hospitality worthy of their rank with no warning. But Thane Ethenan and Lady Bethoc saw none of this. They were focused on the child, who squirmed and cried in her mother's arms. Jenny did not know what to do. She jumped when Cospatric spoke at her ear.

"Lady Isabel told me I might be needed, my lady," he said. "Shall I play for the guests?"

Jenny sighed with relief. "Aye, Cospatric. Do you know any lullabies?"

The harper only nodded. He seated himself at a respectful distance and began to play. The sick child grew less fretful with the first gentle note and was sleeping peacefully with her thumb in her mouth by the time the tune ended. Cospatric immediately began another.

When the harp fell silent, Thane Ethenan leaned toward the harper and said something quietly in Gaelic that made Cospatric smile. Then he turned to Jenny's father. "That's a gold coin for your harper, Sir Philippe," he said. "My daughter has not slept so sound in many days."

"I would give anything to restore the bairn to health," Lady Bethoc said, a tear trickling down her cheek.

"Have you only this child?" Jenny's father asked.

The thane smiled. "No, we have a daughter, eleven

years this spring, and my son and heir, Neis, who will one day be Thane mac Ethenan."

"Ah, I have a son myself, with Sir Robert's household at Lilliesleaf. He lately earned his knight's spurs. Is your son yet a knight?"

Jenny was happy the hall was so dark. Her father's blunt questions made her blush. But the thane only smiled again. "Neis is still a wee lad at home, not yet seven."

Jenny could see this reply left her father puzzled. She realized that, like her, he assumed Brother Bertrand had recommended Jenny as a possible daughter-in-law. But the thane said nothing more about his family, and Galiene soon arrived to show the visitors their quarters.

"Let my old nurse watch over the child while you rest," Jenny whispered to Lady Bethoc as she rose with her sleeping daughter in her arms. "She has a gentle touch."

"Dear lass," Lady Bethoc replied, "you are a treasure, just as we were told." She squeezed Jenny's arm with her free hand. "I have a feeling you may be the answer to our prayers."

Jenny was left to wonder what she meant. Surely they could not want her as bride for a child of six. Such odd marriages were sometimes made, but only when kingdoms were at stake.

Lady Bethoc could not be persuaded to leave her child in Galiene's care until suppertime. Even then, she ate little, glancing anxiously toward the bower all the while as if her love gave her the power to see through walls. Brother Turgis arrived before the meal was over. Jenny had never been so pleased to see him. This was Isabel's doing, of course. She had remained out of sight, doing exactly what was needed all afternoon. With a pang, Jenny realized what a terrible hole Isabel's absence would leave in their lives.

Brother Turgis offered to pray over the sick child. When Lady Bethoc took him to the bower, Thane Ethenan lingered. "How long is the journey to Broomfield Abbey?" he asked.

"Broomfield is closer than Rowanwald," the vicomte replied. "It will take you half a day to walk there, but no more."

"Lady Bethoc wonders if Lady Jeanette would accompany us. We will remain at the abbey for a single night only. You would do us a great kindness. I am torn to see my wife like this. Lady Jeanette may ride, if she prefers."

Jenny did not wait for her father to speak. "I certainly will not ride while you go afoot, my lord, but I will gladly go with you."

The thane smiled as he rose. "I will tell my lady so. Thank you, child. You will help ease her burden, and we may know you a little better by the journey's end."

As soon as the thane left the hall, Jenny's father said, "I think they mean to make a match for you. The king holds court at Thane Ethenan's hall each year. They must know many who would make fine husbands."

"Aye, Papa, but I wish they would tell me." Jenny looked down to discover she was wringing her dress. She quickly stopped and smoothed the cloth.

"You must not ask. A girl seems unmaidenly if she is too eager to wed."

"I am not eager to wed. I only wish to know what manner of man they propose, whether he be kind or cruel."

"A match such as Thane Ethenan might suggest could make our fortune, child. The young king would know me by name."

Jenny knew her welfare was not uppermost in her father's mind. This could be his chance to regain everything lost with Isabel's downfall. But she could not help imagining the worst a husband might be.

Jenny slept poorly that night. The inner wall of the bower was little more than a partition, and Brother Turgis's nasal prayers droned on and on. Late in the night, she woke from a light doze to hear Lady Bethoc crying. Soon after, Jenny fell into an uneasy dream. She was back in the forest, but there was a great gathering of knights with horses and banners and tents. Jenny found herself dressed in a gown of scarlet silk, a finer dress than she had ever seen. "Come forward to meet the king," Lady Bethoc said, taking her hand. Jenny knelt before the throne. When she looked up, Tam Lin was smiling down at her with a crown on his head. He stepped down and put his arms around her, and Jenny was flooded with a strong feeling of belonging.

Jenny woke to the weak gray light of dawn with a headache. The dream had been so vivid, she wondered if it held some portent for the future, as Galiene said dreams often did. Could it be that Thane Ethenan and Lady Bethoc were looking for a wife for Tam Lin? No, that made no sense. A Scot from the north would not be acting for the Norman earl of Roxburg. She snuggled into the warm bed beside Isabel and was almost asleep again when Galiene shook her foot through the blankets. The old nurse had the bleary look of someone who had not slept all night. "Time to be up, my honey," she whispered. "The thane and his lady are anxious to be gone. Hawise packed some food to eat along the way."

When they left the bailey, a light drizzle was falling, but it burned off with the morning mist soon after they passed through the village of Langknowes. The day was going to be warm and clear. Under other circumstances, the trip would have brought Jenny joy. But the child seemed even worse now, and the journey took on an air of urgency. They traveled quickly, without speaking.

The great forest of the fairies rose untouched across the River Tweed, but the land on this side was tame. The plowed riggs were now softened with the green of new oats and barley. The road followed the Tweed, but not closely. Sometimes they lost sight of it for long stretches. Then, at the crest of a hill or a bend in the road, it would appear again, weaving through the countryside like a sinuous black serpent, the ripples on the surface flashing like scales. The sun was high overhead before the cultivated fields gave way to forest again. By then, it was so hot that Jenny was grateful for the shade. They did not stop to eat, but traveled on.

Early in the afternoon, Jenny heard a strange new noise from the litter, somewhere between coughing and choking. Lady Bethoc ordered the men to put the litter down and took the child in her arms. "I know that rattle well.

Death comes to take my child," she said.

Jenny heard sadness in her voice, but relief as well. Lady Bethoc rocked her child and crooned to her. A few moments later, the child's eyes lost their depth, and Jenny knew her soul was taken. After a long moment, Lady Bethoc laid the child on the litter with great tenderness, closing her eyes and covering the small body with a blanket. Then she drew herself up and folded her hands.

"The Lord has answered our prayers. Her suffering is ended."

The grieving mother walked on in silence, but Thane Ethenan spoke softly to Jenny. "Death is no stranger to my house," he said. "Three of our bairns died at birth, but this is the first time one has suffered so. Poor wee mite, she took her pain with the courage of a warrior."

Soon after, the trees parted and Broomfield Abbey could be seen in a sheltered river valley below. The clean, strong walls of a stone church were just beginning to emerge out of a confusing maze of wooden huts and outbuildings. It looked more like the encampment of an army than a holy place. Near the first buildings, a smiling man in the plain brown robes of a lay brother came to meet them, but the smile fell from his face when he saw the small bundle on the litter. "Follow me," he said. He led them to a wall of wooden palings as high and strong as those of a bailey. "No visitors pass beyond," he said. "I will fetch the guest master." And he disappeared behind the stout gate that cloistered the monks from the world.

When Brother Turgis had spoken of Broomfield, Jenny had pictured a quiet and secluded place, but the abbey grounds were thronged. Dozens of lay brothers buzzed about like brown worker bees. The unmistakable stench of a tannery drifted over from distant buildings. Masons came and went, distinguished by the funny hose that buttoned outside their jerkins and the fine white rock dust that covered them. Peddlers hawked their wares to the crowds. Every unused space was littered with pilgrims who had come for the well, some far advanced in their infirmities. Jenny looked away quickly to avoid the gaze of a leper with no nose.

The noise and smells mixed in the hot sun. It was too much after the child's death. Jenny felt faint. Just when she thought she might have to sit down, the lay brother returned with a white-robed monk, a tall, stooped man with thinning hair.

"Welcome, travelers," he said in heavily accented English. "I am Brother Marius, the guest master. You bring us the body of a child for burial?" His straightforward manner made lengthy explanations unnecessary. As they introduced themselves, Jenny could see how grateful the grieving parents were for his tact. Brother Marius made a gesture that encompassed the grounds around him. "The nature of our abbey has caused us to have a kirkyard before we have a church. The child's body will rest in consecrated ground. Follow me, my lady, and tell your men to bring the body."

Thane Ethenan opened his purse and pressed a generous heap of coins into Brother Marius's hands. "To pray for the soul of our Avece," he said.

The monk took the coins but said, "Please, hide your

purse well within your tunic, my lord. Some who came as pilgrims remain as beggars, and not all are honest. We will send for you when the body is ready to be committed to the ground. Brother Freskyn," he said to the brother who had brought them to the gate, "show the thane and the young lady to our hospital."

"In time, we will have a proper hospital for visitors, and an infirmary too," Brother Freskyn said. "But now, everything is makeshift. The abbey was founded eight years ago, but since the well gained its reputation, the place has grown beyond control." His pride was obvious.

"How long have pilgrims been coming to the well?" Thane Ethenan asked.

"Not yet a year. A lame shepherd boy dipped his foot in the water of the well one hot day last summer, near Lammastide, and his foot was miraculously restored. News spread. Now, we even see pilgrims from far away, like yourself." He hesitated. "Would you like to see the well?"

Jenny understood his hesitation. It could be bitter for the thane to see the well that might have saved his child. But he simply nodded, and Brother Freskyn led them to a small wooden hut. The ground outside was littered with the ill and infirm, some lying on pallets. The door was barred. When Brother Freskyn nodded to another lay brother to open it, the crowd surged forward. He spoke sharply to the pilgrims. "Leave off. The noble lord and lady wish to see the well. It will not be open again until dusk." He added more quietly, "The pilgrims would tear the place apart in their zeal if we did not control them."

Jenny was blinded by the sudden dimness, but as her

eyes adjusted she saw the walls were covered with fine wall hangings. "Scenes from the life of Saint Coninia," Brother Freskyn said, knowing their eyes would be drawn to the colors. "After the church is finished, a worthy shrine will be built here."

The well itself was a plain circle of stones, now covered with canes, crutches, and even some eye patches, attesting to cures. There were also dozens of little ex-votos, wax or wooden images of body parts or organs pilgrims left to indicate where their illnesses lay.

"It is wonderful that pilgrims can gain relief from their suffering here," Thane Ethenan said after a long silence.

"Aye, though some are cured and some are not. It must depend upon the depth of the sin that caused the illness, I think," Brother Freskyn said, leading them outside again. "Perhaps ills caused by the sins of ancestors are more readily cured than those due to the pilgrims' own misdeeds." Then he seemed to remember himself. "This is my own thought, of course. The brothers in monastic orders would know better."

The hospital where they would spend the night was just two long sheds, one for women, one for men. Jenny barely had time to glance around before a novice arrived to take them to the gates of the kirkyard, where Lady Bethoc and her servants waited with Brother Marius and a priest.

Wrapped in a linen winding sheet, the child's body looked more like a bundle than a mortal being. The thane lifted it from the litter. Jenny had never seen a weight that looked so hard to bear. Two lay brothers were still digging a hole in the soft red earth as the small procession approached. The child was laid in the ground with little ceremony, and damp earth showered onto the taut linen cloth, pattering like falling rain.

"Heaven will surely smile on one so innocent and young," the priest said as they left the kirkyard.

"She is safe in the hands of God now," Lady Bethoc said. "A mother could ask no more."

Even without the child's death, Jenny would have found the crush of folk, foul smells, and constant activity at Broomfield oppressive. She felt she had been away from home for months. So she was relieved when Lady Bethoc nudged her awake at first light the next morning. "We have food enough from yesterday," she whispered to Jenny. "Let us leave now."

The servants were sent ahead with the empty litter so Jenny and the child's parents could travel on without being reminded of the death. Tears trickled down Lady Bethoc's cheeks from time to time as they walked, but she said nothing of her grief.

With Broomfield behind them, the thane and his lady began to ask Jenny about herself. Did she hunt? Did she like to ride? Had she ever traveled abroad? Could she read Latin? This was more than idle curiosity.

When they stopped at noon, Thane Ethenan excused himself. Lady Bethoc wasted no time. "The ways of God are mysterious," she said. "We came seeking a cure, not a bride, though we knew both were needed. We found no cure, and yet, we may have found the bride."

Jenny wondered if Lady Bethoc could hear her heart

beating as she waited to learn more.

"My child, you may know the king has sworn he will never marry. This is not a wise choice for a king, but he will not be swayed. This year, his sister Adeline is to wed the count of Holland, so both sisters will be happily married. But there are two younger brothers, David, who is yet a lad, and William, who is nineteen, only a year younger than King Malcolm." She paused, searching for words, it seemed. "I must be frank. Earl William does not share his brother's saintly virtues. He is hot-blooded, in more ways than one, if you take my meaning."

Jenny wondered what Lady Bethoc meant. She was too embarrassed to say she did not understand, so she nodded, blushing in confusion.

"The king desires his brother to wed, but of course, the choice must be William's. King Malcolm has charged his most trusted nobles with the task of finding suitable lassies. The almoner at Rowanwald spoke well of you when we told him this, and he did not mislead us. You may not be the only one to be considered. What do you say to that?"

Jenny took a deep breath. "Lady Bethoc, the night you came to our hall, I dreamed I was presented to a king," Jenny said. She did not mention Tam Lin. That part of the dream was too confusing and too secret.

Lady Bethoc laughed. "If you were a Scot, I would say you have second sight."

Jenny squared her shoulders. "But I am a Scot. My mother's folk have always lived here."

"Forgive me, lass. We find it hard to think of anyone

who lives south of the Forth as a Scot. Even Edinburgh itself is not properly Scottish in the eyes of my folk." Jenny knew there was no point in arguing. Lady Bethoc continued. "William's mother is a Norman, like your father's people. He has taken the name of his mother's family, de Warenne, and he is very much the Norman knight, with virtues and sins that you may well understand."

Jenny thought of a husband with her father's flaws. She shook her head without realizing.

"Are you unwilling to tame our young lion, then?" Thane Ethenan said, returning.

Jenny smiled. "Not unwilling." She remembered something else from that dream, the way she had felt in Tam Lin's arms. She lifted her chin. "Earl William would have to please me as well."

Thane Ethenan clapped his hands. "Well spoken, lass. Our young earl needs a wife with mettle. But he is handsome enough to please the ladies, is he not, Bethoc?"

Bethoc nodded. "Rufus, they call him, for his copper-colored hair, and in our language he is called *garbh*, which means 'brawny.' But there is more to him than his looks, Jeanette. Our king has always been delicate in health. He may not, God forbid, live out his years. Earl William is his brother's heir. We are not only seeking a bride for a powerful earl. We may be looking for the queen of Scotland."

Chapter Eight
❧

W HEN JENNY WAVED GOOD-BYE to Thane Ethenan and Lady Bethoc at the gates of her father's bailey the following day, she felt she was parting with friends. Her father stood beside her, beaming. He had not stopped smiling since the thane told him the news on their return from Broomfield Abbey. Thane Ethenan's description of Earl William at supper that evening was highly flattering. "The flower of Scottish manhood," he had said, "skilled in battle, fair of form."

Jenny's father had wished to arrange a meeting at once, but Lady Bethoc calmed him. "In good time," she said, "The royal house is much occupied with the marriage of Lady Adeline."

When they parted, she had whispered in Jenny's ear, "I will arrange to be present when you meet the young earl. Our clerk will write Brother Bertrand when things are settled." Jenny was grateful to Lady Bethoc. For once in her life, she would have a proper chaperone.

"You shall marry one of the most powerful men in

Scotland," her father said as soon the bailey gates were closed. "What do you say to that, little one?"

Jenny smiled. "It would be lovely, Papa." The thought of being married to the king's own brother did appeal to her.

Vicomte Avenel began to travel to Rowanwald regularly to discuss Jenny's future with Brother Bertrand and the abbot. Anticipating the meeting, her father's generosity seemed limitless. The merchants of Rowanwald grew to know him well and began to come to Langknowes with their finest wares. Jenny was not entirely surprised when the bolt of scarlet silk arrived.

"Oh, Jenny, feel it," Isabel said, running her hands over the heavy fabric. There was no envy in her voice. She was taking Jenny's good fortune with her usual grace.

Galiene draped a length of the cloth over Jenny's shoulder. But the touch of the silk brought Jenny's dream back to her vividly, and with it, all the misgivings she was trying to hide from herself. "If Earl William is not to my liking, how will I be able to refuse?" The words rushed out without warning.

Isabel looked alarmed.

"There, there," Galiene said, putting her arm around Jenny. "Many a bride-to-be has cold feet before she meets her betrothed. It will all come to rights. Wait and see, my honey."

Everyone was speaking as if the betrothal were already accomplished. Jenny felt trapped. Would an earl's wife ever be able to ride in the woods alone? Would the queen of Scotland, if it came to that? Suddenly, the bower walls seemed to press in on her.

"I need time to think," she said, pushing the scarlet cloth away. "I will take La Rose for a ride." No one tried to stop her. That was something else she noticed. Everyone was treating her as if she were already above them.

At least La Rose was no longer trapped in the dark stable. The horses had been turned out to pasture in the warm weather. The mare cantered over when Jenny whistled for her, tossing her head in delight. Jenny led La Rose back to the stable, had her saddled, and was on her back before anyone had time to object.

The grain stood high in the fields now, tasseled oats and barley just beginning to turn gold. Summer was passing without her, it seemed. Would she always feel so trapped and confined if she were the wife of an earl? Jenny nudged La Rose with her heels, urging the mare to a gallop. Her hunger for the forest was suddenly overwhelming. How could she have lived without it all these weeks? The canopy of trees was full and green, sunlight falling in golden shafts through rare openings. Without stopping to think, she turned La Rose toward Carter Hall, where she had always imagined herself living with a husband.

The gardens at Carter Hall were overgrown now, but the hardiest flowers still bloomed in their seasons. Bluebells carpeted the ground in spring, and there were roses all summer. Jenny's favorite had pale pink buds that opened into cream-colored blossoms. Those roses would be blooming now. Perhaps she would feel better if she could gather some and breathe their scent. La Rose crossed the Tweed at a broad, shallow ford, and

Jenny guided her into the fairies' woods.

Soon after fording the river, Jenny rode into a small, steep-sided glen, where a fast little brook called Lin Burn tumbled down toward the river. Rocky, treed hills rose on either side, giving the place a sheltered, peaceful air. Jenny had played here with Eudo since she first took to the saddle. Over the years, the forest had reclaimed the land, so the ruined buildings now emerged suddenly from the new growth.

The first thing Jenny saw was a white horse tethered to the old stone well. Snowdrop, Jenny remembered he was called. Tam Lin's horse. Jenny kicked herself down off La Rose. How dare he treat this place as his own? Carter Hall belonged to her. All the mixed emotions she had been trying to contain boiled to the surface, and she burst into tears. She launched herself at the roses in a fury, ripping the flowers, letting the brambles scratch until she bled. If this place was not hers, it would be no one's.

"Is this how the wood sprite tends my garden?" a voice behind her said.

She turned, prepared to fight, but there was no anger in his voice or his eyes, only mild amusement that made her even more angry.

"My father gave this place to me. You have no right to be here. Go home." She knew she was shouting.

He raised an eyebrow in response. "Something has upset you, I think. Come and sit down."

His kindness defeated her. Suddenly, all her anger was gone. She felt heavy and drained. He took both her arms in his hands and gently led her to an old stone bench. "Stay here," he said, and he disappeared.

Jenny's face burned with shame. She could not believe she had behaved so badly. She vowed that when Tam Lin returned, she would act like someone worthy of a royal household.

He came back with a clean, wet cloth, sat beside her, pushed up the sleeve of her kirtle, and began to wipe the blood from one arm, patiently, gently. The cold water stung, but Jenny did not pull away. Instead, she tried to maintain her dignity.

"Other arm," he said after a few minutes. The cloth was streaked bright red. Jenny obeyed in what she hoped might seem a regal manner. When he finished, he rose again. "When I come back, perhaps we can talk."

He was gone so long, Jenny wondered if she should search for him. But then he returned, carrying a horn cup and another length of clean, wet linen. "Drink this," he said. The cool, sweet water soothed her throat. "Now, stay still." He took her chin in his hand and wiped her face. She was surprised to see how dirty it had been. "You go all blotchy when you cry, you know," he said. Then he sat back and studied her, as if inspecting his work. "You really are the strangest creature."

His words stung as much as the rose brambles. "A fine one to talk, you are," Jenny said. "Do you know what folk say of you?" She immediately regretted her words.

His face went stony. "That I do. I doubt you could add anything that would be new to me."

There was a long silence while Jenny stared at her lap. "Sorry," she said finally in a very small voice. "I seem to be a bit daft today." Then, after a pause, "Thank you for your kindness."

When she looked up again, he was smiling. "Everyone acts daft from time to time. Can you tell me what the trouble is?"

"I may have to marry a man I have never laid eyes on."

"Nothing strange about that for a lass of your rank, is there?"

"I suppose not, but, you see, he is a powerful noble. And I may not be the only lass."

"He would have to be a fool to pick another over you," he said.

Jenny looked at him in surprise. How could he tease her when she was so upset? "Stop your silly Norman flattery. What if I disappoint everyone? My father most of all."

He drew back as if she had slapped him. "It was not my intention to vex you. You are a bit like a thorn patch yourself, you know." If this honesty was an attempt to make her feel better, it failed. He must have noticed, because he hurried on. "Perhaps I can help. Would this powerful noble be anyone I know?"

Jenny suddenly remembered that Tam Lin was not just a strange man in the woods but the earl of Roxburg's grandson.

"Earl William de Warenne. The king's brother," she added, in case there was any doubt.

Tam Lin smiled. "In that case, he may act the fool and choose another. For he is one."

Jenny burst out laughing. "No one else speaks of him like that. 'The flower of Scottish manhood,' they say."

"Oh, aye. If knocking a knight off a horse with a stick

makes the man, Earl William is one. Jousting seems like such nonsense to me. Now Malcolm—King Malcolm, I should say—would make a good husband. Kindly, scholarly, the flower of chivalry. But he has sworn himself to celibacy. A notion more suited to a monk than a king, but it seems to run in the family. His father's family, not his mother's. Young William favors his mother's folk. A Norman through and through."

"So they say," Jenny replied.

"Well, now I understand your temper. The thought of marrying William would put any young woman out of sorts." Before Jenny could protest, he continued. "But why did you say this place is yours? I was born here, you know."

Jenny nodded. "Aye, but you must know my father owns the land now. He gave Carter Hall to me, to be my tocher."

"This is all you possess?"

Jenny nodded, and Tam Lin smiled. "Well, that brightens your lot considerably."

"Why do you say that?"

"Earl William has debts. He has no earldom to support himself, you see. He was given Northumberland when his father died, but the king of England demanded it with other lands soon after Malcolm was crowned. The border lands are always in dispute. Malcolm probably avoided war by giving in. That was prudent, but William is very bitter. Our young earl will be looking for a lass with a grand tocher. Mark my words."

Jenny looked down. "My father will be very disappointed," she said after a long silence.

When she looked up, Tam Lin searched her face. "And you? The thought of being queen-in-waiting is not entirely abhorrent to you, is it?" He seemed to look right into her soul.

She could not lie to him. "I find it hard to know what I feel. Maybe I would like to be the wife of an important noble. If I could meet Earl William, I would feel more certain. But the meeting is weeks and weeks away." A tear trickled down her cheek.

"Now, now. I just got you all tidy. Your tears will spoil my handiwork." He sighed. "The wife of a powerful man is more an ornament than anything else, lass, like the falcon on his wrist. You seem too spirited to content yourself with such a role."

Jenny knew *spirited* was too kind a word for the way she had behaved today, but she silently accepted his kindness. "That may be. I feel I am being pulled in all directions at once, until I have no notion what I want."

He put his arm around her. If any other man had done such a thing, Jenny would have pulled away, but the action was so natural, so gentle, she could not take offense. Instead, she leaned against his shoulder. As in the dream, she felt as if she belonged.

After a long moment she asked, "Why do you live out here alone?"

She felt his shoulder stiffen, as if the question shocked him. Then he relaxed and sighed. "I suppose I can tell you some of it. I find myself in a bit of trouble. I need to think. This place is so peaceful. It seems to help."

Jenny nodded against his shoulder. "This place is

peaceful. More than anywhere I know." She wondered what kind of trouble he could be in, then remembered what he had said about Earl William. "Are you in debt too?"

He laughed. "You could say so. There are many kinds of debt, after all."

Could he be talking about the fairies? Jenny found it impossible to ask. He seemed so levelheaded, and she had already made herself look silly enough today. She suddenly realized she was sitting alone in the woods with her head on a strange man's shoulder. This would not do. She made herself stand.

"I must go."

Now it was his turn to look down. "I understand," he said, but she thought she heard regret in his voice. It must be terribly lonely out here. She tried to think of something that would comfort him as he had comforted her.

"If I had money, Tam Lin, I would give it to you."

He smiled and stood beside her. "Thank you, Jeanette Avenel. But what I need would cost you more than gold. Go now, and try to decide where your heart lies."

Jenny smiled. "Thank you for your kindness. I feel better."

"Of course you do. I have a talent for healing. Whistle for that little mare of yours. I like to see how she comes to you."

So Jenny did. As she started down the path, she turned to wave, but Tam had already disappeared.

While she rode home, the scratches on her arms vanished like water splashed on stone in the sun. He must have a talent for healing indeed, she thought.

Chapter Nine

"SINGING LESSONS! BUT PAPA, you say yourself I have the voice of a crow."

Behind her father, Jenny saw Cospatric try to suppress a smile.

"If you think this is maidenly modesty, Cospatric, you will soon think again. Galiene says I need a bucket to carry a tune."

"A lady of your rank should know the old Norman songs," her father said.

"I know the songs by heart, Papa. To sing them, I would need a voice."

The vicomte's expression darkened. "It will please Earl William to hear them."

"How is it that you are so well versed in Earl William's desires," Jenny said, "without ever setting eyes on him?"

Isabel placed herself between them. "I will help Cospatric with her lessons, Papa. She may learn in spite of her voice."

"Very well. My huntsman has seen signs of a boar in the woods. We will be gone all day. You may work here in the hall."

When he left, Isabel said, "Jenny, you should not provoke our father so. He only wishes you to win Earl William's favor. Besides," she added, "this will give us a rest from sewing."

For the last week, Galiene had kept Jenny, Isabel, and a young servant girl named Hilde working almost constantly on the scarlet silk dress. "I will be glad to rest my eyes, but you know I have no ear for music. For all we know, Earl William may hate music."

"He would be a strange knight indeed if that were so," Cospatric said. "Even those who have no ear for music learn to pretend they do, and so may you, my lady." He turned to Isabel. "You know the Norman songs. How should we teach your sister?"

"The *rondes*, the line dances, always use two singers. One repeats each line after the other so that the rhythm is unbroken. We could start with those. If Jenny learns to sing for the dances, that might satisfy our father. Some of the tunes are monotonous. That will help."

Jenny made a face. "So I am to be schooled in monotony. No doubt that will win Earl William's heart." Isabel looked as though she might cry. "Oh, Isabel, forgive me," Jenny said at once. "I should be better." She knew most sisters in Isabel's place would not be so kind.

Isabel gave a tired smile. "I will be glad when word comes of your meeting with Earl William, Jenny. You and our father both grow more grumbly by the day."

"Perhaps you could sing a song for your sister, my lady," Cospatric said, "to show her what they should sound like."

So Isabel sang a *ronde*. "Now, we can try it together," she said when she had finished.

Even knowing her limitations, Jenny was amazed to discover her voice could stray so far from the tune in a single line of song. Isabel came in at the end of each line to guide her, but Jenny could tell from Cospatric's face that she was not doing well. After a few verses, he stopped them.

"Perhaps it would be best if you sang with your sister, my lady, in unison."

Jenny felt like crying, but she tried. Buoyed by Isabel's fine, clear voice, Jenny finished a whole song without going astray.

"Well done," Cospatric said when they finished.

"Now we should try it the proper way," Jenny said.

"Not yet. And no faces, please." The harper surprised Jenny with his sudden sternness. "We will do the songs until they are perfect, then do them again. This is how music is learned."

Behind him, Isabel nodded. She understood him completely.

So every afternoon for a few hours, Jenny did as they wished. After the first day, Jenny saw Alric, the lame boy, steal into the hall. He kept to the shadows but listened intently. Jenny wished she could share his interest.

"All music is about monotony," she said one day. "Even the most interesting songs must be sung to death."

Isabel smiled. "But you are learning. You can carry a tune now."

"Aye, but my voice will never be like yours, Isabel. Give me my reward," Jenny demanded.

Isabel smiled again as she sat on the bench beside Cospatric. She was teaching him the Norman songs too, the long, complex ballads that Jenny would never master. The tunes came easily to him, but the words were harder. Jenny and Isabel laughed at his awkward French, and Cospatric laughed with them, for he was not a proud man. Jenny marveled at his patience and skill. At the end of the lesson, Isabel always sang one song just for joy. Her beautiful voice reminded Jenny of the free flight of some graceful bird. Cospatric and Isabel sounded perfect together.

The music lessons provided only a brief release from sewing. The scarlet silk dress seemed to take forever. But it was almost finished when the messenger arrived from Rowanwald three weeks later. Jenny looked up as the boy entered the bower. Her eyes burned and she rubbed her fingertip with her thumb. She had already broken three bone needles.

"Well, boy," Galiene said, "eager as we are to hear your words, we must wait for Vicomte Avenel." Jenny's father arrived, red-faced and out of breath, before she finished speaking.

"Out with it, boy," he commanded, but the messenger's words were for Jenny.

"Brother Bertrand sends you greetings and news from the Lady Bethoc mac Askil, my lady," he began. "The blessings of our Lord be upon you. Lady Jeanette Avenel is asked to travel to the household of Comte Robert de Burneville at Lilliesleaf, one week hence, to meet Earl William de Warenne. Lady mac Askil is newly with child and cannot travel. She begs you forgive her."

The bower erupted into cheers and laughter, as if Jenny had won a prize. She tried to smile, but the news that Lady Bethoc would not be there alarmed her. Whenever Jenny pictured herself with Earl William, it was always under Lady Bethoc's watchful eye.

"Who will go with me to Lilliesleaf?" she asked when the commotion died down.

"Why, I will," her father replied. "It will be good to see my old friend Sir Robert. And I can make sure Eudo is known to Earl William as well. We can make plans this evening. Right now, the miller is here to discuss the state of the millstones. I must return to him." But then he paused. "Oh, Jeanette, Ranulf says there are two eyases in the aerie you found at the top of the knowe. One looks to be a falcon. You may have a peregrine for Earl William this fall."

"Back to work. We must finish the dress." Galiene patted Jenny's shoulder. "You know I cannot travel, hen, but Hilde's bones are young enough to make the trip. She will attend you."

Jenny tried to enjoy the excited chatter around her, but she longed to speak alone with Isabel. Galiene would keep them in the bower all day unless she acted.

"Galiene," she said, "the day is fair. Isabel and I will sit outside where the light is good and finish these sleeves."

Galiene looked as if she would protest, then stopped. "As you wish, my lady," she said, "but please keep the cloth out of the sun. It will fade."

Jenny was pleased to get her way, but dismayed as well. "*My lady!* When has Galiene called me anything but

Jenny?" she said as soon as they were out of earshot. "We can sew in the shade of the chapel. Oh, Isabel, I do wish you could come with me."

Isabel said nothing until they had settled themselves on the grass. Then, she kept her eyes on her work. "I would love to see Eudo, but everyone in Lilliesleaf must know of my disgrace, Jenny. I would only harm your chances with Earl William."

Jenny sighed. "Isabel, you bear all this with such good cheer. I cannot think I would do as well in your place."

Isabel smiled. "Your good fortune has given me time to think, at least."

"And are you ready to confess now?"

Tears came to Isabel's eyes. "Jenny, if I confess, I will be sent to Coldstream. The more Brother Turgis tells me of the life there, the more I fear it. The Cistercians feel that bathing delights the flesh too greatly. They wash only their hands and faces. What a harsh life it will be."

"There must be some way out of this."

Isabel shook her head. "Father will not keep me forever. A man would have to want me for his wife, just as I am. No one will." Her shoulders sagged. "Especially now that—" She stopped abruptly.

"Now that what? Please, let there be no more secrets between us, Isabel," Jenny coaxed.

"Father learned from Brother Bertrand that Earl William will not consider a lass without a fine tocher. He has taken most of my tocher for you."

So Tam Lin had spoken true. "But Isabel, will the

Church allow this?"

Isabel nodded. "The king is a great friend of the Church and he wishes Earl William to wed, so the abbot at Rowanwald sought permission for Father and it was granted. I only know because Brother Turgis told me, to help me appreciate the mercy of the Church. Taking me without a tocher is a great kindness, he says, though it will lower me within the priory."

Jenny knew that everyone's position within the Church was determined by rank and wealth, just as it was in the world at large. "Then you will be little more than a servant. Oh, Isabel, I have left you without hope."

"Jenny, hope left me the day I returned here alone. All the way back, I imagined what I did might be understood. But when I told my story to Father, I knew I would be disgraced forever in the eyes of men."

"No, Isabel, not in everyone's eyes. Do you know there are folk who think you a hero?"

"How can that be? How could you know such a thing?"

"Cospatric told me. He came here because he heard the stories. The folk even sing of you."

Jenny could see Isabel struggling to take this in. "But no one will forgive me for what I did. You see how Father treats me, how Brother Bertrand did."

"Aye, Isabel, among the nobles you are disgraced. But why? We are taught that a woman should always bow before a man of her rank or better, even when he means to harm her. But what of those who must always bow? They see you with different eyes. Isabel, to them you acted with honor. You should believe them."

Isabel took up her sewing and Jenny said nothing, giving her sister time to think.

After a long silence Isabel said, "The harper is a good man, Jenny, is he not?"

"Aye, Isabel, I think he is," Jenny said.

Isabel smiled a little. "I never knew he came here because of me. Do you suppose he cares for riches?"

"I think he cares for them not at all."

Nothing more was said, but that afternoon at her singing lesson, Jenny looked at Cospatric with new eyes. He was older than Isabel, but no one ever thought that a drawback in a man. He was fair enough to look upon, with kindly brown eyes and a face creased by laughter, his curly dark hair and beard just touched with gray. He was a patient and gentle teacher, serious about his music and skilled, but not vain. Under any other circumstances, his rank would have placed him beyond consideration as a match for Isabel. But now, Jenny wondered. It was next to impossible, but the things that had already happened to Isabel seemed even less likely.

And what of Cospatric himself? How did he feel about Isabel? As the singing lesson progressed, Jenny watched for some sign. He was kindly and polite as ever, but beyond that there was nothing. His feelings were hidden under a heavy cloak of proper deference. She sighed to herself. Cospatric would behave exactly the same whether he loved Isabel or loathed her. That was part of his role.

Combing her hair at bedtime that night, Jenny thought about her new tocher—a real tocher, for most of her father's wealth that was not bound up in land had gone to

Isabel's marriage fee over the years. If things had not changed so, nothing could have persuaded Jenny to accept what was rightfully Isabel's as the elder daughter. But if Jenny's thoughts about Cospatric were not too wild to be real, the loss of the tocher might help free Isabel from a life in the cloister. The Church would not fight to receive a lass without wealth.

And what would this tocher do for Jenny? Surely it would make her more appealing to Earl William. Aye, Jenny thought, but what lass wishes to be loved for her wealth? She wondered what Tam Lin would say if he knew she was now a lass with a tocher. *He* would not love me for my wealth. The thought surprised her so, she dropped her comb. I know nothing of him, really, she told herself, as she fumbled after it. She went over their last meeting in her mind. What was it he had said to her? "What I need would cost you more than gold." What could he mean by speaking in riddles like that? Maybe he was mad, just as everyone said. Jenny had not gone back to Carter Hall since that meeting. I will not, she told herself now. Not ever. This was only proper for a lass who might soon be betrothed.

As she climbed into bed beside Isabel, she was surprised to find that doing what was right could make her feel so miserable.

Chapter Ten

ᴈ

THE STRANGE, HALF-FLOATING motion of the horse litter made Jenny slightly sick. She felt suffocated and confined under the cloth tilt that covered her. She longed to put her head out to gulp some fresh air, to ask Hilde what she could see, but her father had commanded her to stay hidden as they approached Lilliesleaf.

She had been shocked when her father had forbidden her to take La Rose.

"You must appear gentle and ladylike when Earl William first sees you," he said.

"But Papa, only the old and infirm travel by horse litter—," she began, but her father cut her off.

"No argument." This was new. While most of the household had grown more deferential to Jenny over the past few weeks, her father had become arbitrary and commanding. But the thought of riding to Lilliesleaf in a horse litter was more than Jenny could bear.

"Why do you order me about, Papa?" she demanded. "You never treated me like this before."

The hardness in his eyes as he met her gaze was new

as well. "Do you think great men allow their wives to do as they please? If you would be the wife of an earl, you must learn to do as you are told. I have failed you sadly in this regard, and now we must correct that." It was useless to argue.

Jenny almost cried when she saw the awkward litter. The horses that carried it, one before and one behind, were almost hobbled by the cumbersome thing. The trip to Lilliesleaf would take forever.

New noises floated in through the heavy cover now—a blacksmith's hammer, the cries of children at play—muffled but distinct enough to recognize as the sounds of a town. Lilliesleaf. Jenny hoped Sir Robert's hall was not far, but the journey dragged on long after the sounds had faded. Finally, Jenny felt the litter stop. She waited. Nothing happened. Am I supposed to sit here forever? Jenny wondered. Apparently so. She longed to push the hated tilt aside. They must be waiting for Earl William, she thought. But when the cover lifted, her father was beside her.

"You may come down," he said. He sounded disheartened. "Earl William is busy. His steward says he will meet you at supper this evening."

Jenny only nodded, lifting her chin so that the servants would see no reaction. She did not expect Earl William to love her on sight, but she had not guessed he would ignore her. Her disappointment and humiliation quickly turned to anger. She had to force herself to smile as a lady in fine clothes came toward them.

"Sir Philippe, Lady Jeanette, I am sorry your host

cannot greet you. Sir Robert and Earl William have matters of grave importance to discuss. I am Lady Margaret de Burneville." She suddenly stopped and looked past Jenny. "But here is one who has awaited you most eagerly."

Jenny found herself in a warm hug. "Eudo!" she cried. Her brother lifted her off the ground. "Can it be that you are even taller than you were at Christmas?" she asked, laughing and pushing him back for a better look as he put her down. He was clearly Isabel's brother, dark like her with the same fine features, though unclouded by sadness.

"And you, little one, I think you are smaller than ever," he teased. Then he turned to hug his father.

"See what a jewel my sister is, Lady Margaret," Eudo said when the greetings were over. "Earl William is bound to fall in love with her, is he not?"

Jenny smiled and blushed.

Lady Margaret smiled, clearly fond of Eudo, but said nothing. Her silence disconcerted Jenny.

Sir Robert's holdings were far finer than Vicomte Avenel's. Away from the other buildings, a stone keep sat proud and alone. "Sir Robert must have borrowed stonemasons from the abbeys," the vicomte said.

"We would not think to slow the work at the abbeys. Sir Robert's masons came from England." Lady Margaret smiled, but her tone was disapproving.

"The keep is fine and strong, Father," Eudo said quickly. "If anyone dares to attack Sir Robert, it will be a wonderful base of defense. No enemy could burn us out in there."

Jenny studied the keep. The high stone tower had no

doors or windows on the ground level. It looked inde-structible. "But what use do you make of it in the mean-time?" she asked.

Eudo looked surprised. "Why, none. It is provisioned with food and water, so it can be manned at a moment's notice, but otherwise, it sits empty."

Jenny said nothing, but it seemed like a terrible waste of money and labor. She knew that if Earl William had greeted her, smiling, if Lady Margaret had not made her family look like backward country folk, she might have thought this stone tower a marvel. Coming here was a mis-take, she thought.

Eudo, at least, was delighted to see them. He talked excitedly while they ate a cold lunch under Lady Margaret's cool gaze. They were otherwise alone because they had arrived so late in the day. Jenny was sorry for that, because it was clear Lady Margaret had no intention of befriending her.

When they had finished their meal, Eudo offered to show them Sir Robert's lands. "If we can find a horse for my sister . . . ," he said, looking to Lady Margaret for per-mission.

"There are some ponies in the pasture that the chil-dren use," she said.

This was such a deliberate snub, Jenny could not bear it meekly. "I would think, Lady Margaret, that a household of this size might have a horse to suit a lady."

The shock on Lady Margaret's face told Jenny she had hit her target. She must have expected me to be as harm-less as a rabbit, Jenny thought. But the older woman quickly recovered herself. "Very well, Eudo. She may have Le Vent." And she left without another word.

"Jenny, it will do you no good to make an enemy of Lady Margaret," Eudo whispered as they approached the stables. "Where are your manners?" Between them, their father said nothing, but Jenny could feel the anger rising off him, as palpable as heat.

"Let us talk while we ride," she said. Like her father, she had no wish to be overheard by the servants.

Le Vent proved to be a large, unruly charger. Jenny barely reached his shoulder, and Eudo had to boost her onto his back. She felt ridiculous astride such a huge mount, but not afraid as she was sure Lady Margaret had intended.

His name, Le Vent, meant "the wind." "Very well," Jenny said. "We shall ride like the wind." She kicked her heels with more force than she would ever have used with La Rose. Le Vent surged into the stable yard, where Jenny almost ran down a group of men who seemed to have appeared out of nowhere. She saw them for only an instant, but it was easy to guess which was Earl William; the other men were all arranged around him. Jenny watched him lunge for safety as she flew past. He might have been handsome had he not been red-faced with fury. He shouted something Jenny could not hear over Le Vent's hoofbeats, but she could guess what he might have said. Fine, she thought. My first impression of you is not good either. She rode through the wide bailey gates at full gallop, leaving her father and Eudo to follow.

It was such a relief to be out in the open air that Jenny

made no effort to rein in Le Vent, who was well named indeed. Bondsmen working in the riggs stopped to watch them fly past. Jenny clung to Le Vent's neck, low in the saddle, savoring the wind that sent her hair flying like a banner behind her. The horse was too big for her, but he seemed to share her love of freedom, and she found him surprisingly easy to manage.

Not until Jenny finally slowed did she remember her father and Eudo. When she looked back, they were gaining ground. Even before she could see the look on her father's face, Jenny knew she was in trouble.

"What did you think you were doing?" her father demanded. "You might have killed Earl William. We had to stop to apologize."

"There was no one in the stable yard a few moments before," Jenny said. "How was I to know it would be full of men?" Then she stopped herself and took a deep breath. She was not among friends here. It would not do to fight with her father as well. "In truth, Papa, I urged the horse on more strongly than I intended. I will apologize myself when I meet Earl William." Her father seemed mollified. "But Eudo," Jenny said, turning to her brother, "why is Lady Margaret so cold to me?"

Her brother shrugged. "She has acted the same with every young woman who has come into the household in my time here," he said, and then he grinned. "You should be flattered, Jenny. They say, the prettier the girl, the colder Lady Margaret is. It seems she has judged you a beauty." He laughed, and so did their father.

Jenny tried to smile, but in her heart she longed for

Lady Bethoc. How different everything would be if she were here to smooth the way.

"Look around," Eudo said. "All this land belongs to Sir Robert." The landscape spread out around them like a blanket, the plowed riggs neatly stitched together by small burns that meandered through the land, cutting deep into the rich soil.

"Sir Robert is a wealthy man," Jenny said.

"Yes," her father replied. "We were young together, in Earl Henry's cavalry." He sighed. "Sir Robert and I were both without land then. Who would have thought life would treat us all so differently? Earl Henry is dead, Sir Robert is a powerful man, and my daughter may wed Earl Henry's son."

Jenny blushed. "That seems unlikely, Papa."

"You will have your chance with Earl William yet, Jenny," Eudo said. "Tonight, at the banquet, you will sit with him and share his dish. Lady Margaret should have told you."

Jenny's heart raced faster even than Le Vent could gallop. "But we never share dishes at home, Eudo. You know our ways are not so fine. How will I know what to do?"

"I had to learn when I came here, Jenny, and so shall you. The one of lesser rank helps his better. You shall break the bread, pass the cup, and choose and cut the finest meat, so Earl William may eat without effort."

Jenny groaned. "I wasted all this time on singing lessons when I should have been learning table manners. I am bound to make mistakes, Eudo."

"Never mind. Let me tell you what I can as we ride back. If you have a pretty gown and a maid who can dress your hair, Earl William may notice little of the food on his plate."

Suddenly, the scarlet silk gown seemed worth all the trouble it had taken to make.

By the time Jenny returned to Sir Robert's, her mind was focused on matters of great importance: hot water, the location of the walrus ivory combs that Isabel had lent her, whether the scarlet silk dress was badly wrinkled by the journey. She had asked Eudo every question she could think of, and still felt unprepared. As the afternoon progressed, she grew less and less like the wild-haired rider who had charged through the gates a few hours before and more, to her dismay, like Lady Margaret. She snapped at Hilde when the nervous young maid tried to comb the tangles collected on her ride with Le Vent.

"Galiene would not hurt me so," she cried, snatching the comb from the poor girl. Jenny knew she was behaving badly but could not bring herself to apologize. She almost cried when she discovered that one of the ties for the sleeves of her dress had gone astray in her luggage, and did burst into tears when it was found.

It seemed hours before the *assemblée* sounded for supper. Sir Robert himself greeted them as they entered the hall. "Welcome to my home, old friend," he said to Vicomte Avenel, grasping his arm with both hands. He talked with Jenny's father a few moments before taking Jenny's arm. "Your radiance puts the sun to shame, my dear," he murmured in her ear, leaning far too close.

Suddenly, Jenny could understand why Lady Margaret was so unkind.

Sir Robert showed her to her place himself. "And this," he said with a flourish, "is our king's own brother, Earl William de Warenne."

Earl William had been talking to a man down the table and turned only when Sir Robert said his name. He was indeed handsome, broad-beamed with red-gold hair, high color, and piercing blue eyes. He raised an eyebrow at Jenny. "Can this be the young Amazon who tried to run me down this afternoon? You are much changed."

Jenny would have apologized, but he turned back to his companion and continued his conversation. Sir Robert was gone, so Jenny sat without a word.

After the blessing was said, Jenny did everything according to Eudo's hasty instructions, catching the butler's eye when the cup was empty without drawing attention to herself, selecting and cutting the best joints of meat, and breaking Earl William's bread. The food was excellent, but she hardly tasted it. Earl William ate steadily, talking to the men around him about Scotland's trade with Holland and how it might be changed by the forthcoming marriage of his sister. He did not speak to Jenny again. No one seemed to think this unusual.

In spite of the earl's indifference, Jenny found herself at the center of attention. Everywhere she looked, someone was ready to give her a smile or a nod, except Lady Margaret, who looked as if she would gladly have poisoned Jenny's food if it were not being shared by the king's brother. Because she envies me, Jenny thought.

Even though her disappointment at Earl William's rudeness was sharp, the attention she received from others was flattering.

Earl William did not turn to her until the sweets were served. Then, suddenly, he said, "Where did you learn to ride like that?"

"At home," Jenny said. She wanted to make a good impression, but this was hardly brilliant conversation. "My brother Eudo taught me," she added.

"Ah, yes, Sir Eudo Avenel. Comte de Burneville speaks highly of him. Is your father a wealthy man?"

This was such a bald question, Jenny dropped her eyes. "My father is not as wealthy as Sir Robert," she said truthfully, but pride pushed her on. Her chin went up. "I have a fine tocher, though, my lord."

"Do you indeed? Well, that counts in your favor. And you are not ugly by any means."

Jenny was grateful to the man down the table who called to Earl William just then, for her face burned with shame. This was not courtship.

When the meal was over, she rose to escape to her father and Eudo. "Where are you going, *demoiselle?*" Earl William demanded.

"I thought you would prefer the company of your friends, my lord," Jenny said.

"But you are my companion for the evening." To Jenny's surprise, he grabbed her hand as everyone moved outside. Jenny glanced over her shoulder to her father, who gave her an encouraging smile. Jenny's spirits lifted a little. Perhaps this was how an earl courted after all.

An almost full moon had risen and the breeze was gentle. Sir Robert had ordered a fire built in the bailey yard. Someone tried to seat Earl William in a heavy chair that had been dragged outside for his benefit, but he waved it away. "Come, sit, so I might know you better," he said to Jenny. She sat on a bench beside him. He pressed his leg against her far too closely, but she knew she could not remove herself.

And still he ignored her, seeming to prefer the entertainment. Sir Robert's harper played, but not nearly so well as Cospatric, Jenny thought. Then he told a story of King Arthur. When he finished, Earl William turned to Jenny and said, "A fine story, was it not?" She could see he did not expect her to disagree, so she said nothing. Jenny found she cared very little for the stories of King Arthur and his court. The women were all either evil or passive. She preferred the old ballads, where women often won the day through bravery or virtue. She wondered what Earl William might make of her opinion. The thought of disagreeing with him made her smile to herself. Earl William caught her eye just then and thought she was smiling at him. He clapped his hand on her knee in a companionable way. Jenny would have moved if he had not taken his hand away at once.

"Let us have some dancing, the night is so fine," Sir Robert called.

"My daughter sings the old *rondes*," a voice called out. Jenny was mortified to hear her father. "Do you sing, my lady?" he addressed this question to Lady Margaret.

Until that moment, Jenny had supposed "looking down

116

your nose" was just a figure of speech, but Lady Margaret did indeed manage to look down her nose as she replied. "We keep a serving girl for that sort of thing," she said. "Send to the kitchens for Mary."

The girl arrived, wiping her hands on her skirt and ducking her head in shyness. She had flaming red hair and a lovely face, a pale oval in the moonlight. Jenny had no choice but to go to her. The party took up riddling games to amuse themselves while the music was sorted out.

Jenny quickly discovered that Mary had been well schooled in the old dances. She knew every song Jenny had learned, and more. "Can you lead?" Jenny asked.

"Lead you, my lady?" The girl looked appalled.

"Aye, Mary, if you would. My sister always leads at home, and she is not here tonight."

The girl must have heard the plea in Jenny's voice, because she did not argue.

When the riddling was over, everyone called for dancing again. Lady Margaret quickly arranged them in a huge circle around the fire. "Start with something simple," Jenny whispered to the girl.

Mary began a simple *ronde*. Her French was so awkward, Jenny was fairly sure the girl had no idea what she was singing. But that hardly mattered, because her voice was beautiful. It soared into the gentle night air like the song of a lark, leaving Jenny to hop behind like a sparrow with a broken wing. The simple round dance that went with the song created a rhythmic shuffling—one-two-three, *one*, one-two-three, *one*—that helped hide Jenny's voice, but she knew she was outclassed. Earl William's eyes shone, but he looked at the servant girl, not at Jenny.

The dancing went on and on until Jenny finally begged to be relieved. Another singer took her place, but Mary kept singing as if she were born to. Jenny joined the line beside Eudo. Earl William did not claim her again. His admiration for the serving girl was so obvious that Jenny saw other men exchanging winks.

The eastern sky was bright before the dancing ended and Jenny was finally able to bed down among the other visitors in the great hall. She fell asleep almost before she closed her eyes, too exhausted to feel the disappointment she knew was waiting for her.

Sunlight streamed into the hall as the servants made a show of setting up the tables, so that the visitors would know it was time to get up. Jenny blinked in the bright light on the way to the chapel to hear mass with everyone else. The place of honor set aside there for Earl William was empty. He did not appear at breakfast, either.

As soon as Jenny could, she spoke to her father alone. "Papa, we should leave this place."

He did not argue. "I will tell my men to make ready and bid Sir Robert good-bye. Meet me in the stable yard."

Soon after, Jenny hugged Eudo good-bye. As she did, she realized she had been too taken with her own concerns to find time to talk to him about Isabel. Looking past her brother's shoulder, she saw the servant girl, Mary, in the distance by the kitchen shed. She was slumped against a wall, looking exhausted. When she saw Jenny, she quickly looked away. She fears she has shown me for the bad singer that I am, poor girl, Jenny thought. She cannot help my voice. But she liked Mary even better for her modesty. Life must be hard for such a pretty girl in Lady Margaret's household. Well, I am not Lady Margaret and I never will be, Jenny thought. She pulled a long white ribbon from her hair and called to one of her father's men.

"Give this ribbon to the servant girl with red hair who stands by the kitchen door," she said, "with my blessings for her lovely voice."

The girl took the ribbon and looked at Jenny, her face white and stricken. Then she turned and fled. Jenny was puzzled. She must be overwrought from so much work with so little sleep, Jenny thought. I feel much the same myself.

Jenny was happy to climb into the hated horse litter. Here, finally, she could be alone with her disappointment. Lady Bethoc and Brother Bertrand had been mistaken to think that Earl William would take a wife. Still, all the attention had pleased her—even to feel Lady Margaret's jealousy and know it could not harm her while she sat in Earl William's shadow. With regret, Jenny realized she might have enjoyed being the wife of the king's brother.

Before they could move, Jenny heard a commotion. The tilt was flung aside, and there stood Earl William, red-faced and angry. "Do you mean to go without bidding me adieu, Lady Jeanette?" he demanded. "What manner of trick is this?"

Jenny was too shocked to reply. After a moment, she managed to close her mouth, but words had somehow deserted her. Her silence seemed to calm Earl William.

"Bide a bit," he said more kindly. "I would speak with your father." And he drew the vicomte aside.

When they returned, Jenny's father was smiling broadly. Earl William bowed to Jenny, who had recovered enough to remember it was not polite to remain seated while he stood. She climbed down from the litter. He was not as tall as he had seemed the night before.

"Give me your hand, Lady Jeanette," he commanded. Jenny could not have disobeyed if she had wanted to. The full force of his attention was totally compelling. "Let us part as friends," he said, and he kissed her hand.

Jenny climbed back into the litter in a daze.

Chapter Eleven

⁘

JENNY LONGED TO KNOW what Earl William had said to her father, but her pride would not let her ask while the servants could hear, and servants were always near on the journey home. She amused herself on the long ride by reliving the scene in the stable yard over and over, with different witnesses. She tried to envision the look Lady Margaret might have worn had she seen Earl William kiss Jenny's hand. She did not allow herself to think about the night before.

Her father smiled always when he saw her. On the second evening, as they stopped to demand hospitality at a small fermtoun, he dropped a hint. "Next time you go to Earl William, he says you should ride." Jenny longed to know more, but she wanted to prove she could behave like a lady.

That night, she was almost too excited to sleep. If I were married to Earl William, she thought, perhaps I could keep Isabel with me, as a companion. And she fell asleep dreaming she would be her sister's salvation.

When they arrived in Langknowes, Jenny saw everything with new eyes. The town was just a slapdash collection of wattle huts. Even her father's hall seemed small and poor.

Isabel was waiting for them by the stable. "What word do you bring me from Eudo?" she asked.

"Why, he sends you love, of course," Jenny said, kissing her sister to avoid meeting her eyes. She did not want Isabel to know that she had not even thought to ask Eudo for a message for their sister.

But it was not in Isabel's nature to focus on herself. "And Jenny, what of you? How did you fare with Earl William?"

"Our father knows better than I," Jenny said, glancing over her shoulder. "But I suppose we must wait until he has spoken with the men to hear what he has to say." Walking to the bower, Jenny told Isabel, "I sat by Earl William's side at the banquet. I ate from his dish, and everyone smiled at me." Jenny knew she was changing the story in the telling, making things sound better than they had been. She found she could not tell Isabel how Earl William had ignored her, or how the servant girl had outshone her at the dance. She had already learned never to think about the way Earl William had looked at Mary. If I am to be a great lady, she told herself, such thoughts will be beneath me.

When their father finally joined them, Jenny grabbed his hand. "Now tell me, Papa, for I have been good and waited until we could speak alone."

Her father smiled. "You were a lady in all things, Jeanette, once we got you off that horse. Earl William said he likes a lass with spirit. He bids you come see him next week at Roxburg, where he will ride in a tournament."

"Next week! Why so soon?"

"Afterward, he says, he will be away to his sister's wedding."

Jenny stamped her foot. "But I have no time to prepare. I should at least have another new dress." Too late, she realized she had yelled the words. Half the household must have heard her. Isabel and her father stared. Jenny looked at the floor, but did not apologize. Someone of my standing should get out of the habit of offering apologies, she told herself. "Did he say nothing of marriage, Papa?" She could not keep the disappointment from her voice.

Her father seemed willing to forgive her. He shook his head. "No, but we may hope."

Jenny wrung her hands. "How can I prepare myself? Do you know anything about the tournaments?"

Her father shook his head. "They have changed greatly since I was young. King Malcolm and his brother learned the new ways in France when they rode with the king of England to Toulouse to defend Queen Eleanor's claim to lands there."

Jenny sighed. "If only Eudo were here to teach me what I should know." Her father and Isabel suddenly seemed useless. And she could not bring herself to be schooled by her father's knights.

"Come now, Jenny, smile," Isabel said. "You will travel all the way to Roxburg."

"Yes," her father said, "and you may ride."

Jenny lifted her chin. "Aye, and Earl William shall wait for me."

But in bed that night, Jenny fretted. How would she know how to behave at Roxburg? She was drifting off to sleep when her eyes suddenly opened wide. Of course! Tam Lin knew about tournaments, and Roxburg as well. The promise she had made to herself never to visit Carter Hall again seemed silly now. Tam Lin could be useful to her. But she would need an excuse to visit the forest. She remembered what her father had said about the young falcons. Tomorrow she would see Ranulf in the mews.

Jenny did not manage to escape from Galiene and Isabel until the afternoon. The mews was dark, to keep the hawks calm, but clean and airy. Unlike the sheds that housed the other animals, it was not smelly. Her father's hunting hawks rustled quietly on their perches at the back of the mews.

Ranulf sat on a bench in a shaft of sunlight, tying small bells onto strips of leather. When he saw her, his disfigured face creased into a smile. "I will need new bells and a hood and leather to make new jesses for that young falcon, my lady."

Jenny smiled. "Could you find what you need in Roxburg?"

"Yes, certainly. The royal burghs have all manner of goods."

"We are going there next week, my father and I. Ask him if you may come too. Now, I would like to see the aerie. Take me there, please."

"Yes, indeed, if you could just wait until—"

"No, now," Jenny said. She tried to make her voice sound commanding. If she waited, someone might see her and stop them.

"Yes, my lady, if you wish." Ranulf was not pleased.

Jenny felt badly for treating him so, but quickly pushed her feelings aside. My father is entirely too soft with his servants, she thought, which was fine, perhaps, for a man of his rank, but not for her.

Ranulf said nothing while the horses were saddled, but Jenny pretended not to care. If sullen silence went with obeying commands, she would have to get used to that as well. She did not ride La Rose as hard as she would have before her trip to Lilliesleaf. Instead, she tried to imagine herself riding by Earl William's side. The little mare would have preferred a gallop and was restive, but Jenny ignored her. Surely the wishes of a servant or a horse should mean nothing to me, she told herself.

"How do you view the aerie without disturbing the birds?" Jenny asked when they reached the foot of the knowe.

"I found a ridge below the aerie at a distance from it. It gives a good view, but they seem to know I cannot harm them from there," he said as he tethered his horse. "We will have to be quiet, of course, my lady, or they might take fright." He turned his back and started up the hill without waiting. "The birds recognize no rank."

Jenny could only dismount and follow as quickly as she could. He had said nothing that might allow her to accuse him of insolence, yet she felt the rebuke in his words. As the climb grew steeper, Ranulf did not slacken his pace for her. Jenny bit her lip, remembering how friendly he had been in the spring.

She crested a ridge to find Ranulf waiting at the edge of a sudden precipice. He motioned for her to crouch near him, their backs to a ridge of stone. Without speaking, he pointed across the chasm and up to a crag. There, at the base of a stunted rowan, was the aerie. Jenny would not have found it without his direction.

The two birds on the ledge beneath the rowan looked so big that Jenny wondered if the eyases had already fledged. But then a falcon arrived with a limp swallow in its talons, half the feathers already plucked from the body. The two birds in the aerie began bobbing and screeching, jostling each other in their efforts to attract the bits of meat their mother was stripping from the swallow's body. Although they were already the size of fully grown birds, these were indeed the eyases. The falcon looked across the chasm directly at Jenny and Ranulf just once, as if to show she knew she was being watched. She did nothing else to acknowledge their presence, but did not leave the aerie when her young finished their meal.

Ranulf finally motioned Jenny to follow him down the knowe. She left the birds reluctantly. The path was steep and difficult, and Jenny did not try to speak at first.

"They are wonderful," she finally said when they were near the horses. "I could have stayed there all day."

Her enthusiasm seemed to thaw him a little. He grinned. "I come here whenever I can. They scarcely take note of me now, as you saw. One of those eyases is a falcon, I am certain."

"When will you take her?"

"Not until after they fledge. We call them branchers then because of the way they fly from branch to branch in the forest, still uncertain of their wings. The dame and sire fly about with prey in their talons, teaching the branchers to hunt. That is the time to take them, when they have learned much, but are not yet ready to hunt alone. Those eyases will take to the sky any day now, but it will be weeks before the young falcon is ready for the mews."

"You must train her well, Ranulf. She may fly with the king of Scotland himself one day," Jenny said.

As they reached the horses, Jenny remembered the real reason she had come to the forest. "You have been good to bring me here. Now, I would like some time in the forest alone." She turned her face to La Rose as she spoke so that it would not betray her. Once, she had promised him she would not go to Carter Hall.

"My lady, your father would not wish you alone in the woods, I am sure."

She turned to face him. "My father is not here now. You must do as I wish."

"But he is my master. If I were to cross him—"

"You have already crossed him, Ranulf. Remember? The last time we rode out this way. It would not please him to know that."

The falconer looked shocked but simply said, "As you wish, my lady." He left without saying good-bye.

Jenny felt slightly sick. She had never threatened to tell her father anything about a servant's behavior before. And this was doubly bad, because Ranulf had been reluctant to let her go off alone in the spring. She waited before mounting La Rose so that she wouldn't have to face Ranulf again. She sighed as she tugged her mare's reins. Would it be this way with all servants if she rose to a higher station? Sullen silences and resentment on their part, bullying and threats on hers? She had a sudden vision of how lonely such a life might be, ignored by her husband and disliked by the servants who filled her household.

It may not be like that at all, she told herself, wiping away a tear. The excitement of the past few days has left me overwrought. I should think about Roxburg instead. Which dress should I take? The red wool, which was once her best dress, seemed a poor choice now. I shall have to wear the red silk again, she thought, and Earl William will see how little I possess.

The forest was now at the height of its midsummer glory, but Jenny hardly noticed as she passed through. Just before the ford in the river, the sound of voices ahead abruptly caught her attention. She guided La Rose off the path, careful not to trample the undergrowth as they went. Behind the trunk of a great oak she dismounted, holding La Rose's reins. Soon after, she heard men on the path. When they were past, she peeked around the trunk.

Jenny counted six. They were not her father's men. They were clothed like bondsmen, but everything they wore was unwashed and unmended, the clothing of men who lived without women to tend to them. They were freebooters. Even though she was safely hidden, Jenny's heart pounded. Until this moment, they had hardly seemed real to her. When she was sure they were gone, she led La Rose, keeping off the path, afraid to ride in case the thumping of her horse's hooves should reach the freebooters' ears. She did not begin to breathe again, it seemed, until she was safely across the river.

What would they have done if they had found her alone on the path? Her rank would have given her some protection, for they would forfeit their lives if they harmed her, but they might have been tempted to hold her for ransom. With La Rose, she might have been able to outpace them, but she was glad she had not had to try. I should not come this way again, she thought.

Chapter Twelve

CARTER HALL LOOKED ABANDONED. Jenny had been
sure Tam Lin would be there. She sat on the edge of
the old stone bench, La Rose's reins in her hand. The freebooters had unsettled her so, she was afraid to let go. The
thought that she might have made this trip for nothing
was more than she could bear.

"We will have to wait a while, La Rose, to let those
men go away, for I would not meet them for the world."
She sighed. "I wish we were safe at home. I should never
have come here." She pulled a white rose from a bush
beside her and began to pluck at the petals.

"There you are, ruining my roses again," said a voice
close behind her.

In the half second before she could understand what
she had heard, she was on her feet and facing the sound,
terror driving every reasonable thought from her head.
Then she saw Tam Lin. Of course. She felt shaken and
ridiculous all at once.

"Is something wrong?" he said.

She nodded, still trying to catch her breath from the

scare he had given her. "Freebooters. I saw them just across the river."

He came over and put his hand on her shoulder. "Did they see you?"

His concern comforted her. Her fear was not silly. She shook her head and explained how she had heard them at the ford and hidden.

"I would not like for them to meet you," he said when she had finished.

She looked at him, puzzled. "Do you know them?"

He blushed. "Aye. They bring me things I need from time to time. In fact, they were coming from here when you saw them."

"But they are outlaws. How can you trade with them?"

He shrugged. "Sometimes, you pick the lesser of two evils."

"What does that mean? Buying stolen goods is better than stealing yourself?"

He looked surprised, but nodded. "You could think of it that way. Now, tell me, have you met young William yet?"

Jenny sat down again with a sigh. "Aye, and he wants to see me again. We are to go to see him ride in a tournament next week."

"Swept you off your feet, did he?"

Jenny looked up at him. He was not teasing, but the contrast between being swept off her feet and what had happened was so absurd, she burst out laughing. Her relief at escaping the freebooters and her pleasure at finding Tam again bubbled up, and she laughed until she had to hold her sides from the pain.

"I must seem mad," she gasped at last.

"I prefer this to crying. Can you tell me the joke?"

She found she could. William's indifference, which seemed such a shameful secret at home, was suddenly something she could laugh at.

"And after we sang," she finished, "his eyes were only for the servant girl. Her voice was much better than mine, and she was pretty, but I felt shamed. He could have been nicer to me."

"And should have," Tam Lin said, sitting beside her. "You deserve better, lass. How is it you agreed to meet him again?"

"I wanted to slip away unnoticed, but Earl William heard we were leaving. He came to the stable yard to find me and told my father to bring me to see him again. It was flattering, but I did find it odd." She had not admitted this, even to herself, until that moment.

Tam Lin frowned. "This is no surprise to me. William only wants a thing he cannot have. He has always been that way. I had a dog once, a bonny terrier who was a good ratter. Hardly a dog for a nobleman, but she followed me everywhere and I loved her. William was ten and I was twelve. I remember because it was the year his father died. He whined for that dog. Everyone prevailed upon me to give him what he wanted—my grandfather, even old King David himself. So finally, I did. Soon after, I went off hunting with the men. While I was gone, William tied the little dog to a tether and baited her with a sharp stick. By the time I came home, she was dead."

"But boys are often cruel to animals," Jenny said.

Tam Lin nodded. "Aye, they are. But you see, William only wanted the terrier when he could not have her. The devotion that made me love her so was only tiresome to him."

"But he was just a child. He is now a man of nineteen. Surely he has changed." Jenny found herself wanting to believe this very badly.

Tam Lin opened his mouth to say something, then stopped himself. "That may be," he said, without conviction. "Now, tell me what brought you here." He was deliberately changing the subject, and Jenny was glad. The story she had just heard was something she did not want to be forced to think about too carefully, like so many other things about Earl William.

"I hoped you might tell me about the tournaments, for I have never seen one. I do not wish to seem unschooled when I go to Roxburg."

"Roxburg? The tourney is there?" He looked alarmed. "Will you tell anyone you have spoken with me?"

"How could I? I steal off to visit you without anyone's knowledge. My father would be terribly angry if he knew."

"But my grandsire may ask. Even if he seems sad and you are tempted, will you promise not to tell?"

"I swear," she said. Why was it so important? If the old man was worried sick about him, why should he hide himself away like this? She found she was afraid to ask, because, suddenly, it seemed possible that his answer might make no sense at all.

But her promise seemed to return him to himself.

133

"Well, what shall I tell you? The war games played at a tourney are called *hastiludes*. Most tournaments have two parts, the joust and the melee. The joust is the new part, the sort of thing Malcolm and William brought back from France. The knights try to knock one another off their horses with long sticks called lances. Daft, really. If a knight is unhorsed, he forfeits everything to his opponent—weapons and horse and all. It can easily beggar a man. In the melee, everyone is divided into two companies, like mock armies, and they fight in a sort of free-for-all. A captured knight is held for ransom. If he has not the means with him to buy his freedom, he is released on his word to fetch the fee. You know the French word *parole*? Of course you do. Well, he is released on his word, on parole.

"My grandsire's hall, Marchmont, stands on a hill with the Teviot hard by on one side and the Tweed just a field away on the other." He fell deeper into his memories until his eyes seemed to be looking back into the past. "They will surely choose the fine flat rigg that lies between Marchmont and the Tweed to hold the tourney.

"When enemies meet, the knights fight *à outrance*, with real weapons, dealing real blows." He shook his head. "But King Malcolm would not allow such hard play among friends. So, they will fight *à plaisance*, with blunted weapons, and due care for life and limb, though injury is still possible. The tourney itself will hold little interest for you, but Roxburg is a fine place." He turned to her with shining eyes. "Have you ever been there?" She shook her head. "It sits just below Marchmont, where the Tweed and the Teviot finally meet. Kelso Abbey is just a stone's throw beyond. King David made it a king's burgh, you know. My grandsire gave him the whole earldom, so they could show what a royal town might be. All the free men who live there, the burgesses, are king's men. The riches made in the town go straight into the king's coffers."

Jenny knew land was everything to a nobleman. "It must have cost your grandsire dearly to do such a thing."

Tam shrugged. "He and King David were boyhood friends in England. The king gave him the land to begin with. Marchmont is still his home, and he houses the king's court when they travel to Roxburg, but he no longer foots the bill. I think he came out on the better side of the bargain." It occurred to Jenny that the earl had also given Tam Lin's birthright away, but he harbored no bitterness. Jenny remembered what Tam had said about William having no earldom to support himself.

"It was more than a bargain to both of them, you see," he continued. "They believed Scotland could only increase her prosperity through trade. Foreigners trade only in the royal burghs. Roxburg was the very first king's burgh, with Berwick. I remember how they used to stay up late, my grandsire and King David, talking about the good that could be gained. I would fall asleep at Granda's side, and he would carry me off to bed." He sighed.

"But I thought . . . ," Jenny began. As soon as she spoke, she realized she should not have.

He smiled. "What did you think?"

She knew she was blushing. "I thought, at least, I heard, that . . . that you had lost your memory. In a hunting accident." Then she remembered his story about

William and the dog and blushed more deeply. Of course he remembered his past. Galiene's gossip must be wrong.

But he surprised her. "I did forget," he said, "for a long while. Things came back to me slowly. I remember most of my past now, but there are still holes." He sat back and studied her until she wished she could vanish. "You seem well versed in the story of my life, lass."

She had not known it was possible to blush even more deeply, but she did. "The folk about here care for you. You must know that. They remember your father and all." She hoped this sounded like a reasonable explanation. That she might care for him herself was not a thought she wished to explore. Perhaps it was time to leave. She rose. "Thank you. I feel prepared for Roxburg now." She sighed. "If only I had a new dress."

"You need a dress?"

"Aye, but they take weeks to sew, and the tournament is only a few days away."

"Just wait here." And he disappeared before she could stop him.

Why would Tam have a dress? Finery was valuable and rare. Good clothing could be traded for things he would need—food, for example. He might have brought some from Roxburg with him for that purpose. The ruffians she had seen on the path today would not be able to trade fine stuff locally without arousing suspicion, but they might know a peddler who would take such things for a fraction of their worth without questions.

Of course, she could never accept a gift of fine clothes from a man she was not to marry, she told herself. But she could hardly bear the thought of going to Roxburg without a new dress. I must see what he has, she thought. I can always return it to him.

He was gone a long time. She looked around on tiptoe, but the land was now so overgrown that she could see very little of Carter Hall itself. She forced herself to stop looking. Where he lives is of little interest to me. Where he lives, what he feels, what he will make of his life, all these things matter to me not at all, she told herself. She was just beginning to grow angry with herself for refusing to accept this when he finally returned.

"Here," he said, holding a dress up. "This should fit."

Jenny gasped. It was as if all the colors of the forest at midsummer had somehow been captured in the cloth. The green, shimmering as if alive, was shot through with gold and hints of warm brown. She ran her fingertips over it, but gently, as if she feared her touch might somehow ruin it. "By heaven," she said, "I never hoped to see a thing as fine as this."

Her delight was echoed in Tam's laughter. "Take it," he urged. "It will not fall to pieces in your hands." The cloth flowed when it moved, lighter than silk. Jenny held the dress against her and looked up for his approval. "You should always wear green," he said. "It makes you look like the wood sprite you are. Every young nobleman who sees you in this dress will fall in love with you."

The smile fell from Jenny's face. "But everyone will wonder where it came from."

"Who goes to Roxburg with you?"

"Only my father and his men, and a young maid to

tend to me. My nurse is too old to travel, and my sister is . . ." Embarrassment stopped her.

"I know about your sister's troubles," he said gently. "We need not speak of that. What if you hide the dress until you are in Roxburg? Men know very little of women's clothing. If your father takes note, tell him you bought it from a peddler. Would that not do?"

Jenny looked down at the dress. She could not bear to leave without it. "It would be a risk," she said slowly. Then, in a rush, "But I am willing to try. Oh, thank you. No one has ever given me anything so fine." She suddenly felt shy. "I will return it, of course."

He waved this away. "No need for that. I mean for you to have it."

Jenny suddenly had a terrible thought. What if the dress had belonged to his mother? "Will anyone in Roxburg know this dress? Your grandsire, perhaps? Surely anyone who saw it before would remember."

"That dress was never seen in Roxburg. I promise you." Something in his tone made it impossible for Jenny to ask where the dress did come from.

"Can I give you nothing in exchange?" She spoke innocently, but immediately blushed to think what her words might mean to a young man.

He did not misunderstand her. "I still love Roxburg, and my grandsire too, though I cannot be there. When you return, come and tell me about it. That is all I ask."

"Aye, certainly, I will." It seemed a small price for such a dress.

"Good," he said, warming to the thought. "Come by

the full of the moon and dine with me, and tell me everything." Jenny nodded numbly. "Is something wrong?" he asked.

Jenny hardly knew where to begin. Even if she could slip away unnoticed at night, she was still shaken by her near encounter with the freebooters. "Those men . . . ," she began.

"Will not harm you. I will see to that, lass. I promise." He looked at the sky. "They will wonder where you are at home. You must go." And he kissed her on the forehead.

A brother's kiss, she told herself as she rode home. He is not like anyone I have ever known. Gentle and kind and thoughtful. When I speak to him, all my troubles seem to vanish. A brother's kiss, she told herself again, but it felt like something very different.

Chapter Thirteen

BEFORE LEAVING LANGKNOWES, Jenny had been eager to see Marchmont. But when they finally came out of the forest, the hill where it sat was shrouded in a curtain of rain and river mist.

La Rose kept her dripping head down, following Jenny's father on Bravura of her own accord. Jenny had done nothing to guide her these last few hours. She had given up after they came to the rain-swollen burn that turned the forest road into a riverbed. When La Rose had stumbled in the mud, the saddle girths shifted and Jenny had slid into the dirty water. Ranulf had quickly righted the saddle, and Hilde had done her best to fix Jenny's clothes, but the care that Galiene and Isabel had put into her grooming was wasted. Jenny was soaked to the bone. She smelled of earth and wet wool and leather. But she smiled to herself in spite of everything, for the green-and-gold dress was safely stowed in the bottom of a stout wooden trunk. No matter if I look like a drowned rat when we arrive, she thought, as long as that dress is safe and dry.

Now, Jenny could see that Tam had guessed rightly.

Tents ringed a large open rigg by the Tweed. This must be the lists where the tournament would take place, though it was abandoned in the rain. Jenny's attention came back to La Rose abruptly as the little horse turned off the road. But La Rose was still following Bravura.

"This is the back path to Marchmont," her father said. "On a fine day, we might have gone ahead to Roxburg and followed the road back along the Teviot to make a grand entrance. But the riverbanks are soft and the Teviot may be swollen with the rain. This path is humble, but it will spare you another ducking."

Jenny was touched by this unaccustomed thoughtfulness. "It will please me to wash and change before anyone sees me, Papa."

"Your temper is much improved, little one. You seem more like yourself than you did when we returned from Lilliesleaf."

Jenny was glad La Rose was behind Bravura, so her father could not see her face. What he said was certainly true, but she did not want to consider why. It was only the dress, she told herself. The dress made all the difference.

They rode up a steep path that edged the ditch beside the bailey wall. Even from here, Jenny could tell that Marchmont was the finest place she had ever visited. By now, Earl William had probably forgotten his rash invitation at Lilliesleaf. But even if Jenny should be ignored again, she would not have missed this trip for the world.

The main gate appeared abruptly at the crest of the hill. Once in the bailey, Jenny was glad to slide from La Rose. Her father's small, bedraggled entourage must compare poorly with others coming for the tournament, but servants took the horses to the stables immediately, and a well-dressed man came to greet them.

"I am Brice," he said, "the steward of this house. My lord is sorry he cannot be here to welcome his visitors. This weather has thrown our plans for the tournament awry. Come this way, sir. We have set aside one of the bays in the hall for all the young ladies. There are so many, it seemed best to keep them together. Your daughter may make herself comfortable there."

Jenny had not expected this. Who were these other girls?

The great hall seemed chilly after the open air, and somehow damper than the rain. Jenny began to shiver. On either side of the main hall, she saw large bays that were almost rooms in themselves. Ahead, one was curtained off. She heard the other girls before she saw them.

"We leave the young lady here, my lord. I will show you where the men are quartered. At the top of the hall is the court, where you may eat at any time. With parties arriving at all hours, it seemed useless to try to keep mealtimes today."

Jenny did not want to leave her father. She knew no girls her own age aside from Isabel. Would these other girls be unkind?

Her father seemed to read the apprehension in her eyes. "Go now, little one, make friends with the other ladies. The servants will bring your trunk presently." And he was gone.

Jenny looked at her maid. Galiene would have swept

into the thick of everything and claimed a place for her lady, but Hilde stood wringing her hands.

"Have you my combs?" Jenny whispered.

"Aye, my lady." The girl looked miserable. Jenny realized that Hilde was probably remembering the way she had railed against her at Lilliesleaf, and she blushed at the memory. Hilde was little more than a child. Why had she been so unkind to her?

"Come then," she said.

There were at least a dozen young noblewomen, most with mothers, all with servants. Jenny could see they had established a pecking order, as chickens would. The most forceful were ringed around a brazier that had been set up for warmth. These girls regarded Jenny, in her muddy clothes, with frank disdain. There was no hope of a place at that inner circle. Jenny looked around. A pretty girl with blond hair smiled from a corner. That one spark of encouragement was all Jenny needed.

"Come, Hilde," she said, and she set her course for that timid smile.

"Is there room here?" Jenny asked, but only to be polite. This dark corner of the bay was almost empty.

"I think so," the girl replied. "My name is Adèle," she added quickly. "Lady Adèle de Montgommeri of Maxwell, to be proper. Who are you?"

Jenny breathed a sigh of relief. This girl put on no airs. "Lady Jeanette Avenel of Langknowes."

"You may use my table if you wish, until your things arrive," Adèle said, "and my mirror."

Jenny accepted the offer gratefully. She had neither

143

table nor mirror. Adèle must come from a fine family to travel with both.

"Hilde," she said, "you may comb my hair."

Hilde produced the fine walrus ivory combs that Isabel had again lent Jenny. Adèle admired them greatly and insisted on sending her own maid to the kitchen to fetch warm water. She sighed. "I find it hard to be here without my mother," she said. "I would certainly fare better in her care. But she just had another child and is still in her bed. Even Nurse stayed home to care for them. Is your mother ill too?"

When Jenny told Adèle she had no mother, the girl's eyes filled with tears, as if Jenny's mother had just died. "Then we must care for each other."

None of the other girls had made a move toward Jenny. Adèle's generosity warmed her like a flame. Jenny smiled. "We shall," she said.

When Jenny's clothes arrived, she put on her good wool tunic, leaving the special dress hidden at the bottom of the chest. Then she sat on the chest, facing her new friend.

"You look lovely," Adèle said. She leaned closer and whispered, "Tell me, who are you here for?"

Jenny did not understand at first, then realized that all these young noblewomen were here to be courted. But how many had been invited by royalty? She raised her chin as she replied, "Earl William de Warenne, the king's brother." To Jenny's satisfaction, Adèle's mouth formed a small O of pure surprise.

"And who are you here for?" Jenny asked. She could

not keep a slight condescension from her voice.

Adèle dropped her eyes and blushed. "I have come," she said, "for the king himself."

"But how can that be?" Jenny's voice was louder than she had intended. She moved closer to Adèle to deflect the attention she had attracted and whispered, "How can that be? The king has sworn to take no wife."

Adèle nodded. "Yes, but his mother does not accept that. My mother says it is Lady Ada's duty to put young women in his way, hoping one may tempt him into marriage, as befits a king." Adèle lowered her voice until Jenny had to strain to hear her. "My mother says it is my duty to be one such woman." Jenny began to think it was lucky Adèle's mother had been unable to make the journey. Adèle looked as if she would cry. "I fear the king will not even glance at me."

Jenny's false pride vanished in the light of such honesty. "To be truthful, Earl William paid no court to me at all the last time we met. I am sure he cares more for his horses than he does for me. You are very pretty, Adèle. If anyone could tempt King Malcolm to relent his vow, it would be you." Adèle smiled through her tears. "Take heart, now," Jenny continued, sounding much bolder than she felt. "We will face this together. Perhaps we should snub the king and his brother ourselves." Adèle ducked her head and giggled. Jenny guessed that no one had ever made such a scandalous suggestion to her. "Tell me, Adèle, do you know how things are to go? We were told nothing when we arrived."

Adèle nodded. "Four of my brothers have come for the

hastiludes, and the old earl is a great friend of Father's. The tournament was to begin tonight with a procession to the lists, and then some hastiludes for show. The vespers, they call it. But in this weather, that seems unlikely. When we arrived, everyone was rushing about, making plans to keep the knights amused if they cannot tourney, so that they will not quarrel among themselves.

"Tomorrow, if the rain stops, they will joust all morning, then fight a great melee in the afternoon. We may watch from the platforms at the top of the bailey wall."

Jenny was taken aback. "That is all? We watch from a distance while they play at war?"

"They say it is not safe for women to be closer." Adèle giggled. "The melee is dangerous, but my brothers joust at home. We could watch beside the lists without fear. They pretend to be concerned for our welfare, but I think they wish to use language not fit for our ears."

Jenny sighed. "We will have a dreary time of it, watching little figures tourney in the distance."

"But it will not be so dull as that. There will be a banquet and amusements, of course. And the town is hosting a fair, I hear."

Jenny remembered how Tam's eyes had shone when he spoke of Roxburg. "Oh, Adèle, we should see the fair. Roxburg is not distant."

"But we could never go without escort. And who would leave the spectacle of the tournament to accompany us?"

Ranulf. He would be going to Roxburg. But Jenny almost winced, remembering the way she had treated him.

She could not bring herself to ask a favor of him yet. Still, to see Roxburg, to share that with Tam. She took a deep breath. "I will find a way." Jenny's stomach growled. "Are you hungry, Adèle?"

"Yes. Father said he would send for me, but I fear he has forgotten. He often does when there are friends about. Mother rages at him sometimes."

Jenny stood. "I have had nothing since breakfast. Let us find the food."

Adèle nodded. "I will faint if I wait for Father. He will not mind when he realizes he forgot."

None of the other women even glanced at them as they left. Jenny knew that would change when they learned why she and Adèle were here. But then it would be her turn to snub them. How lucky she was to have found a sincere friend like Adèle.

When they were out of the women's bay, Adèle took Jenny's hand. "You can see the court ahead. Behind it is the solar, the earl's private rooms."

They passed bays that housed dozens of men who had come for the tournament. Adèle kept her eyes down out of modesty, but Jenny could not resist looking around. No one was bold enough to speak to them, but a few winked, and one leered almost indecently. Jenny realized how sheltered her life was. Adèle was right. Any trip outside would require an escort.

In the court, Jenny saw her father almost immediately, sitting with some other men, but her new friend held on to her hand.

"Oh good. I see Father," Adèle said. "I was afraid he

might be hiding in the solar." She made straight for the head table with Jenny in tow, stopping before two elderly men at the very center.

"Adèle, my child," one said, "I forgot you once again. You must forgive me." He certainly looked too old to be the father of a newborn child, but Jenny was only mildly surprised. Nobles often took much younger brides. "You remember my daughter, my lord," he said to the other man. Jenny knew this could only be the earl of Roxburg. His silver hair parted just like Tam's, and his eyes held the same gentle humor.

"Indeed," he said. "Lady Adèle has flowered into young womanhood since last I saw her." Even his voice sounded like Tam's. Jenny could hardly take her eyes off him.

Adèle's father sighed. "Lady Ada herself summoned the child. And where is the lady? I have not seen her today."

The earl of Roxburg glanced behind him in a way that, in a lesser man, might have seemed almost fearful. "She is in the solar, in council with her sons," he said. Then he corrected himself. "Rather, the king is in council with his mother and his brother." He seemed embarrassed by his slip, but Adèle's father was not.

"Well, what mother is pleased when her sons refuse to marry? The lady has good reason to be cross with them. Lady Ada and my good wife wish Adèle to entice the king into thoughts of marriage. A fool's errand, I fear." He was just as open as his daughter.

The earl of Roxburg laughed at his honesty. "We may

hope not. Such a pretty child. King Malcolm may yet relent and take a wife."

The comte de Montgommeri noticed Jenny. "And you have found yourself a friend, my dear." Adèle smiled and introduced Jenny.

"Who would have guessed so many young ladies would come to a tournament?" the earl of Roxburg said.

"The knights like to have the ladies watch their feats of valor, I think," the comte replied.

The earl sighed. "Well, jousting may be fit to watch, but I fear the melee is too rough."

Jenny saw her chance. "My lord, Lady Adèle and I would like to visit the fair in Roxburg tomorrow if you would allow. Perhaps while the melee is held?"

"Yes," Adèle broke in. "We really would. Please, Father?"

Her father laughed. "Of course, child. This trip will be tedious enough for you, I fear."

"They will need an escort," the earl said. "I will send a man with them tomorrow afternoon, if the weather ever breaks." The earl cast an anxious glance at a window, still dripping with rain. Then he turned to Jenny. "So you are the daughter of the vicomte Avenel. Where is your father, my child? I find myself in his debt."

Jenny knew he was referring to Tam and hoped the earl would think she was blushing out of shyness as she led him to her father. She liked the earl at once and had no wish to lie to him, but she had a promise to keep. As soon as the earl shook her father's hand, she hurried back to Adèle, barely speaking. She hoped to seem timid rather than rude.

When they had eaten and were returning to the dreary ladies' bay, Jenny saw a figure far down the hall. Without stopping to explain, she sprinted away from Adèle, straight into his arms. Eudo lifted her high above his head, then wrapped his arms around her. When they had finished hugging and laughing, she turned to find Adèle looking shocked and shy.

"Lady Adèle de Montgommeri, this is Sir Eudo Avenel, my brother."

"Oh," Adèle said. "Your brother. I should have guessed."

Eudo was suddenly speechless. Jenny had to nudge him. "Yes," he said. "I have been for sixteen years now. Her brother, I mean. Since she was born. I am older, of course."

Jenny stared at him. He was babbling. Adèle put a hand to her mouth and giggled.

Eudo blushed. "Do you know where Father is?" he asked.

Jenny took his arm. "I will show you. Do you tourney tomorrow? Papa will be so pleased. Adèle, I will join you shortly."

Eudo took his eyes from Adèle only with difficulty. "She is a beauty," he whispered when they were out of earshot. "Is she here for anyone?"

Jenny nodded, surprised that her brother would know so much. "The king himself," she said. "That is to say, in the eyes of everyone *but* the king himself."

"Then I dare not even speak to her."

The disappointment in his voice surprised Jenny. Until that very moment, she had never thought to picture Eudo with a wife.

Chapter Fourteen
꒰꒱

DARK GRAY CLOUDS GLOWERED the next morning, but the rain held off. The brisk wind carried enough of a chill to make Jenny glad of her cloak as she stood by the top of the bailey wall. She and Adèle had taken a corner for themselves. The other women would certainly have been friendlier now if Jenny had given them an opening, but she took some pleasure in rebuffing them.

"I believe these knights will tourney today, even if it pours," Jenny said.

"I hope so," Adèle replied. "Nothing else will deliver us from their foul tempers."

Jenny only nodded. After the vespers had been canceled because of the rain, last night's gathering had soured. The royal family stayed in the solar. All the young men had avoided Jenny and Adèle, for the sake of the king and his brother, Jenny supposed. But even Adèle's brothers and Eudo had acted like strangers. As the night wore on, insults were traded around the fire more often than jokes. Finally, a fistfight broke out. The earl of Roxburg declared the evening over and ordered everyone to their lodgings. It was dismal.

Now, the mounted knights appeared to be milling around aimlessly in the lists. "What do you suppose they are doing down there?" Jenny asked Adèle.

"If the joust is well ordered, the outsiders, the *venants*, may choose the men they wish to joust against by touching the shields of knights from the home company, the *tenants*."

"But which are *venants* and which are *tenants*?"

"A good question. When one earl's men meet another's, you always know. But here, all are the king's men. They may group as they please. You can be sure that some of the surliness we saw last night had to do with the drawing of those lines."

"You know a great deal about this, Adèle," Jenny said.

Her friend sighed. "I have six brothers—no, seven now. The baby has not yet taken his knight's spurs, though he howls in a most warlike way. My brothers visit often, and my father takes any number of young men to live with us. They seem to think hastiludes are the only fit topic for conversation. My mother says my knowledge of the tournaments is most unladylike. If I had a sister, we might turn the talk to other things, but I am overwhelmed."

Jenny smiled to picture Adèle in a household full of men. Down by the river, the knights were moving out of the lists.

"But how will we know who is jousting?" Jenny asked.

Adèle frowned. "In France, they say, households dress in colors so that everyone knows whose men are jousting, if they wish to be known. Here we are not so splendid. We may not even know who is fighting."

She proved to be right. They spent the morning watching mostly anonymous knights tilt at one another with blunted lances. When one was unhorsed, the men crowded into the lists to watch the fight. Then Adèle and Jenny could see nothing at all.

Jenny did recognize Eudo when he took position with his charger. "There is my brother," she said. Her heart pounded. On the second charge, Eudo unhorsed the knight who stood against him. "Is he winning?" she cried as the crowd obscured the view. She clutched Adèle's arm. Their father would be hard-pressed to replace Eudo's horse and armor should he lose it.

When the crowd cleared, Jenny saw her father hugging Eudo while other knights slapped him on the back. She sighed in relief. "He must have won."

Adèle looked puzzled. "The knights are gentle today. Even if he lost, he would not be harmed." Jenny realized that such a loss would mean little in Adèle's household. Adèle craned her neck. "He is handsome, Jeanette. Is he betrothed?"

Jenny remembered how Adèle's beauty had reduced Eudo to an idiot when they met. "He is not," she said, "and he will have my father's lands one day. He would make a good husband for some lady, once she has spurned the offers of the king."

Adèle blushed scarlet, laughing. Then she frowned. "My mother means to marry me to a powerful man. She thinks it her life's work."

Jenny pictured Adèle with her brother. They would make a fine match. But poor Adèle might easily end up

153

with a man closer to her father's age. "I wish," Jenny said, "that we were free to marry men of our own choosing, just like the common lassies. Do you ever wish that, Adèle? To marry a man just because you like the sound of his voice and the way he smiles? To marry a man who would make your troubles seem to vanish simply by listening to them?"

Adèle looked shocked. "Our marriages must advance our fathers' alliances. That is our role."

Jenny sighed to herself. As the only daughter of a powerful man, Adèle could not be expected to think otherwise.

"That looks like Earl William coming into the lists now. Do you know a man who would suit you better?" Adèle asked.

Jenny quickly peered down to avoid Adèle's eyes. Even in her own heart, she was not ready to answer that question. The strong and stocky figure on a fine gray horse did look like Earl William. When they tilted, his opponent slid off his horse at a slight touch of the lance.

"Did you see that?" Jenny said. "I believe that knight unhorsed himself."

Adèle nodded. "A wise man would rather lose his worldly goods than risk Earl William's wrath. His temper is legendary." She suddenly remembered Jenny's reason for being there. "Forgive me; that may very well be false. You know what gossips men are."

"You are not the first to speak of Earl William's faults," Jenny said, to put her at ease.

"Yes, but a crown may cover a multitude of sins." Adèle's hand flew up to her lips. "Oh dear, now I sound like Mother." They both laughed.

At noon, the tables were set for the ladies only. "The men will eat by the lists in their companies, so they may plan for the melee," Adèle explained. "Just as well. They are too sweaty and surly to be fit company now."

"Every man here is entranced by the tourney," Jenny said. "I suppose the earl of Roxburg will forget to give us an escort into town."

Adèle nodded. "Most likely. Father would." But a man was waiting when the meal was over, a lame old guard who could barely hide his disappointment at missing the day's main event.

Adèle was delighted. "Wait a bit, man," she said. Then she turned to Jenny. "Come, I want to wear something pretty to the fair."

Adèle searched through her trunks for a dress to suit her mood while Jenny tried to pretend to share her interest. She had planned to save the green-and-gold dress for the evening, but she could not bring herself to admit she had no other fine dress to wear. She cursed herself for leaving the scarlet silk at home just because she had not wanted Earl William to see it again. Reluctantly, she dug to the bottom of her trunk. But as soon as she touched the dress, her mood changed. How could anyone who owned such a dress be unhappy? It weighed so little, it might have been spun from spiderwebs. She slipped behind one of the dressing screens.

Adèle gasped when she saw Jenny. "That is the prettiest dress I ever saw," she said. "Where did you find the cloth?"

"A merchant in Rowanwald brought it to us. It may be Flemish," Jenny lied.

"You look enchanting. Perhaps you should save it for tonight."

Jenny found she could not lie again. "In truth, Adèle, I have no other. No one will see it under my cloak."

But outside, they found the wind had gone, taking the clouds away. The August sun shone brightly. Jenny and Adèle shucked off their cloaks and handed them to the grumpy old guard.

"It was good of you to sacrifice your afternoon," Adèle said, as if the man had been given a choice. "Take this for your trouble." She slipped him a coin, and his temper improved visibly. Jenny noticed Adèle was always kindly with servants, in spite of her rank. Jenny was ashamed to remember how she had behaved the past few weeks.

The short path to Roxburg followed the Teviot, a dark river now sparkling in the sun. The girls had to lift their hems to avoid the mud from yesterday's rain. Jenny heard crowds and music even before they passed through the gate in the stout town wall. The narrow streets hid the fairgrounds from view, and stalls were set up everywhere, selling a confusing array of goods, everything from new ribbons to chipped crockery. They passed a piper busking in the street. The skirl was deafening, but the man played well. Adèle threw a few coins into his hat.

"Why are the stalls set up here and not on the fairgrounds?" Jenny asked the guard.

"Saint James Fair Green is set aside for the *behourds*

this day, my lady," the man said, and Jenny looked to Adèle, knowing she would explain.

"The behourds are a kind of play tournament set up for fun. Anyone can join in, even small boys." She turned to the guard. "Will there be a quintain?"

He nodded. "The pile, they call it here, my lady, but aye. They have a fine one."

Adèle laughed. "This should be fun. Oh look, a bee-keeper. Let me get some honeycomb." They chewed the honeycomb until all the sweetness was gone from the wax, then spat it out. Jenny was careful of her dress, but she relished the rare treat.

Roxburg was everything Tam had said it would be, a real town with some timber-frame buildings, even a few with an upper story. Houses belonging to tradesmen hung signs outside. A wooden boot indicated the shoemaker's house, a candlestick marked the chandler's, and the many signs with sheep on them showed where cloth merchants lived. Jenny could not imagine how Tam could bring himself to leave such a wonderful place. His troubles, whatever they were, must be serious indeed.

As Adèle promised, the behourds were more fun than the stuffy tournament. At the edge of the fairgrounds, a swing hung from a great ash tree. One man sat on the swing, with his opponent on a stool nearby, and the men attempted to "unhorse" each other, using their legs in place of lances. The quintain proved to be a kind of manikin on a pole that swung around when men tilted at it, unhorsing the rider more often than not. One man was knocked out when he was hit by the flat "arm," and had to be brought around with a bucket of water. The jousting was conducted on docile old nags with padded lances so blunt they appeared to have pillows at the ends. Best of all, fools wove in and out of all the games. They snatched shields or helmets or wooden swords away from unwary combatants and used them for outrageous parodies of battle. They were so nimble and skilled, Jenny was sure they must be clowns by trade. Adèle rewarded them with silver coins from her apparently bottomless purse.

"We had better return to Marchmont," Adèle said finally.

Jenny looked around. She could hardly believe the shadows had grown so quickly. "I hope tempers will be improved from last night."

"We shall see. Some tournaments end on a merry note, others are sour through and through," Adèle said. "Oh, I see a woman with remedies. Let me speak to her. The baby has colic, and nothing Nurse can do will stop him from howling."

Ahead was a booth covered in bundles of dried herbs. The woman tending it was neither old nor young. Her manner was polite but independent, reminding Jenny that these burgesses owed allegiance to no one but the king himself. Adèle explained what she needed as the woman gathered herbs on a clean cloth.

"Peppermint will ease the gas, my lady, and give him just a touch of these poppy seeds, ground fine. No more than will fit on your baby finger. Your nurse should find wild lettuce and press the juice. It will help as well, but it cannot be dried."

When Adèle handed her a coin, the woman turned,

unexpectedly, to Jenny. "And what are you doing here, my lady, dressed in cobwebs and old leaves?" Her tone was so civil, so conversational, that Jenny did not realize at first what she had said. Then Adèle's mouth fell open, and both girls froze.

The old guard finally spoke. "Give the lady no trouble, Meg. Good evening to you." He took Adèle's parcel and walked away.

Jenny fell into shocked silence, but Adèle said, "That woman should be whipped for speaking to Lady Jeanette like that." The guard said nothing. "The king would say so too, I feel certain," she persisted as they left the town.

The guard shrugged. "Meg is midwife to Roxburg," he said. "She sees the bairns into this world and is godmother to more than half the town. The folk here think much of her."

"But she must be mad to speak like that. My friend's dress is beautiful."

The guard sighed. "Meg has gone odd. No one would quarrel with you on that. A few years ago, she disappeared for a month or more. She often goes far afield, gathering weeds for her cures, and everyone thought her lost forever—fallen into the river, maybe, or eaten by a wild beast. But suddenly she was back, no worse for wear. She told anyone who would listen that she had gone with two men who came to fetch her for a birth. The place they took her was under a hill, but finer than a lord's hall inside."

Adèle gasped. "You mean to say she was taken by the fairies?"

The guard nodded. "So she claims. She said, when she

came into the hall, the men dipped their hands into some water and touched their eyes, so she did the same, and suddenly, all the finery disappeared. She could see it was nothing more than old leaves and bits of moss, fairy glamour as they call it. Since then, she claims she can see anything made by the fairies for what it is. I suppose she fancies your dress to be fairy glamour, being so finely made," he said to Jenny.

"At home, anyone would get a thrashing for speaking to a lady like that," Adèle said. "Jeanette, you look so frightened. You must not let such nonsense trouble you." She took Jenny's arm as they walked back to Marchmont. Jenny felt weak in the knees.

They could hear crowds down by the lists when they returned. Marchmont seemed empty. "The melee is over," Adèle said. "Everyone is out congratulating the knights. We should go too."

Jenny excused herself. "I have a terrible headache."

Adèle patted her hand. "No wonder, after the way you were treated. Do you want me to send for your maid?" Jenny shook her head. "At least you may rest alone," Adèle said.

As usual, Adèle was right. The bay where the women slept was empty. Even the maids were gone. Jenny dragged a pallet from a stack and laid it behind one of the screens. She slipped out of her dress, carefully hanging it on the screen, and lay down in her kirtle.

The dress shimmered in the gloom like a shaft of sunlight in the forest, as lovely as ever. She raised her hand and touched the fabric, soft and fine. It looks so real, she thought. Because it is, she told herself. The midwife was daft. She must be. The other possibility—that the dress was nothing more than cobwebs and leaves bound together by fairy magic—was too bizarre to consider. But she could not stop herself from wondering. What if that midwife were right? That would mean this dress was an unearthly thing, the devil's work, something to be shunned. If I really believe that, I should burn it right now, she thought. But Jenny knew she never could. It would break her heart to destroy it.

And what of Tam? She shook her head, remembering his kindness and his gentle ways. Could he be capable of such a trick? Jenny closed her eyes to shut out her confusion. Like a boat loosed from its mooring, she drifted away.

"Jeanette, Jeanette, wake up."

At first, Jenny did not know where she was. Then she remembered. "Adèle?"

"You fell asleep. Get up now, for the banquet is starting soon. Most of the women have already left. I thought their noise would waken you. Is your headache better?" Jenny nodded. "Your maid laid this out for you." Adèle handed her a clean kirtle.

Jenny rose and changed, still groggy with sleep. What had happened that afternoon seemed so distant now. The green-and-gold dress flowed over her fresh linen kirtle, as beautiful as ever. How could she have thought to destroy it?

Jenny's hair was tangled from an afternoon in the air, but Hilde had become more skillful. When she was finished, Isabel's fine walrus ivory combs swept Jenny's hair from her face.

"You look enchanting," Adèle said. This was kind of her,

for Adèle was far more beautiful. "Come now," she continued, "or we will be late. I talked to my father while you were resting." They hurried along the hall. "There was no end of bickering about the seating for tonight. The king wanted the banquet to be held in the French style, with separate tables for the ladies, hosted by his mother. Lady Ada, apparently, saw this as a ploy on his part to avoid having to deal with the ladies. Me in particular, I suppose. In the end, she won her way, as she often does, but not before harsh words had been exchanged."

"Adèle," Jenny said, "they seem a most unhappy family."

Adèle nodded. "The earl of Roxburg says Earl Henry's death was akin to knocking the most important chess piece off the board in the very middle of the game. King Malcolm has grown to be a fine man and a good leader, but the hole that was left in the family never mended." Adèle's voice dropped to a whisper, for they had entered the crowded court.

Jenny saw her father and Eudo, but the earl of Roxburg claimed the girls before she could catch their attention. "You look like two flowers tonight, my dears," he said. "I trust you enjoyed your visit to the town."

"It was wonderful," Jenny said quickly, hoping Adèle would follow her lead and not mention the unpleasantness.

"Come now, Lady Ada is most anxious to see you. That is a lovely dress," he added, turning to Jenny. "You remind me of my daughter tonight. She favored those colors."

Everyone turned to look as they passed and, strangely, as they did, all fell silent. Jenny wondered if she or Adèle had done something wrong. By the time they reached the head table, the entire hall was as quiet as if it were empty.

It took someone as forceful as Lady Ada to break the spell. "Lady Adèle," she said, "you grow lovelier by the month, my child. And this must be Lady Jeanette. I have longed to meet you, my dear." Jenny thought this odd from a woman who had hidden away in the solar for the whole of her visit, but she smiled politely and said nothing.

Lady Ada was a commanding woman, with Earl William's red-gold hair and his features writ fine. She was, Jenny realized, far too young for the role fate had forced upon her. She should be queen, not the king's widowed mother. Past Lady Ada stood her sons. Earl William and King Malcolm seemed afflicted by the same strange malady that was bothering all the other men in the hall tonight. They stared, mouths slightly open, saying nothing at all.

No one could sit until the king did, but he seemed rooted to the floor. Jenny saw at once that he was not like his brother and mother. His features were spare and straight, his body slight. He was beardless, with brown hair as fine as feathers. His pale blue eyes were fixed on Jenny in a way that seemed quite out of keeping with his vow of celibacy. She blushed and bowed her head.

"Malcolm," his mother said, "everyone is waiting to be seated."

To Jenny's surprise, Earl William stepped past his mother to take her hand. "You are the loveliest lady in the room," he said, loudly, so that everyone nearby would hear. It was a true Norman compliment, intended to aggrandize the bestower as much as the recipient, careless of anyone else's feelings.

Jenny blushed, in anger more than modesty. "What nonsense. Lady Adèle is much prettier. Anyone can see that," she said, forgetting her manners completely.

"No, my brother speaks the truth. You are enchanting," a soft voice said. They all turned to King Malcolm, who looked as astonished by his words as everyone else.

"Adèle, my child, you sit here," Lady Ada said, indicating the chair beside the king. She gave Jenny a look of pure annoyance. Although he still looked flustered, King Malcolm took the hint and sat down. Everyone in the hall followed. Jenny noticed that Earl William seemed to enjoy his brother's discomfort.

Jenny found Earl William changed since Lilliesleaf. He scarcely took his eyes off her and he spoke to no one else. "Please, keep that breast of pheasant for yourself," he said when she selected it for him, "for you deserve as good as any." Jenny was both flattered and unsettled. But, for all his attentions, Earl William's conversation was not engaging. He mainly boasted of his winnings. "Five knights I unhorsed, and took seven ransom. No one else did nearly so well. I took your brother single-handedly."

Jenny dropped the pheasant breast. "My brother?"

"Yes. He is on parole to me. Did you not know? He must return with his fee within a fortnight."

"But sir, I do not think my brother can raise whatever sum you require."

Earl William laughed. "Why do you look so pale, lady? Give me a kiss and I will release him."

How could he be so cruel? "This is hardly a joking matter, my lord."

He leaned close, his hot breath brushing her cheek. "You think I jest?" he whispered. "I will release him from his bond for just one kiss. His fate is in your hands."

"Very well, my lord," Jenny said, leaning toward him, but he laughed and ducked away.

"Not here. Not now. Let me claim my forfeit as I wish, my lady."

Jenny nodded miserably, wondering if "just one kiss" was likely to become more.

Earl William failed to notice her discomfort. "Even without the Avenel money, I will do well. Five fine chargers, all the knights' weapons and armor, and six more on parole."

Jenny remembered what Tam had said about Earl William's debts. "Is it enough, my lord?" she asked.

He frowned. "How do you mean, Lady Jeanette?" His tone was suddenly stern.

Too late, Jenny realized she had stumbled onto forbidden ground. "Enough, I mean," she faltered, "to make the tournament worth your trouble."

He roared with laughter. "Worth my trouble indeed. You are sweet to ask, my lady"—he leaned toward her again—"and far more beautiful than I remembered."

Earl William launched into a blow-by-blow account of his victories. The banquet dragged on. To make things worse, whenever Jenny looked around the hall, she found far too many young men gazing at her with sickly longing. What was the matter with them?

Jenny supposed things could not be worse, but she soon discovered she was wrong. When the tables were finally put away and everyone gathered at the fire, young men crowded around, vying for her attention. "Lady Jeanette, let me give you this cushion to soften the bench." "No, please, sit here. You will see better from here." "Lady Jeanette, allow me to sing you a song." Jenny noticed that Earl William was not annoyed. Their envy pleased him. Jenny guessed he would feel the same if she were a fine charger or a suit of clothing. She glanced around for some escape. Adèle looked pinched with the strain of sitting between the king and his mother all evening. Poor Adèle. Jenny caught her father's eye and he smiled broadly, delighted to find his daughter the center of attention.

Jenny sighed to herself. She would have to handle this alone. "I am accustomed to a bench without a cushion, thank you. I can see perfectly from here. I care little for music. Some other lady would better appreciate your song." She tried to sound as abrupt as she could, without actually being rude. But somehow, her tactic failed. The young men laughed and nodded as if she had flattered them, and pressed upon her more than ever.

"Enough," Lady Ada said. "Anyone would think Lady Jeanette was the only girl in the hall tonight. Give her some room." Her tone was so commanding, the young men fell back.

Jenny looked to her with gratitude, but Lady Ada's gaze was anything but sympathetic. Without meaning to, Jenny knew she had made an enemy of this powerful woman.

Chapter Fifteen

❧

J ENNY WOKE EARLY the next morning, before anyone else in the ladies' bay stirred. Her head throbbed. Even the light hurt her eyes—her punishment, surely, for lying about a headache the day before. She wished the banquet had been nothing more than a bad dream. She had sometimes wondered what it would be like to be beautiful like Isabel or Adèle. Now, she knew the attention was suffocating.

Turning on the pallet, she found herself facing the dress, draped over her trunk where she had cast it the night before. Such a lovely thing, but it was magic, she was certain. I can never wear it again, she thought with regret. When I am home, I will throw it into the fire.

Then, in spite of everything, she smiled. All the attention had at least served her in one way. Earl William had found it impossible to get her alone and claim his kiss. Jenny knew the kiss would have to be given, for Eudo's sake, but she felt sure it would not be claimed with nearly as much ardor when that dress was safely packed away.

She shook her head, thinking of Tam Lin. She found

167

the malice of his trick harder to accept than the magic itself, for surely, the way men had treated her when she wore the dress had been nothing more than a cruel jest on his part. She suddenly realized how much she had come to depend upon Tam's friendship. And now, she thought, that friendship is over. He must be very different from the way he appeared to me. Twisted with magic and malice. By the time the other women began to stir, Jenny's heart was aching just as fiercely as her head.

"You look so pale," Adèle said when she saw her.

Jenny nodded. "I may not be able to eat. I rarely get these headaches, but they make me sick to my stomach as well."

"Your maid can fetch some hot milk from the kitchen. Rest as much as you can, for the journey home will be hard with a sick headache."

Adèle was so thoughtful. Jenny realized she had asked her friend nothing of herself. "How did you fare with the king last night?"

Adèle laughed. "No better than I feared. Lady Ada did her best to draw him out, but he said very little. She is such a forceful woman. I think she should accept her son's decision and leave him alone. He is king, after all. But Jeanette, it might be best for you to stay out of her path. Lady Ada does not like to find herself outshone."

Jenny gave a shaky laugh. "I know she was not pleased with me. But she is not difficult to avoid, and I will do just that. Adèle, you have been so kind. I will miss you."

"And I you," Adèle said, and they embraced.

After Hilde returned with the milk, Jenny gave her a

message for her father. "Tell the vicomte to send for me when it is time to leave, for I am sick with a headache." Remembering Lilliesleaf, she added, "Tell him, too, that I will see Earl William before I go if the earl wishes. And tell my father I am sorry." Then she lay down with a piece of wet linen over her eyes.

When it was time to go, Earl William was waiting with her father in the stable yard. He looked angry, but when he saw her, his expression softened. "So you really are ill," he said. "I thought this might be some game to keep my interest. You look so pale and very . . . ordinary. Hardly like the lady I sat beside last night at all." He sounded disenchanted.

Jenny remembered how he had misinterpreted her leaving at Lilliesleaf as well. Can he wish to marry me, she thought, when he knows me so little? She lifted her chin. "My lord," she said, "it is not my way to win a suitor with ploys. You must take me for myself, or not at all." Then she remembered the dress and blushed hotly.

He laughed. "You speak bold words, my lady, but your cheeks betray a maidenly modesty. You are not well enough to deliver my forfeit. Give me the kiss of peace. I will claim my prize when next we meet. But your brother is released from his parole."

Jenny felt an overwhelming rush of emotions—annoyance, because it seemed Earl William would never see her as she really was, but also gratitude for releasing Eudo from his debt, and for deferring the kiss. As she received his brotherly kiss, her eyes filled with tears.

"There now," he said, "be not sad at our parting. We

will meet again." Once again he had misunderstood her.

The journey home had the quality of a nightmare. Not long out of Marchmont, Jenny had to dismount to throw up her meager breakfast. "We should stop and let you rest until you feel better," her father said as she came unsteadily back to La Rose.

"No, Papa," Jenny said. "This headache may last for days. I will be better off at home."

"You are lucky to see these headaches so seldom, my child. Your mother was plagued by them."

As they traveled on, Jenny noticed that something troubled her father. He should have been happier. Earl William wished to see her again, and Eudo was relieved of the debt that would have put a strain on the entire household. Yet he brooded as he rode, his chin on his chest. What could be wrong?

When they stopped at noon to eat, Jenny saw Ranulf going to fill water bottles at a stream. She slipped after him with a piece of clean linen in her hand, unnoticed in the general confusion.

"Your maid should be doing that, my lady," Ranulf said as she dipped the cloth into the stream.

"Sunlight makes my headache worse. This shade is soothing. Did you find what you need for the new falcon in Roxburg?"

"Yes. I should be able to take her soon. Perhaps next week." His tone was chilly, reminding her of the shameful way she had treated him.

"I want to apologize for being so rude when you took me to see her. I was not myself."

"Courtship is hard on a young woman, my lady. I noticed that the last few days."

This was all he said, but Jenny knew she was forgiven. And he had given her the opening she was looking for. "Hard on their fathers too, I fear. My father frets today. Do you know why?"

Ranulf filled the rest of the leather bottles before he replied, meeting her eyes with reluctance when the task was done. He plainly knew more than he wanted to say. "My lady, it would be best if you ask your father. It is not my place to discuss his money with you."

"His money? But Earl William released Eudo from his parole. My father should have no worries about money today."

Ranulf grimaced. "I have already said more than I should, my lady." He hurried down the path leading back to the encampment, but Jenny followed, speaking urgently.

"Ranulf, if I am the cause of my father's unhappiness, will you not tell me?"

He stopped and turned. "If I tell, my lady, you must promise never to reveal what you know to his lordship. Give me your word."

Jenny knew he would never have insisted she promise if she had not threatened to betray him before. "I vow on my life."

"Very well," Ranulf said. "I overheard your father and Earl William this morning in the stable yard. The earl will betroth himself to you only if your dowry is increased."

"But all my father's wealth has already gone to my tocher. How can he add more?"

He spoke with great reluctance. "The earl has recommended certain moneylenders."

"No!"

"Hush, please, my lady. Someone will hear," Ranulf begged.

Jenny lowered her voice. "This cannot be. Earl William is deeply indebted to moneylenders himself, but he is the king's brother. My father would have no such protection. He cannot ruin himself for my sake. Tell me, Ranulf, is this bargain sealed?"

"I cannot say for certain, but it seemed to me they had not bound themselves yet."

Jenny heard Hilde calling for her. "Thank you, Ranulf, for your honesty. I will not forget my promise," she said in a rush. "Wait a bit before you follow me."

Now, Jenny was almost grateful for the headache, which neatly masked her new distress. While the others ate, she rested in the shade of a great oak tree, trying to sort through her feelings. I may be wife of an earl, she thought, even queen of Scotland. But this provoked no joy, only a wave of panic. She would be trapped in that suffocating role forever, married to a man who seemed to misinterpret her every move. She thought of her father. I cannot allow him to ruin himself for my sake. But she knew he was not doing this for her alone. Her father craved the company of powerful men, a place at court. Until this moment, she had not realized how much he would sacrifice for these things. Not only her future, but everything he possessed. She pressed the wet cloth to her eyes.

Jenny thought they would never reach home. As soon as they entered the bailey, she slid from La Rose into the waiting arms of Galiene and Isabel. Galiene saw at once what was wrong. "Poor lamb. What a time to take one of your headaches." Jenny was in bed with a tansy leaf tucked into the cloth on her forehead to cure the headache before her trunk was returned to the bower.

"What in heaven's name is this?" Galiene cried as she opened the trunk. Jenny winced, remembering the green dress. She would have to explain it now. But Isabel said, "Jenny, how did these dead leaves get into the trunk with your clothes?"

"I shall have words with Hilde about this," Galiene said. "That girl is worse than useless."

"No, it was my doing." Jenny struggled to think of a lie. "There were clowns at the fair in Roxburg. They threw leaves at the crowds for a joke. I came back late and had to hurry to dress for the banquet, so I just tossed my clothes into the trunk. I thought the leaves had fallen off. Hilde never saw them."

So there was the final proof of magic. The fairy glamour that had held the dress together had vanished on the way home, leaving only the things the midwife had seen in Roxburg. I never want to see Tam Lin again, Jenny thought, turning to the wall so that no one would see the hot tears spill down her cheeks.

Her headache was gone the next day, but it was harder to forget Tam than Jenny had expected. Working at her loom, she would suddenly think of something he had done or said and smile before she could remember to be angry. She had to remind herself that the real Tam Lin was very different from the man she had thought she knew.

She could not console herself with thoughts of Earl William. She was angry with him as well for tempting her father to ruin himself with moneylenders. Even without her anger, memories of Earl William offered meager comfort. He was a boastful man who gained his way at any cost. She realized now that his kindness when they parted was probably sparked by the fact that he was getting far more from her father than he should.

"Jenny, look to your weaving," Isabel said. "Everything is awry. You must be unsteady from the headache. I can look after this."

Jenny was grateful to surrender the shuttle and sit down. Her head felt fine, but she could not keep her thoughts on the loom.

As Isabel worked, she sang a song about a girl waiting for her lover to return from Paris for their marriage. The line at the end of every verse, *"Marchons, joli coeur, la lune est levée,"* was filled with joy. "Come, sweetheart, the moon has risen." Jenny smiled to hear her sister sing a happy song again. She had been so wrapped up in her own concerns, she had not really looked at Isabel for weeks. Now, she noticed a new lightness in Isabel's movements, a pride in the tilt of her chin that had been absent for too long. But Isabel might soon be leaving. Suddenly, Jenny could not bear to think she might never see her sister sing for a dance again.

"Isabel," she said when the song was over, "do you think

we might have a dance before the summer is past?"

"Why, Cospatric and I spoke of that very thing while you were gone," Isabel said. "Remember how we used to dance every month on the full of the moon?"

Jenny's smile faded. What was it Tam Lin had said the last time she saw him? "Come by the full of the moon and dine with me." She could recall how his voice had sounded, his smile, the light in his eyes, and every detail filled her with an almost unbearable ache.

"What do you say, Jenny? The full moon is only a few days away," Isabel said. "I thought you would be pleased."

Jenny realized she had been silent too long. "Aye, Isabel. A dance would be just the thing." To her surprise, Jenny found herself close to tears. She was relieved that Isabel was facing the loom. "I think I will take some sunshine," she said, and she was gone before Isabel could turn to question her.

Outside, Jenny clenched her fists. I cannot walk around crying, she told herself. Tam Lin is nothing to me. I must forget him. When she looked up, she saw Ranulf. He looked so grim, she wondered if he thought she had broken her promise. At least I have nothing to fear on this account, she thought, for she had said nothing to her father. But Ranulf was not looking for her.

"Is your lord father in the bower, my lady?"

"No, he must be in the hall. Is something wrong, Ranulf?"

He nodded. "I went to look for that young falcon this morning. She is gone."

"But how can that be? Perhaps you missed her?"

"No, my lady. The dame and sire are teaching the tercel how to hunt. But the young falcon is not with them."

"Where could she be? Would someone take her?"

"I think not. Your lord father has the right of all the creatures on his land. A man who took a hawk could be punished by branding. But young birds often die, my lady. They are fragile creatures. I must go tell your father." And he was gone.

The tears Jenny had struggled against spilled over. At least I have a reason to cry now, she thought. There was only one place she might find comfort. La Rose was saddled and out the bailey gate before anyone saw her.

The fields were gold with ripening grain in the fullness of summer now. A few had already been stripped of their harvest. In the fallow band on either side of the road, bramble flowers bloomed in a thorny tumble, attended by humming bees. Orange butterflies drifted from flower to flower. Jenny tried to take some of the peace of this place for her own, but she could not. The fierce ache in her heart refused all comfort. I will feel better in the forest, she told herself.

The great trees were heavy with greenery, and their shade was cool and deep. The few sunbeams that broke through the thick cover looked strong enough to climb, and the bracken ferns on either side of the road were as tall as La Rose. But the forest no longer eased her heart. This was the place where she had met Tam Lin. Everywhere she looked, it seemed to speak of him.

She had not intended to go to Carter Hall again, but now she knew it was the only way she could help herself.

I have to see him as he really is, she thought, to see his malice and his cruelty. That will give me a memory to overshadow all the others.

She remembered the freebooters only when she came to the ford, but there were no signs of tracks in the soft mud near the river. She urged La Rose on, hoping that seeing Tam Lin would give her a kind of release. At the well, she sprang from her horse and called his name, but only the birds replied. She looked all around, even into the old hall itself. There was no sign of him. The place was abandoned and empty. She was not even to be granted this one chance to free herself from him.

"Damn you, Tam Lin," she cried. "Damn you to hell." Then she realized that his use of magic might well damn him.

She threw herself on the cold stone floor and burst into tears. Even as she did, a small part of her half expected to feel his hand on her shoulder at any moment, hoped he would gather her into his arms, kiss her tears away, and make everything better. But she cried herself out alone, and lay there long after, like an empty husk. For she knew now that she loved him, but he was gone.

Chapter Sixteen

❧

"GALIENE, GALIENE, get the lady, please. Tell her to come to the stables, quick." Alric's high voice pierced the thin wattle shutters of the bower, forcing itself into Jenny's ears. After a long, sleepless night, she had finally drifted off with the wicked wish that she might never wake again. Now she pried one eye open. From the light, it was just after dawn.

"There are two ladies in this household, Alric. Which do you want, and why must she come to the stable before mass?" Galiene's voice was calm and firm.

"Lady Jeanette. The groom sent me. Something has happened to her horse."

Jenny's feet were on the floor before Alric could finish. "Tell the boy I am coming, Galiene," she said, slipping a dress over the kirtle she had slept in. She came out, pulling on her shoes, her hair still in braids. "La Rose was fine yesterday. Is she ill?"

"No, my lady, not ill, exactly. Come see."

Outside, the air was filled with wafting river mist, lending an air of magic to the commonplace buildings of the bailey. Jenny overtook the lame boy in her rush to reach the stable. She had to push through a crowd of servants to reach La Rose.

"Ah, there you are, my lady. Do you know how this happened?" Gilchrist, the groom, stood beside La Rose. Jenny gasped. The little horse's mane was a mass of tangles.

"Not at all. After I rode her yesterday, one of your boys took her for me. Thurstan, I think. She was fine then."

"You see?" Thurstan said. He was a large boy with short-cropped hair. He was sullen at the best of times but looked so miserable now that Jenny was sure he had played no part in this mischief. Gilchrist was a dour man. Jenny guessed he could be a harsh master.

Galiene pushed her way through the crowd and stood beside Jenny. "Oh my," she said. "Elflocks." She looked shaken.

"Come now, Galiene, are you giving us that old wives' nonsense?" Gilchrist asked.

Jenny knew Galiene did not like to be taunted about the unseen. She squared her shoulders. "I say the wee folk entered here by magic and tangled the mare's mane, Gilchrist. You can accept that if you wish"—she paused— "or we can wonder how you could be so slack with the guarding of your lord's horses as to let some prankster in."

The groom's frown deepened. "I will bar the bailey gate and set a guard upon the stable tonight. We will see who dares breach it."

"Fine," Galiene said, "and when you find that brawn alone is not enough to stop the wee folk in their mischief, maybe I will help you. Now, I must prepare my ladies for mass." A queen could not have made her exit with more majesty.

But Jenny could not bring herself to leave yet. She stroked her horse's neck. "Poor La Rose. Set someone to groom the tangles from her mane, and do not leave her alone today. I will return as soon as I am able."

At mass, Jenny paid little attention. Tam had to be behind this magic too. But why would he torment her so? She had done nothing to harm him. Jenny knew Galiene would soon realize that the magic was aimed at her and start to ask questions. The full moon was only two nights away.

Jenny clung to the faint hope that Tam would honor his invitation, that she might find him at Carter Hall then. Could she possibly slip away from the dance? She felt she could find peace only by seeing him. Her feelings were as deeply tangled as La Rose's mane.

As they left the chapel, Galiene whispered to her, "Put a silver coin in some water and give that to your mare to drink. It will help."

When Jenny returned to the stable, she found the two boys, Thurstan and Alric, had made little progress with the tangles. She slipped a silver coin into a bucket of water and set it before La Rose. "Let her drink a bit before you go on," she said. After that, the elflocks did come loose more freely.

"The boys will sleep in here tonight, my lady," Gilchrist said. "And your father's best men will guard the doors."

The next morning, Jenny woke early and went to the

stable right away. Before the guards could unbar the doors, she heard Alric cry, "What happened to me? Oh, what happened?" Jenny rushed inside to find the boy in a panic. His fine, fair hair was just as tangled as La Rose's mane had been. He was close to tears.

Thurstan's hair was too short to tangle. "Stop squalling, you sookie bairn," he said, and he raised his arm to give the smaller boy a clout.

"Leave him be," Jenny cried. "Go check the horses." She put her arm around Alric's shoulders. He was trembling. "Never mind," she said. "I will look after you." She felt as if she had harmed the boy herself. He said nothing, but leaned on her for comfort.

"Only your horse again, my lady," Thurstan reported when he had toured the stalls. "Same as yesterday."

Gilchrist arrived and frowned at the boys. "Are you two the pranksters?" he asked.

"No!" Thurstan cried. "This is beyond my ken, sir. I thought my eyes were open all night." His indignation was sincere. Alric still looked terrified.

"And the men at the door swear the same. I suppose we should ask your old nurse what to do next, my lady." Gilchrist looked anything but pleased.

"I will send her to you myself," Jenny said. "And the boy can come with me to get his hair combed."

"Never mind, my lady. We can cut those knots out."

Jenny felt Alric flinch beneath her arm. "No. Leave the boy to me."

As they crossed to the bower, Jenny said, "I must go to mass, but wait in the bower for me. We can hardly bring you into the chapel like this." She hated to have to leave him alone. He still looked like a frightened rabbit.

In the bower, Galiene took everything calmly. "Lucky your hair is not as thick as a horse's mane, boy. We can set you to rights at once." She sat Alric on a stool and fetched a comb.

"But what about mass?" Jenny asked.

"A child came from Langknowes while you were gone. Old Jemmy in the town is drawing his last breath. Brother Turgis is with him, so we will have no mass today. Poor old Jemmy."

"May heaven bless him," Jenny said, but her thoughts were not on the farmer. "Give me the comb. Gilchrist is ready to take your advice." And she began to work on the boy's hair.

"So, he has more sense than I thought." Galiene chuckled as she sat down. "I am in no great hurry to help him, but it will be easy enough to fix. And no one seems to have told Brother Turgis, which is just as well. He would want to bless the stables, and that would not work."

"Galiene! How can you say that?"

"The wee folk do not fear God. The Church has no power over them."

Alric, who had been silent all this time, suddenly pulled away from the comb and faced them. "Am I cursed by the fairies, then? Will I be odd for the rest of my life? Will they come for me?" His eyes were large in his pale face.

"Oh, hush," Galiene said. "What would the wee folk want with a scrawny lad like you? The only lad I ever heard of who was taken by them was the grandson of an earl."

Jenny knew this was Galiene's way of being kind, but the words made her heart lurch. "Turn around now, Alric," she said, more sharply than she had intended. "Let me deal with this mess." A long moment passed before she trusted herself to speak again. "Galiene, if someone were taken like that, could he ever be freed?"

Galiene paused to consider. "There are plenty of stories of those taken by the wee folk, hen. Most are never right in their minds again, never really of this world."

"But could it happen? Could the enchantment be broken?" As Jenny struggled to keep her voice calm, her hands worked convulsively.

"Ow!"

"Oh, Alric, forgive me," Jenny said. A clump of the poor boy's hair lay in her comb.

"I fancy it could," Galiene said. "But it would take a powerful charm. Such things are beyond my ken. I have only the simple charms that anyone knows. Now, I suppose I should go lend my lore to Gilchrist. He only needs to put iron bars in all the stalls, but it will take the smith all day to forge them."

"Wait a bit, Galiene," Jenny said. "Alric, does Thurstan bully you?" The boy nodded slowly, reluctant to tell. Jenny grinned at him. "Galiene, be sure that Gilchrist puts Thurstan on the bellows. The smith will need a stout pair of arms." For the first time that day, Alric smiled.

When Galiene was gone, Jenny worked at the elflocks silently. Could the spell that held Tam Lin be broken? If

183

Galiene's stories were true, Tam had been little older than Alric when the fairies first took him. How much hope could there be, after such a long time?

Isabel came into the bower. "Gilchrist told Papa everything while we ate. Is Alric all right?"

"Almost as good as new," Jenny said. "See, only one patch of tangles left to sort out."

"Oh, good. Alric, will you still sing at the dance tomorrow?"

The boy blushed. "Aye, my lady."

"Alric, have you been keeping secrets from me?" Jenny hoped a little gentle teasing might help restore the boy's humor, but he looked appalled.

"I never tried to hide my voice from you, my lady. They call me the Reed because of it."

"It takes nothing at all to keep a secret from you this summer, Jenny," Isabel said quickly, to ease the boy's discomfort. "You are always gone. Alric has been working with Cospatric and me, learning the old Norman songs. He has a fine voice."

"There you are, Alric. All untangled. So you sing, do you? It will be a relief to leave that to someone else. Now, Isabel, please excuse us. Alric has to go back to the stable, and I want to see to La Rose."

As soon as they were outside, Jenny drew close to the boy, speaking in an urgent whisper. "Alric, I think I know why this happened, but it must be a secret between us. Can you keep a secret for me?" The boy nodded, and Jenny continued. "I must have offended the fairies when I was riding in the forest. I want to make peace with them." This was only half a lie. "Galiene says the fairies go abroad by moonlight. Tomorrow, when the moon is full and everyone is busy with the dance, I will steal away. You must help me. Can you take La Rose to pasture tomorrow afternoon, and make sure she is not returned to the stable in the evening?"

The boy frowned. "Not if Thurstan comes with me, my lady, and he will."

Jenny smiled. "Leave Thurstan to me. When the smith has finished with the iron bars for the stable, I will find a way to keep the boy at the bellows tomorrow as well."

"What if Gilchrist checks and finds La Rose gone?"

"Gilchrist will be busy. It will surely take all afternoon to put the wood for the bonfire in place. I will tell him La Rose is fine." Jenny paused. Alric could never carry her saddle any distance. "I will take my saddle from the stable, but you must be sure the bailey gate is not barred so I can return home."

"But, my lady, the groom makes sure it is barred these nights."

"Just slip away sometime in the night and remove the bar. Everyone will be too busy with the dance to notice. This is important, Alric. If I am caught, it will go hard for me, but I must make sure nothing like this ever happens to La Rose or you again. Do you understand?"

The boy nodded, his eyes large. Jenny knew she was asking him to take a risk as well.

They met Gilchrist and Galiene just coming out the stable door with a very sullen-looking Thurstan in tow. "Very well, then," the groom said. "Off you go to the forge, lad." He looked at Alric. "Lucky you are to be so lame, laddie, or you might be at the forge all day yourself. As it is, you can see to the lady's horse. She needs grooming just as badly as she did yesterday."

By the end of the day, each stall was outfitted with its own iron bar, and old horseshoes had been hammered above all the stable doors for good measure. "You can be sure the wee folk will stay away now," Galiene told Gilchrist.

"Seeing is believing," the groom replied in his terse way.

Jenny wondered why iron bars and horseshoes would keep the fairies away when the horses were already shod with iron, but she knew better than to ask in front of Gilchrist. The groom's barely concealed scorn gave Galiene an uncertain temper.

Jenny went to bed that night knowing it would take a miracle to get her to Carter Hall and back unnoticed, even with Alric's help. She was amazed by her own guile. She had spent half the afternoon in the kitchen shed convincing Hawise that they needed new grills for the kitchen, and the other half at the forge, praising Thurstan's work at the bellows until the smith thought the boy the best helper he had ever seen. She was fairly sure the smith now planned to use Thurstan for another day's work at least while he forged the new grills. Jenny smiled to herself. If he decided to claim the boy for good, it would serve Thurstan right for being mean to Alric. Jenny tried to keep her mind on the practical problems of getting out of the bailey unnoticed. She did not allow herself to consider what would happen after that.

* * *

The sun rose the next morning on a perfect August day. Jenny breathed a sigh of relief. The dance would surely go ahead in such weather. Everything was as it should be in the stable, the horses perfectly groomed in their ironclad stalls. The guards had left. Jenny hefted her saddle and hid it out by the pasture unseen. After mass, she strolled close enough to the forge to see Thurstan hard at work. These small victories cheered Jenny so much that Isabel noticed while they worked.

"Carding wool is not a task that makes you glad enough to hum, as a rule," she said.

"I feel pleased with life today. It must be the weather, or maybe the thought of the dance."

"Or perhaps you are thinking of Earl William?" Isabel said. "How do you feel about this betrothal? It seems as good as sworn now."

Jenny put down her carding combs and sighed. "Lady Ada will be a harsh mother-in-law. She overshadows all around her, and she seemed to dislike me on sight."

Isabel gave her a quizzical look. "You are not marrying the mother. What of her son?"

"Earl William fancies himself the center of the universe," Jenny said. "Like the earth, he believes the sun, the moon, and the stars orbit around him. Even when he tries to be kind, he can find no better subject for conversation than himself. He is not the man I would marry if I were free to choose." She was alarmed to hear herself speak so truthfully.

"Jenny, it may be better this way. I chose Bleddri, and look how it went for me."

Jenny had waited so long to hear Isabel's story. Now, she was afraid she might tell Isabel everything if they continued to talk this way. She quickly changed the subject. "How is the wood for the bonfire, do you know? I asked Gilchrist to see to it."

"Then it will be done properly, you can be sure. But go see if you want. Some sunshine might do you good. You look a bit pale."

Jenny hoped Isabel would not notice how quickly she fled. Could Tam Lin be a fiend like Bleddri, luring her away from home to do her harm? Surely not. Bleddri had always made her uneasy, but the Tam she remembered was gentle and kind. Aye, she told herself, but who played that cruel trick on you with the dress, and who tied the elflocks in La Rose's mane and terrified Alric? Could that be Tam as well? She had to know.

In the open part of the bailey, the pile of wood was growing higher, carefully stacked under Gilchrist's watchful eye.

"Mind where you place that log, boy. Not like that. We must be sure none of the wood will roll when everything is aflame." He was totally absorbed by the work.

Alric limped around a corner of the stable with an armful of bark for kindling. When their eyes met, Jenny knew he would not fail her.

Chapter Seventeen

◈

HIGH ABOVE THE MOON-SILVERED forest, a wind rushed though the tops of the great trees with a song like the voice of a river, but here, far below, everything was hushed and still. Jenny kept La Rose tightly reined, afraid the little horse might stumble in the dark. She had never been alone in the forest at night like this. It was more beautiful and more terrifying than any dream.

It had been easy to slip away unnoticed. The bonfire Gilchrist had made was so large, it was impossible to tell who might be on the other side, and just beyond it, darkness fell like a curtain. Now, if only Alric could make sure the bailey gate would be open when she returned. If only no one noticed she was gone. She tried not to let her thoughts run too far ahead.

Before she came to the river, she dismounted and led La Rose cautiously, straining for any sound that might alert her to the freebooters. There was no reason why she should meet them here rather than anywhere else on the path, she knew, but she could not shake the feeling that this was a dangerous place now.

She mounted La Rose to cross the river and urged her mare on to Carter Hall, her heart pounding. Tam Lin might be completely changed, a cruel, malicious man she did not know. But the thought that Carter Hall would again be empty frightened her even more.

He was there, though, waiting by the well. He even smiled when he saw her.

"You came," he said. "I was afraid you might not be able to."

She dismounted but pulled La Rose close, using the little mare as a barrier. "Able to? Did you not wonder if I would want to see you again?" She shouted the words.

"But I thought . . . I hoped . . . we were friends," he stammered.

"How could you, after the way you treated me?"

"What do you mean?"

"You sent me off to Roxburg in a dress made of dead leaves. It was a cruel trick. How could you be so heartless?"

"Heartless! It took years to learn how to make that glamour. You have no inkling how hard it was to cast a charm that would last that long and travel so far from its maker. And the dress was beautiful. You said so yourself." He looked crushed.

Jenny took a step back. "How can you speak that way?" Her voice dropped to a whisper. "As if magic were part of everyday life?"

"It is part of my everyday life. It has been for almost seven years. I wanted to give you a gift no one else could give you. I forgot how strange it might seem." He looked lost. "Jenny, I can hardly remember what it must be like to

190

live in the world of men."

Jenny's anger vanished. "But it was more than just a dress, Tam. Why did you beguile it so that every man would fall in love with me? I thought you were mocking me."

"Mocking you? Jenny, I have to make you understand." He ran both hands through his hair. "I hardly know how to begin. Will you come to the hall? I made you a meal. Please?" He held out his hand to her.

Jenny hesitated. She had not dared to hope she would find him like this, calm and reasonable as ever. She was still uncertain she could trust this man, whose life might be more terrible and strange than she could imagine. But she knew she could not leave him now. "I will," she said, and she took his hand.

Carter Hall was transformed. A cheerful fire blazed on the floor very near to the place where she had cried herself out a few days before. A hare was roasting over the fire and a table was set for a meal. Jenny was amazed. "Is this fairy glamour as well?" she asked.

"No, it is not." For the first time, Tam sounded annoyed. "Hunting without hounds is no easy sport. I was off in the woods for days, getting that hare to make you a good supper. Everything you see here is the product of my hard labor, I promise you that. Except the bread, which came by the good grace of those freebooters." Then he gave her a smile that was more than a little mischievous. "And the fish, which I robbed from one of your father's weirs. He has so many, I was sure no one would notice."

"You took all this trouble for me?" It was hard to imagine any man making a meal, especially one of noble birth.

He looked embarrassed. "That I did. Will you sit?"

She sat on the only bench while he went to the fire and brought the dishes, a crock of stewed salmon, and the roast hare. Then he set out bread and water. "I wish it were ale," he said, and he sat beside her.

The food looked very real, but then, so had the dress. If this were fairy food, she might be captured forever if she so much as tasted it. She spooned some salmon into her bowl. His presence beside her on the bench was such a comfort, such a relief, she knew she must trust him. She took a deep breath and tasted the salmon. "This is very good," she said.

He smiled. "Eat now, then we will talk."

So Jenny did. Most of the hall was deep in shadow. Somewhere, under the eaves, she thought she heard a sound like the ruffling of feathers. Off in a far corner, she could see the pallet where Tam slept. Since returning from Roxburg, she had been too upset to eat. Now, the food tasted wonderful.

"Do they not feed you in your father's house?" he asked when she emptied her bowl the second time. But he seemed pleased.

When the meal was over, they both fell silent. Jenny wished they could sit here forever, like two ordinary people with no terrible secrets to disclose.

"Are you betrothed yet?" he asked finally. His voice was tight, as if the words hurt him.

"No," she said. "But it seems I soon will be." She looked at him. Everything about him was dear to her—the shape of his cheekbones, the way his hair fell over his brow. She wanted to gather him into her heart and keep him there forever. "Tam, will you tell me how things are for you, and how they came to pass?" she asked.

"I will tell you what I can." He paused and sighed. "When I was a lad, I went out hunting one winter's day and fell from my horse. I hit my head, badly. When I awoke, I was among folk I had never seen before. They cared for me, and I thought all was well, until I tried to return home. Then I understood these were not earthly folk, and I was in their thrall. They were kind to me, Jenny. They treated me well. They wanted me to stay with them forever, but I knew my granda had only me, and I could not bear to think of his grief. So I begged her—*them*," he corrected himself, "to let me return. Finally, my wish was granted. But the charm they had placed on me when they saved my life—for I would have died without it—was too strong. I can be in the land of men, but I am no longer earthly myself. It seems as if I have one foot in both worlds, and I am torn apart by the distance I must stretch to stay that way. If I give up, they will take me forever."

Jenny noticed that, like Galiene, he never spoke the name of these people, as if the word *fairy* alone had power. "Can nothing break this spell?" she asked.

"Nothing I would ask of another. I am a danger to everyone now, especially those I care for. I came here to keep myself away from earthly folk. I should never have spoken to you. I should not have used my magic to give you that dress. I should not have asked you here tonight." He sounded angry with himself.

"A stronger man would have sent you away just as you

came, thinking you were tricked out of malice." He sighed. "But I have fought so hard and so long. And I grow weary of lying. For once, I want to tell the truth. So let me tell you why the dress was beguiled. I hoped it might win a better man. One who would love you and treat you well. William de Warenne is not the man for you."

"I know that," Jenny said, looking away so that she might not betray her feelings.

"But my magic is not strong enough to do just anything," he continued. "I made that dress so that every man would see you as I do. That was the only way I could seal the charm."

"What do you mean?"

He left the bench and went to the fire, standing with his back to her. He spoke so softly, she had to strain to hear him. "If I could come to you as an earthly knight, my lass, if I could court you at your father's hall and win you for my own, I would. But that cannot be. I want you to find someone who will love you as I would, so I bound the charm with my own feelings. They loved you because I love you."

She rose and stood behind him, leaning her cheek against his back. "Listen to me, Tam Lin. Even if I spend the rest of my life sleeping in William de Warenne's bed, even if you are someplace I can never reach, you are mine. You will always be mine, even if this one night is all I ever have of you." She took his shoulders and turned him around.

He looked alarmed. "You should leave now. We should not . . . ," he began to say.

But anything they should or should not do seemed meaningless to her now, so she put her mouth over his to stop the words. He resisted briefly, then began to respond.

Jenny had never so much as kissed a man, but what happened next seemed so natural. It was as if their bodies continued the kind of conversation they had always shared, each gesture answered by another that matched it perfectly. Somewhere far away, a voice tried to tell her this was dangerous and wrong, that she might pay for what she was doing for the rest of her life. She silenced the voice, knowing that this was not so, no matter what anyone else would think or say.

She had expected a man would be rough and callous all over. The sweet shock of his skin delighted her. She tried to memorize the feel of it, the way he glowed in the firelight, to hold him forever in her mind's eye. She could hardly believe anyone could seem so beautiful. She wanted to breathe his spirit into her lungs. She wished they could become a single being. He tried to pull away, but she drew him back, insisting he stay with her. Time slowed. If he had cast a powerful charm, it could not have been more magical.

He was as gentle as he could be, but what they did, ultimately, hurt till she cried out in pain. He answered with a cry of his own, a long sigh of release and regret. Then, finally, they were back in the real world.

"That should never have happened," he said, stroking her face. "I have ruined you."

She smiled at him. "It was my will, more than yours. If I am to be given away like a piece of property, at least I will know that once in my life I took a man of my own choosing, the man I love. Hush now. Let me lie here in your arms."

Jenny kept the thoughts away as long as she could, but finally, they came creeping in. And then she remembered there was still one thing she did not understand. She propped herself up on her elbow to look at him. "Tam, why did you tie the elflocks in La Rose's mane and in the boy's hair when he was guarding her?"

He sat up, alarmed. "Someone did that?"

"Aye. I thought you were playing tricks on me."

"Jenny, I would never do such a thing." He reached for his shirt and pulled it on, stood up, and began to pace. "She must know. What a fool I am."

"What are you talking about?"

"Jenny, rise up and dress. You must leave this place. You should never return."

She pulled on her kirtle. "You cannot mean that, Tam. Tell me what troubles you."

"I thought I could keep you secret. But the queen of the wee folk must know. Jenny, she will harm you if she can. I will put a charm on you to see you home, but you should never come this way again. If you value your life, please, stay away."

She came to him and took his hand. "I stayed even after I knew you were no longer earthly. I would risk my mortal soul for you. Do not forbid me to see you again."

He put his arms around her and kissed the top of her head. "How can I? You are my only friend. But at least promise never to come back after dark." He frowned.

"Jenny, I cannot say how much longer I can hold to this earth. When the summer is gone, I may be gone as well."

"No! You must be mistaken."

"I wish I were, my love. Now, please, you must go. Dress and let us find La Rose."

The horse was waiting for her by the well. "How can I bear to leave you?" Jenny said.

"You must. There is grave danger here for you now." He kissed her one last time. "I should not work magic, for every time I do, a part of me is lost, but I cannot send you into this night unprotected." When she was up on La Rose, he said, "Close your eyes." She did, and he mumbled something. "There. That should see you home. Godspeed."

Jenny was scarcely out of sight of Carter Hall when her troubles began to press in on her like the darkness. He will never be mine, she told herself. He may disappear forever, and I have ruined myself. How will I face the world tomorrow? The enormity of what she had done was just beginning to come home to her. She felt hot and unclean and angry with herself. At the ford in the river, she left La Rose to drink and walked along the bank to a nearby pool. She stripped off her clothes and slipped into the black water. She felt better at once, cleansed and soothed. She wondered how late it was, and whether they had missed her at home. Moonlight still bathed the forest, so not too many hours had passed.

Jenny was about to climb out of the river when the freebooters appeared on the opposite bank. The noise of the water over the stones of the ford must have hidden the sounds of their approach. Jenny swam in plain sight. She froze, waiting for them to see her, but they crossed the river as if she were not there. She held her breath. La Rose was right by the path. They passed close enough to reach out and touch the little horse, and still, they seemed to see nothing. And then they were gone.

Jenny's teeth chattered as she climbed up the riverbank, but not from cold. Tam's charm must have protected her. Nothing else could have kept those men from seeing La Rose on the path beside them. She wrung the water out of her hair and patted herself with her kirtle, then quickly dressed.

"Come, La Rose," she whispered. "Take me home."

Chapter Eighteen

❧

"Your lord father says come hear the messenger from Rowanwald, you and your sister both, my lady." Alric looked around. "Is she not here?"

Jenny arrived back at the kitchen garden just in time to hear the boy speak to Isabel. She leaned unsteadily against the garden fence and tried to swallow down the acid taste of vomit. She had been gathering herbs for winter with Isabel until a wave of nausea sent her running to the manure pile behind the stable, where she might hide what was happening. Just as she had become accustomed to avoiding breakfast, this sickness had expanded to fill most of her day.

Isabel gave her an anxious glance. "Here she is, Alric. Tell my father we will come presently." When the boy left, she said, "Were you sick again, Jenny? I wish you would tell Galiene. I fear all your travels this summer have left you ill."

"It is nothing, Isabel. Galiene's remedies are sometimes worse than the illness they cure." Jenny hoped her smile was convincing. At first she had allowed herself to believe that she had, in fact, been taken with some illness. But now, at the end of September, she could no longer pretend. If Galiene knew, she would guess at once what ailed Jenny, and she was not yet ready to own the secret. She would pay for her night with Tam for the rest of her life. Each day she managed to hide her pregnancy now would be one less to bear.

"Come," Isabel said, "we must not keep Father waiting."

They passed through the bailey without seeing another soul. Every able-bodied servant was down at the big barn in Langknowes, helping to thresh the harvested grain. Even Galiene had gone.

"Do you suppose this is about your confession?" Jenny asked.

Isabel nodded. "I hope so. I am ready now. It will be a relief to have it over with, no matter what comes next."

Jenny wished she could feel the same way. She had avoided confession herself for weeks.

Their father was waiting in the bower with the same boy who had brought Jenny's invitation to Lilliesleaf only a few months before. "The message is for both of you," the vicomte said, smiling broadly. Jenny's stomach lurched so, she was glad it was already empty.

The boy took a deep breath and launched into his memorized speech. "Brother Bertrand of Rowanwald sends greetings to the house of Vicomte Philippe Avenel and the blessings of our lord abbot. Brother Bertrand begs you prepare for him, a week hence, when he will hear the confession of Lady Isabel and solemnize the betrothal of Lady Jeanette to Earl William de Warenne. Earl William will travel to Rowanwald and thence to Langknowes with

Brother Bertrand to pledge his troth to Lady Jeanette and decide the day of their wedding."

Jenny eased herself onto a stool. Everything swam before her eyes, and she was afraid she might faint.

Her father noticed none of this.

"Boy, carry a message back to Rowanwald," he said. "Ask Brother Bertrand, would he please send a message to my son Eudo in Lilliesleaf, so he may come witness his sister's betrothal." He clapped his hands together. "What a fine day this will be for all of us. Isabel, we must make ready for the royal party." He suddenly frowned. "Has anyone gathered oak galls for the abbey?"

Jenny took a deep breath. "I took a few in the spring, Father. I can get those for you. But this year's crop should be ready. They are not hard to find. Tell your men to look in any of the great oaks."

"Very well. I will go to the threshing barn myself to send someone out today. Otherwise, we might forget in the heat of preparations. You two can begin your planning."

When he was gone, Isabel took up her shuttle. "I will work here now so you may rest, Jenny. You are as green as glass." She worked in silence for a moment, then put the shuttle down and came to sit with her sister. "To think I will make my confession on the day of your betrothal. As you commit yourself to the man who will make your life, I will finally free myself from the one who ruined mine."

The question Jenny had kept to herself all these months was on her lips before she could stop herself. "Isabel, did you never think that Bleddri was not what he seemed? I confess I did. I only saw his true nature once, but it frightened me. He seemed another man."

"It has always been your talent to see folk as they are, Jenny. And you saw the truth, for he was another man." Isabel stared at her lap. "I saw only what I wished to see. The scales did not fall from my eyes until he brought me to that cliff by the sea. Then he told me to get down off my horse, for it was too fine a beast to be covered in my blood.

"He said he loved only gold," Isabel continued, her voice a whisper. "That he had already killed six maidens for their wealth, and I would be the seventh. He said all our blood and all our riches could not give him back the lands he had lost because of the Crusade to the Holy Land. He said I could not imagine the blood that was spilled there, the brutality. He was already bound for hell and nothing could change that, so he took whatever he wanted."

"But how did you keep your wits about you?" Jenny asked.

"I knew then he had never loved me. I still loved him, for love cannot be put aside so quick as that, but I also knew, however much I loved Bleddri, I loved my own life more. So I told him to turn around, to let me take off my finery, for it was too good to be ruined by his knife and my blood. I hoped he would be greedy enough to do so, and he was. It was so odd. I felt as if it were happening to someone else. As I took off my cloak, he stood close behind Bravura with his back to me, so certain I would never harm him. I took my cloak pin and stabbed the horse in the flank. I was lucky, for Bleddri was caught square in the back. He could not rise or speak. If any kind word had passed his lips then, I might still have relented. But he turned and gave me a look of such scorn and hate, it steeled me for what I had to do. I threw my cloak over him, so I would not see that face again, so he could not grab to stop me. I rolled him to the edge, which was not far, and pushed him over."

"How could you be so strong?"

Isabel thought Jenny was speaking of physical strength. "I could not have moved him like that before or after. It was as if angels held my arms. But if they did, they fled too soon, for I was left, standing at the top of a cliff, looking down on the body of the man I loved while the waves and rocks battered it to pieces, knowing he had died by my hand. Knowing too that he suffered the fate he had planned for me. I was farther from home and more alone than I had ever been. I began to shake then. I sank to my knees and cried and cried." She looked at Jenny with large, empty eyes. "To this day, I wonder what kept me from throwing myself after him."

"Oh, Isabel, how can you say that?" Jenny was shocked.

Isabel nodded. "I know. That may be the worst sin of all. It was as if I had split in two when Bleddri said he would kill me. When I came back to myself, I wished I were dead. The man I loved was dead. How could I feel otherwise? You have never loved like that, Jenny. How can I ask you to understand?"

Jenny put her arms around her sister and held her like a child while Isabel cried. The sun still shone, but the light seemed to have gone out of the day. Jenny longed to tell her sister that she knew what it meant to love so deeply, but she could not. Isabel was ready to cleanse her soul, and Jenny's secret would only mar her confession.

Finally, Isabel dried her tears. "I should not have burdened you with my story. I have been rehearsing it in my mind all these days, preparing for my confession."

"No, I am glad that you told me, finally." Jenny knew she should let Isabel recover now, but as she compared Isabel's ruin with her own, curiosity overcame her. "Isabel, you were gone with him three days. Did he . . . did he never touch you?"

Isabel smiled sadly and shook her head. "Not so much as a kiss. At the time, I thought it was a mark of his respect for me. But now I know I was loathsome in his sight. He hated all of us, you see. Somewhere deep in my heart, I felt that coldness. I thought it was his nature, but I never guessed that nothing else remained. I know better now, Jenny. If I could choose again, I would not be so blind."

Isabel said no more. Jenny wondered if she were talking about Cospatric, but it seemed cruel to ask.

The days that followed were so filled with preparations, Jenny could keep her worries at bay as she worked, but each night they overwhelmed her. If she confessed, her father would probably send her to the priory in spring, soon after the child was born, to hide her shame. Jenny wondered if it might be possible for her to take her sister's place. But even in Galiene's care, a newborn without its mother would not be likely to survive, and no one would mourn if it died. No one but Jenny. In spite of everything, she already loved her child fiercely. *If this is all I can have* of Tam, she thought, I must find a way to keep the baby. If she could only convince Earl William to make the vows soon, she might marry him and pretend the baby was born early. She felt sick to think of the guile it would take to trick a man like that. And then, there was the problem of confession. Could she bring herself to withhold everything that had happened with Tam and put her soul in peril? Yes. She already valued the life of her child above her soul. If she had to lie in confession, she would.

She had not gone back to Carter Hall since the full moon of August. Jenny's journey home that night had been so uneventful after she left the river, her absence so completely unnoticed, that she suspected Tam's charm had even worked its way into her father's bailey. She longed for Tam now, thought of him constantly, but she stayed away. Not because she feared the fairy queen, but because she could not bring herself to add to his troubles. She knew he would blame himself for her pregnancy, though she never would. I will honor his memory by protecting his child, she told herself. That may be all I can do.

When Eudo arrived the night before the betrothal, Jenny was surprised to find he had come alone. Surely Sir Robert and Lady Margaret would want to witness Earl William's betrothal. Half of Teviotdale was coming. Jenny noticed that Eudo seemed more serious than usual, but in all the confusion there was no chance to ask what troubled him. Isabel had not seen her brother since Christmas, and she was so happy, Jenny could imagine that nothing bad had ever happened to her.

As the evening ended, on the way to the bower, Isabel said, "I have a surprise for you, Jenny: a song. At least, Cospatric and I do. If you like, I will sing it again at your feast tomorrow evening."

Cospatric seemed a little uncomfortable in the family bower, but he quickly settled himself on a stool and began to play. The song Isabel sang was in his own language, Gaelic. It sounded strange to Jenny's ears, but Isabel seemed to have mastered it without difficulty. Her voice sounded even more beautiful than usual. Everyone in the bower—her father, Eudo, even Galiene—was captivated. Only Jenny looked at Cospatric, so only she saw his face when he looked at Isabel. In that fleeting glance, Jenny found what she had been searching for all these weeks, a love so deep and honest it almost took her breath away.

"Cospatric taught me that love song in his own tongue," Isabel said when they had finished.

"I would love to hear it again at the feast, Isabel," Jenny said. She was more deeply touched than she could say.

When Cospatric left, Eudo said, "I wish to speak to my sister, on this last night that she is truly part of our family. Come, Jenny, let us walk." Only then did Jenny remember how troubled he had seemed earlier.

As they walked along the road, Eudo picked up a stick and hit the bushes. He would not look at her. "Isabel seems fine," he said at last. "I thought to find her greatly changed."

"So she was in the spring. You would not have known her then, but she returned to herself, little by little. The music has helped her greatly."

"That harper is a wonder. I have not heard the like of his music before."

Jenny could not resist praising Cospatric to her brother. "He is a good man, Eudo, forthright and kind, with a heart that would befit a nobleman."

Eudo sighed. "You make it easier for me to speak, for that is the very thing I wished to talk to you about. Jenny, many noblemen do not share those qualities of honesty and kindness. If you were to decide against this match, you need not fear for me. If Earl William were to demand his ransom from the tournament, I would find a way to pay it."

Jenny was so surprised that she stopped walking. "Eudo, I thought this match pleased you." She tried to think what might have caused this change. "Has father spoken to you about the moneylenders?" Perhaps Eudo was worried he would lose his birthright.

"Father told me, but that is not my only concern. Jenny, the more I learn of Earl William's character, the less I am inclined to trust him. If you feel the position he brings you is worth everything, if you think you could love him, I will never speak against him again. But if you wish to change your mind, I will stand by you."

Jenny felt that Eudo was not telling her everything, but she was afraid to probe further. This betrothal was her only hope for the future. She linked her arm with his. "You are a good and generous brother, Eudo. I will always be grateful for your loyalty." She sighed. "But the die is cast. By this time tomorrow, Earl William and I will be betrothed."

That night, for the first time, Jenny dreamed herself

back to Carter Hall. She was standing by the well, and everything was flooded with moonlight, but she was alone. Even in my dreams I can no longer find him, she thought when she woke.

Earl William's party must have left Rowanwald before sunrise, for it was more than half a day's journey, but they arrived at Langknowes just at noon. Jenny was amazed by their number. It would be hard to feed so many guests. Brother Bertrand greeted the family as old friends, but Earl William remained on his horse, looking around. Jenny guessed he was taking the measure of her father's property. He seemed shocked, and she wondered if her father had misled him. Earl William was so aloof and calculating, up there on his fine gray charger, that her heart quailed.

"And where is Brother Turgis?" she heard Brother Bertrand say.

"He thought to take this time to go among the outlying fermtouns, to christen any babies born this summer and perform a few marriages. He sends his regrets, but he knows he leaves us in your good hands," Jenny's father replied. Jenny suspected Brother Turgis had his nose out of joint because the almoner had taken over so many important functions for the family. Whatever the reason, Jenny was pleased. Brother Bertrand would lend grace to the ceremony.

Her father left Brother Bertrand and went to Earl William, who finally dismounted. "I bid you welcome as a son, my lord," he said, clapping him on the shoulder and then looking around. "Where is your lady? Jenny, come greet your bridegroom."

Jenny obeyed. When Earl William looked at her, she thought she saw a flash of the same disappointment she had seen as he surveyed their lands. In truth, he had cared for her only when she wore the enchanted dress. Without it, she might have left Roxburg a free woman. She realized that Tam's confused attempt to bridge the gap between the fairy world and her own had sealed her fate.

"Daughter, show some affection," her father urged.

Jenny leaned forward and planted a chaste kiss on Earl William's cheek, turning away quickly before he could respond. "You have met my brother, Eudo, I believe, and this is my sister, Lady Isabel." Jenny seized Isabel's hand and placed it in Earl William's.

He dropped Isabel's soft white hand as if it were a live toad. "This is the maid who disgraced her family? I cannot believe you flaunt her so." His voice was loud.

A hush fell over the stable yard. Everyone seemed frozen. Eudo moved first, placing his hand on Isabel's shoulder, but it was Brother Bertrand who spoke. "I have come to hear Lady Isabel's confession, my lord. When she has received the grace of God, her sins will be forgiven. Let us not besmirch this day by casting stones in judgment." Jenny heard an unexpected sternness in his voice. This was not the tone a courtier would take with a member of the royal family, but that of a priest addressing someone found wanting. What could that possibly mean?

"Let us go to my hall," her father cried, trying to pretend nothing had happened. From the corner of her eye, Jenny saw Eudo quietly lead Isabel to the privacy of the bower. Jenny found she was shaking with anger. She wished she had the courage to order Earl William to leave, but she knew another scene would only make matters worse.

Whether Cospatric had been present to hear Earl William's slur against Isabel, Jenny did not know, but when they entered the hall, he immediately set to playing. The music was so lovely that Jenny would have guessed it to be charmed if she had not known better. By the time the harp fell silent, the mood of the day was restored, at least until her father spoke.

"Your mother did not travel with you, my lord?"

"No. Frankly, I must tell you, my mother does not care for this match. She feels, as she often does, that I have acted rashly."

Jenny could not believe what she was hearing. "I wonder that you would marry without your mother's blessing, my lord."

He stared at her for a long moment before answering. "My brother is head of the family, as well as king. I have his approval. That is certainly enough for me, Lady Jeanette. It will be your task to win your mother-in-law's affections when you come to court, for she runs the king's household and will until he marries, if he ever does."

While everyone else ate, Jenny picked at her food and pondered her situation. She had hoped that she and William would establish a household of their own, away from the traveling court of the king. It might be possible to trick Earl William into thinking his child was born early, but Lady Ada would be more difficult to fool. How could she spend her life in that unhappy family?

After the meal, Brother Bertrand went to hear Isabel confess, and Earl William drew Jenny aside. "Come walk with me," he said, "and we will discuss our wedding day." He seemed pleasant enough, but as soon as they were out of the bailey, he turned on her. "When you come to court, you will learn to curb your tongue, for there are many there who would use an unkind word against me to their own advantage."

Jenny looked at him, amazed. "I spoke no word against you, my lord."

"Indeed. 'I wonder that you would marry without your mother's blessing, my lord.' What do you call that? I will not suffer your sharp tongue, Jeanette, I warn you. I plan to bring you to court soon. Next month, if that suits your father. My mother will oversee your behavior there, and she will soon bring you to heel if I cannot, I promise you. As for our marriage, that will be delayed a year or more."

"You cannot mean that," Jenny said. Her distress seemed to please him more than anything she had done since he had arrived.

"But I can. My sister's wedding emptied the coffers. My brother is not prepared to pay for another so soon. I am heir to the throne. No expense will be spared when I am married."

Tears sprang to Jenny's eyes. "I cannot wait a year," she whispered.

Flattered by her distress, he stopped walking and put his arms around her. "Come now. After today, we will be as good as married. You still owe me that forfeit from the tournament, you know. When you come to court, I will have the chance to claim my prize in full." And he kissed her. It was a rough kiss, and Jenny's reaction was immediate. Without thinking, she flattened both her palms against his shoulders and pushed. Her strength surprised them both. Suddenly he was an arm's length away, red-faced with anger.

"When I am your lord and master, Jeanette, you will not treat me so," he said.

"When I am betrothed to you, my lord, you may do as you wish. Until that time, I must govern my own behavior."

He gave her a predatory smile. "I think I can wait that long."

She turned back to her father's hall without looking to see if he followed. She tried to wipe the feel of his mouth from her lips with the back of her hand. His kiss was so unlike anything she had shared with Tam that she found it hard to believe it could be called by the same name.

Chapter Nineteen

I T WAS IMPOSSIBLE TO STOP the betrothal ceremony now. Jenny allowed herself to be dressed in her scarlet silk and led back to the hall. The chapel was far too small to hold the crowd of guests that had assembled. Jenny met their smiling faces like a sleepwalker until Brother Bertrand asked her to place her hand in Earl William's. When she looked into William's cold blue eyes, she found her voice.

"Father, I cannot pledge my troth to this man." She tried to speak loudly, but her voice came out in a whisper.

When Brother Bertrand leaned forward and whispered back, she realized that only he and Earl William had heard her. "My child, you cannot mean this. Everything is arranged."

William de Warenne looked as though he would murder her.

Jenny took a deep breath and stepped back. "Father, I cannot marry this man." She spoke loudly enough to be heard by everyone this time. "I am with child by another."

The shocked silence that followed seemed to go on forever. Once again, Brother Bertrand was the first to find his voice. "Do you swear before God this is the truth, Lady Jeanette, and not some falsehood created to deliver you from this betrothal?"

Jenny hung her head. "I did lie with another man, Father, and I seem to be with child."

"This girl has betrayed me," William cried. "I want to see her beaten for her sins."

"And you, Earl William, will you be beaten for your sins as well?"

"Eudo, silence!" their father roared.

Everyone turned to Eudo. His face was white, but he held his ground. "No, Father, let me speak. If my sister is to be punished, why should this man escape unscathed? Mary, a servant at Lilliesleaf, is also with child, and she names Earl William as the father. Lady Margaret has her beaten black and blue for saying so, but her story does not change. And I believe her."

Earl William's face was dark with fury. "I did not come here to be slandered. This girl is as bad as her sister. I am well rid of the lot of you." He stormed from the hall, and his entourage followed.

Everyone else filed silently after them, until only Brother Bertrand and Jenny's family remained.

"Eudo Avenel, you have made a powerful enemy this day," the priest said. "But I admire your courage. If the child at Lilliesleaf is his, that would make three that I am aware of." He sighed. "The king wished to see his brother wed to prevent such shame. That is why he gave his blessing to this union, though it was not as illustrious or profitable as Lady Ada wished. I thought we were going to sacrifice a lamb this day to protect the honor of the king's household." He turned to Jenny. "But you are no lamb."

His voice grew stern, though it was not as angry as it might have been. "I want your confession now. Do not think to delay as your sister did. Childbirth will place you in the very jaws of death, and you must cleanse your soul at once. Come to the chapel with me now."

Jenny knew she would accomplish nothing by resisting Brother Bertrand. In the chapel, she poured out every scrap of bad behavior she had committed over the summer. How she mistreated Hilde at Lilliesleaf, how she bullied Ranulf, how she enlisted Alric to help her steal away the night of the full moon. As she spoke, she felt her burden grow lighter. She did not mention magic or the fairies for fear the priest might doubt her sanity, but she told him about Tam. She finally finished and received her penance and absolution, but Brother Bertrand did not move.

"My child, you have bound yourself to a madman. I hear he lives like some wild beast in the forest." He shook his head in disbelief. Jenny forced herself to remain silent, knowing she could never explain the truth about Tam to him. Brother Bertrand continued. "Still, he is of noble birth. The proper thing would be to see you wed, to give your child a name, even if the man cannot live with you as a husband should. I think your father should send men out to hunt him down at once."

"Oh, Father, no. I could not bear that." The idea terrified her.

"You surprise me, my child. Most women in your state would wish to be wed in haste."

"But Father, he is not like other men. I would not see him frightened or harmed." Jenny suddenly remembered something. "The night we met you, my father swore Tam Lin would come to no harm by his hand. Is he not still bound by that oath?"

The priest nodded. "You remember well. Yes, he is."

"Then, I beg you to keep my secret. I cannot say who the father of this child is until I know he is safe from harm."

Brother Bertrand frowned. "Of course, I can reveal nothing you have told me in confession. But I can hardly counsel you to disobey your father. Knowing that you carry the child of a great household would do much to soften his wrath in the months ahead."

Jenny lifted her chin. "I must see that my father is not tempted to break his oath. But beyond that, I will not lighten my own burden by adding to that of the man I love."

Brother Bertrand rose. "You are every bit as willful as your sister. Like her, you set your feet on the most difficult path. But your wishes are not selfish, and I am bound to honor the sanctity of confession."

Jenny grasped his hand. "Thank you, Father."

He placed his hand briefly on her head in benediction. "You thank me for placing you on a bed of thorns."

Jenny had expected everyone in the family bower to be upset, and she was not surprised. Isabel had been crying, and Eudo was comforting her. Galiene sat in a far corner, no doubt hoping she would not be noticed and dismissed.

Jenny's father rose as she entered with Brother Bertrand. "I blame the earl of Roxburg for this," the vicomte said.

Jenny almost panicked. "What do you mean, Papa?" she managed to say.

"The girls at Marchmont were not properly chaperoned. I will be surprised if you are the only maid who was ruined at that event."

Jenny breathed a sigh of relief, grateful she had kept her wits. "This did not happen to me at Roxburg, Father."

"If not, where?" her father roared. Then, suddenly, his voice broke. "Do not tell me I have harbored another viper in my house."

"No, Papa, no," Jenny said. "No knight about your hall did this."

Eudo spoke. "Then tell us who, Jenny, so that we may find the man and put the shame behind us."

Jenny bowed her head. "I cannot."

"You cannot mean to keep this secret! How can you wish to spare the man who left you so?"

"Father, please, I am not even certain that he lives."

"What nonsense is this?"

Brother Bertrand spoke. "Vicomte, Earl William may be gone, but there are still guests in your hall who have traveled far. They must be fed, and you are their host. Let us see to them now and give your daughter time to reflect on her duty to you." Jenny's father seemed grateful to follow the priest's suggestion. They left without another word.

As soon as they were gone, the three women turned

silently to Eudo. In spite of everything, he laughed. "I know. I am not welcome to stay and listen. But, Jenny, hear me before I go. You got yourself out of that betrothal in the worst way possible, but I am glad to see the back of William de Warenne. I have not slept well in weeks, thinking he would be your husband."

"Eudo, why did you not tell me everything?"

"I thought it would be wrong to ruin your chance to wed such a powerful man. Besides, you heard what Brother Bertrand said. The king knew and so did the Church. Many men sow wild oats before they marry, and no one thinks it a great sin. If you took exception to the match, I was not sure anyone would listen. I would have ruined your happiness to no avail." Eudo blushed. "I questioned Mary myself, when she was left alone between beatings. She was not"—he hesitated, looked down, then plunged on—"she was not taken willingly." He looked directly into Jenny's eyes. "He was not the man for you."

Jenny smiled because her brother had unknowingly echoed Tam's words. She kissed his cheek. "Thank you, Eudo. I will never forget what you did for me this day."

"Before I go, you should know I plan to stay home now. I have lost my taste for Sir Robert's household, and you and Isabel have struggled without me for too long. I should have come home in the spring."

When he was gone, Isabel finally spoke. "Jenny, how could I have been so blind?" Her eyes were red from crying.

It tore Jenny's heart to see Isabel like this because of her. "Hush, Isabel. I thought it wrong to send you into your confession with such a secret. Can you forgive me?" As Isabel nodded, Jenny remembered what that confession meant. "What did Brother Bertrand say about going to the priory?" Jenny was suddenly afraid Isabel might be taken from her at once.

"I begged him to let me stay until after Christmas, and he agreed. I will not leave you yet."

Jenny hugged her sister. "Oh, I am pleased." Past Isabel, Jenny looked at Galiene. She had expected sympathy, but the old nurse looked surprisingly stern.

"Lady Isabel," Galiene said, "could I ask you to go to the chapel and pray for the soul of your sister? I think she was right to keep her secrets from you, for they are grave indeed. I need to understand the depth of her troubles before we can sort them out."

Jenny nodded. As much as she dreaded this talk with Galiene, she knew it was necessary.

"If you are certain," Isabel said. She was reluctant to leave, but Galiene's manner was compelling.

When they were alone, Galiene wasted no time. "If your sister has been blind, I must have had eyes of wood this summer. I knew your fate was linked to his, but I was foolish enough to think you would fight over that piece of land. I let you go traipsing off into the woods whenever you pleased." It was hard to tell if she was more angry with herself or with Jenny. "What manner of charm did he cast to bring you to this?" Jenny noticed Galiene did not speak Tam's name. She looked wretched.

"Galiene, the only magic was that of our honest love for each other. Of that I am certain. He gave me a dress to take to Roxburg that was charmed, but I did not know when I took it. He worked a charm to see me safely home the night of the full moon. That was when I slipped away to see him last. But that was all. That charm was necessary, and the dress was, well, a mistake. He tries not to use his magic. He wishes himself free of it."

"Then there is hope. If he wishes to be freed from the magic, he might yet be."

"But how? I asked you once, remember? While I worked on Alric's hair. You said you did not know."

"And I do not, but he would. Did you ever ask him?"

Every word of their conversations was engraved on Jenny's memory. She thought back. "I did," she said at last. "He said, 'Nothing I would ask of another.'"

"Then it will be dangerous, but you may be able to free him. Would you risk it?"

Jenny did not hesitate for a heartbeat. "Galiene, I would risk anything for him."

"Then you must go back to Carter Hall to find out how. But it will not be easy to get you out of here, and the time may not come soon. Will you trust me?"

"With my life."

Galiene allowed herself one grim smile. "We must hope it will not come to that."

Chapter Twenty

OVER THE NEXT FEW WEEKS, Galiene, Isabel, and Eudo tried to keep Jenny and her father apart as much as possible. The penance Brother Bertrand had imposed required Jenny to spend long hours in the chapel after mass each morning. She had never been so happy to pray. Rare game animals were suddenly sighted all over their father's land, and Eudo organized hunting parties that left early and returned late several times a week. Galiene insisted Jenny take long naps every afternoon. Even so, her father harangued her whenever she was in his sight, trying to discover the father of her child. She suspected Brother Bertrand had said something to her father to temper his rage before leaving Langknowes, and to Brother Turgis too, because neither were as harsh as they might have been. Even so, Jenny had cause to remember Brother Bertrand's words about placing her on a bed of thorns. Her father and Brother Turgis left her alone only if she said nothing. So she learned to hold her tongue, buying their silence with her own.

Autumn claimed the land. The fields were all shorn of

their crops. When the nights were clear and still, they woke in the mornings to find a fine white rime covering everything with diamonds that vanished like fairy glamour in the sun. If she ventured as far as the bailey gate, Jenny could see the forest in the distance, the ash trees yellowing and the great oaks turning the brown of fine leather. Was Tam still at Carter Hall, or was he gone forever, leaving it as empty as her life would be without him? She wondered constantly, but she knew she must wait for Galiene to tell her when she could go. In this way, finally, Jenny learned patience.

One warm afternoon in late October, Jenny woke to find Isabel sitting on the edge of their bed.

"They are hackling flax today, down by the retting pond. Cospatric and I thought we would sing to help the work along." She held out her hand. "Come with us."

Jenny stretched and yawned. The naps were more than just a way of keeping her from her father. She found she could sleep endlessly. It was hard to throw off the weight of dreams and return to life.

Outside, the sun was warm and strong. Cospatric was waiting by the gate with Alric. "Look who I found to help with the songs," the harper said. He made it sound as though he had met the boy by chance, but Jenny suspected he had sought Alric out. Cospatric was kind to everyone.

The retting pond was just a clean ditch below the bailey where rain collected. Weeks ago, after the flax had been hand-pulled and allowed to dry in the fields, it had been brought here to partially rot in the stagnant water.

Then it had been dried again and broken with flails to remove the flax fibers from the woody core of the plant. Now, servants threw the fibers over long iron hackles to comb out the tow that would finally be spun into linen thread. As the last step in this long, messy, backbreaking process, hackling was cause for celebration. Jenny heard a wave of laughter from the retting pond as they walked toward it.

Isabel and Cospatric stood upwind to avoid chaff from the hackling. Isabel began one of the silly, rhythmic songs suited to this work, a song that simply counted down the number of apples in an attic or mills in France, from ten to one, then blended seamlessly into the next, similarly senseless song. Cospatric took up the song at the end of each two-line verse, repeating Isabel's lines so that the music was unbroken. Jenny marveled at how his French had improved. His voice blended perfectly with Isabel's. The servants fell into the rhythm of the songs until their work seemed like a dance, everyone throwing the tow and pulling in time. On the sun-warmed grass beside Alric, Jenny let go of her worries and lay back, letting the mood of the day soak into her soul with the sunshine.

Jenny heard footsteps and opened her eyes to find Eudo standing above her. He knelt and spoke softly. "Galiene said I should tell you that we are going hawking tomorrow, toward Broomfield." Jenny sat up, suddenly alert. Carter Hall lay in the opposite direction. "We will be gone all day. Gilchrist will be happy to spend the day with us, and we are taking all the able-bodied boys to flush out game birds. Galiene says Alric knows how to ready your mare." He smiled. "Whatever you are hunting, Jenny, I hope you find it."

That night, a troupe of traveling musicians arrived. Jenny paid them little mind, except to note they were not half so skilled as Cospatric, but she was glad they kept her father occupied after supper. She barely slept that night. In the morning, she heard her father and Eudo rise before dawn. Without the hounds, the hunting party left more quietly than usual, but Jenny heard them go. She rose and dressed.

Galiene had milk and bread ready for her. "You must wait until the sun is high. Only the day belongs to earthly folk."

A few weeks before, such waiting would have driven Jenny mad. Now, she simply sat and ate. Finally, when the sun was fully risen, Galiene opened the door.

"What will you say to Isabel?" Jenny whispered as they left the bower.

"As little as I can, just as I did with Eudo. She will understand. I packed some bags with food to leave at Carter Hall. It will be best for him to eat our food whenever he can." She placed a silver coin in Jenny's hand. "Do not let go of this as you ride, and promise me, if you see a stranger, no word will pass your lips."

Jenny threw her arms around Galiene's neck and hugged her.

Alric was already in the stable, beside the bags of food. "Galiene said to wait until you came before I saddled your mare, my lady," he said.

"Will the others be out of sight by now?"

"Aye. Sir Eudo said he would lead them straight through Langknowes and keep to the road a good ways after. You need not worry about being seen from the other side of the bailey."

Jenny allowed Alric to help her onto La Rose. Her body had barely begun to change, but the girl who could leap into the saddle was already gone. La Rose seemed to sense this, for she trotted no faster than a man could walk. Jenny allowed her mare to set the pace, even though she felt exposed and wary on the open road, like a mouse waiting for a hawk to snatch it away.

Under the canopy of the forest, she began to breathe easier. The topmost branches of the great trees were already stripped by the wind. Sunbeams penetrated deep into the woods, giving it an open, airy feeling Jenny had not known since spring. Dry leaves rustled like parchment under La Rose's hooves, giving off a spicy fragrance that Jenny took deep into her lungs. Only the holly trees retained their freshness, the glossy dark leaves glowing with the promise that spring would return.

As Jenny came to Carter Hall, she remembered the last time she had seen this place in broad daylight, when she had found it empty and cried on the floor. I will not do that this time, she told herself. If he is gone, I will turn La Rose around and go back to my father's hall and try to face the rest of my life without tears. She braced herself for disappointment.

But she saw him as she came to the well, standing in an open field with his back to her. The sight of him brought an almost overwhelming surge of joy. Jenny knew she would do anything to protect this man from harm.

Before she could call to him, he raised something in his hand and began to twirl it on a rope. Jenny barely had time to recognize the lure before a young falcon swept down from a nearby tree, her small body aimed like an arrow at the bait. Just as the bird brought her talons forward to grasp it, Tam swung himself around, pulling the lure away so that the falcon was forced to fly past, wheel around, and try again. Jenny loved to watch the way he moved. On the second pass, he looked beyond the field and saw Jenny at the well. He was already smiling, but his smile widened. He let the falcon take the lure and left her.

Without a word, he came to Jenny, swept her off La Rose and held her tightly.

"I thought you might be gone," Jenny said after a long moment. "I was so afraid." Until that moment, she had not admitted to herself just how frightened she had been.

"I told you not to come, but I waited for you, every day."

Jenny pulled back to look at him. She laughed from pure happiness. "You have the falcon! My father's falconer watched her all spring. We thought she was dead."

"I took her for company. Training her helps to pass the time. And for food. I try to use my magic as little as possible now. With a hawk, I might at least eat a pigeon or two now and then. I keep her near to me, always. She was here the night you came, sleeping in the hall."

Jenny remembered the sound of wings rustling beneath the eaves. "Show me your falcon," she said. She knew they should talk of more serious things, but she wanted to prolong this moment of unclouded happiness.

The falcon was contentedly ripping the bait, a dead bird of some kind, to shreds. Tam knelt and offered his gloved hand and she stepped up, docile as a dove. Jenny shrank back, afraid the bird might lunge, but Tam drew her closer. "She is gentle as a lamb, for all her fierce looks. I named her L'Avenel, after you. You need not fear her, Jenny."

Jenny saw this was true. The falcon sat calmly on Tam's wrist, looking around with intelligent, yellow eyes. Her bright yellow feet seemed impossibly big.

"She was to be my betrothal gift," Jenny said.

The smile dropped from Tam's face. "And are you now betrothed?"

"No." The relief in his eyes made Jenny laugh with pleasure. "I am free as a bird." For the moment, it seemed true. Her troubles had vanished, as they always did when she was with him, as if there were no world beyond to bother her. "You were right, Tam. William would have made me miserable. He has already fathered children on any number of women." She stopped, appalled by her recklessness, but he did not notice.

"That sounds like William. Sit and tell me the whole story." He let the falcon roost on a hawthorn tree and pulled off his glove. At the stone bench, he took both her hands as they sat.

Jenny had fixed all her energy on getting to Carter Hall, bracing herself for the likelihood that he would be gone. Until that moment, she had given no thought to what she would tell Tam or how. She decided to begin at the end. "I need to know how I can free you from the charms that hold you here, Tam. Tell me. Please."

He rose and stood with his back to her, not speaking for the longest time. "There are things no one can ask of another," he said at last, in a quiet voice.

"But you must!" She took a breath to calm herself. "For the sake of your child." The secret was out. As at the betrothal ceremony, her announcement was greeted by silence. He turned slowly, and as he did, she realized she did not know how he was going to take this news. Not at all.

"There will be a child?" He looked dazed.

She lifted her chin to show him she was not ashamed, but only nodded. She could not speak. She waited for what seemed like a century while he pieced things together.

"And William would not marry you for that? This is wonderful. I have been sick with worry that you would not be able to escape him, and you are safe because of me." He seemed only to care that the betrothal was broken. Jenny remembered how he had responded when she tried to speak to him about the enchanted dress. Brother Bertrand's words came back to her: "You have bound yourself to a madman." Was it true?

"Tam, try to remember the earthly world. What will happen to me if I cannot . . ." Shame stuck in her throat. She swallowed it. "If I cannot find a father for my child."

He looked away into the distance. "They will take the child away and place you in the priory," he said. The words chilled her because she could not tell if he was looking into his knowledge of the past or her future. "But," he continued, "you would still have your life."

"My life means nothing without our child and you." She threw her last shred of pride to the wind. "Would you marry me if you were free?"

He smiled. "You know I would. I told you so, the night you came to me. Jenny, I would be gone by now if not for that night. What you gave of yourself anchored me to this world. I thought it was you, holding me here. Perhaps the child plays a role as well."

"Then tell me, Tam, how I may free you. I beg you." She was near to tears.

He came back to the bench and sat beside her. He brushed her hair from her face. She saw him hesitate. "If I tell you everything, you may think less of me."

"I could think a great deal less of you, and still love you more than life itself. Please."

He rubbed his hands over his face, as if trying to rid himself of something that clung to it. Then he began. "Every seven years, the fairies pay a tiend to hell, just as your father's folk pay a portion of their crops to him, and he pays a tiend to the king." Jenny noticed he had used the word *fairies* for the first time. "The tiend is to be paid in a week, on Halloween." He paused.

"Does this mean something to you?"

"Aye, Jenny. They pay not in crops or in gold as the earthly folk do, but in flesh. They must give someone to the father of evil. I fear it will be me."

"But why would they choose you?"

He sighed. "This is the part I would rather not tell. The queen of the fairies cast a powerful charm over me, Jenny, but that charm is broken now because of you. She knows

229

that and is sick with jealousy. She will not let me go, but she wishes herself rid of me."

Jenny drew back as she understood what he was saying. "You were her lover?" As he nodded, she felt something whole and pure inside her shatter. "Why, you are as bad as Earl William." She tried to draw away, but he held her hands tightly.

"No, Jenny! Think what it was like for me. I was fourteen! Barely more than a child! And she, she is as old as the forest. I was grateful to her for saving my life. But she used me. As long as I loved no other woman, she could keep me in her thrall. But she is nothing to me now. I am held to her world by the finest thread of a charm. She would give me to hell gladly rather than see that thread break."

"But I am not the only woman you have loved," Jenny said. Everything was clouded by her pain.

"You are, lass. Loving and the act of love are not the same. I never knew what it was to love a woman until I met you."

Jenny struggled to see beyond her feelings. If she was going to save him, she could not afford to feel slighted by his past. "Then tell me what I must do, Tam," she said at last.

She saw the relief in his eyes. "I was so afraid you would turn away from me." Then he paused. "But how can I ask you to risk your life?"

Jenny lost her patience. "Tam, I will sit here until you tell me. All night if I have to." She crossed her arms over her chest.

"You must be the most willful lass in Scotland. You know I cannot let you stay." She said nothing for a long moment. He sighed. "All right then, this is what must be done. At midnight, on Halloween, the fairy folk will ride to Miles Cross, the first crossroads between here and Rowanwald. Once the procession has started, they cannot stop for any reason. If you pull me from my horse and hold me, they must pass without me."

"That is all?"

He shook his head. "They will not be able to turn around, but they will use all the magic they possess to make you let me go. You will have to be very brave and very strong to resist their magic until they have passed."

"I do not know if I am brave, Tam. I know I am not strong, but I am willful enough to do this. How will I know you, though, in the darkness, among all the others?"

"A black horse will pass first, then a brown, then you will see Snowdrop. Run to him and pull me off. If I burst into flames, throw me down. Otherwise, hold fast." He paused. "Jenny, if you let go too soon, flee. Never stop for any reason. Take La Rose and ride until you reach your father's gate. I will never see you again, but you must know that I loved you, and only you."

Jenny was terrified she would forget his face. She tried to fix him in her mind's eye as he looked now, tall and fair in the autumn sunlight.

He kissed her forehead. "It is dangerous for you to stay, my love. Go now, while the sun is high in the sky."

As they came to La Rose, Jenny remembered the bags of food. "My nurse sent these, so you would not be tempted to rely on magic," she told him as they lifted them down together.

"Good. The magic grows the weaker with disuse. Now, go quickly."

As she went into the forest again, Jenny carried the feeling of being with Tam like a cloak around her. But the warmth and safety of that feeling suddenly vanished when she reached the river. On the opposite bank, a woman stood, silently watching. The woman's dress was white, but shot through with the colors of a rainbow. This was no earthly garment. Remembering Galiene's words, Jenny said nothing, but once she had locked eyes with the woman, she found it impossible to look away. She was the most beautiful woman Jenny had ever seen, with long, black hair and pale, white skin. But, even at this distance, Jenny could see something hard and cruel about her mouth and eyes.

As Jenny crossed the river, the woman smiled and reached out a hand in greeting. Jenny felt drawn, like iron to a lodestone. It took all the strength she possessed to reach into her sleeve for the piece of silver. She clutched it until it bit into her palm. Only then could she pull her eyes from this woman's face. When they reached the river-bank, she kicked her heels hard into La Rose's ribs and fled without looking back.

Chapter Twenty-one

J ENNY GUESSED BY THE SUN that it was barely noon as she approached her father's bailey. Alric waved from a pasture near the gate, and she rode over to him. "Give the mare to me now, my lady, and I will walk her to the stable. You may follow on foot so anyone who sees you will think you were out walking."

Jenny wondered if this was not overly cautious. "None of the servants would tell my father I was out riding, Alric."

"No, but we have those strangers, the musicians, among us. Galiene says they will know the gossip now, and if one saw you abroad, he might tell the lord to win a coin. Cospatric is keeping them busy in the hall, but Galiene says there is no such thing as too careful."

Jenny smiled in spite of everything. She could almost hear Galiene's voice. She dismounted and handed the reins to Alric, still shaky from that glimpse of the fairy queen. She followed as soon as she dared, relieved to be back where others might protect her.

Galiene would be waiting in the bower, Jenny knew, but she needed time to recover from her fright before she

233

could speak of it, so she let herself be drawn to the faint strains of the music spilling from the hall. Inside, the traveling musicians were sitting with Cospatric, who was patiently showing them some fingerings on his harp. The two who played harps were trying to copy him. The lesson was of no interest to Jenny, but she stayed, trying to think what she would tell Galiene. Without Galiene's help, she could not hope to get away on Halloween, but Jenny was not sure her nurse would let her take such a risk.

When the harp lesson was over, all the musicians played together. One had a set of bagpipes, but he was not as skilled as the piper she had heard in Roxburg. There were plenty of bad notes. Jenny wondered how these men managed to earn a living. When they finished, the leader, a man about Cospatric's age, gestured to his two harpers. "These lads could learn much from you. We travel to Galloway next, for the winter. Do you not long to hear your own tongue again, man? Come with us."

Jenny's heart lurched as Cospatric nodded. "Let me think on it. I was going to stay here until Christmas, but the traveling will be bad by then. Perhaps I should move on now."

The leader of the troupe slapped him on the back. "Good man. A harper of your skill would double our earnings. We will treat you well, Cospatric." They all agreed.

Jenny slipped from the hall. When she entered the bower, Isabel turned from her loom with a smile so sweet and unclouded that Jenny saw at once her sister knew nothing of Cospatric's possible departure. I have often been selfish this summer, Jenny thought, and Isabel has been so good. How can I let the harper go without trying to secure my sister's happiness? Perhaps I can accomplish this one good thing.

But now, her own troubles loomed. Galiene sat in the corner, carding wool as calmly as if Jenny had only been napping.

"I just remembered, the cheeses need turning today," Isabel said. "I should see if Hawise has set someone to the task." She put down her shuttle and left so that she would not have to lie to their father if he asked her what she knew.

"Your sister is a good lass," Galiene said. Jenny only nodded as a lump rose in her throat. Even if things went well, it seemed impossible that she and Isabel could stay near each other. Galiene noticed her distress. "Was he gone then, my honey?"

Jenny smiled. "No, Galiene. He lives, and the magic that binds him grows weaker. I know what I must do to free him." She sat on the floor like a small child with her head in Galiene's lap and told her old nurse everything. Near the end, when she told Galiene about the fairy queen, she felt the old woman's body tense with fear. Then, when Jenny finished, there was a long silence.

"I cannot stop you," Galiene said at last. "No one should. You are a woman now, and you have the right to try to win your love, even if your life is lost in the effort."

Jenny sat up and gazed into the old woman's eyes. "My life or my soul, Galiene, it matters not to me if I lose one or both if I cannot save him."

Galiene stroked Jenny's hair. "A love like this is rare,

Jenny, more precious than gold. It will be your only weapon. Some of us have a bit of magic to work spells, but I have known you since the day of your birth, and a more earthly lass never walked in this world. You have no magic to use against the fairy queen. That is just as well, for our magic would shrivel like grass in a fire before her. But you have your love to guide you"—she touched Jenny's belly briefly in blessing—"and the proof of your love for protection. I will get you safely out on Halloween. After that, everything depends on you."

Somewhere deep inside of Jenny was a little girl who had dared to hope that Galiene would forbid her to go out alone on Halloween, who would lock her up and keep her safe. Jenny said good-bye to that little girl forever as she rose. "I must do my penance now. I had no time this morning." Then she remembered something else. "Galiene, he has been so long among the other folk that he is hardly like us now. If I release him, will he return to himself again?"

"Maybe not right away, hen." Galiene looked away, then she seemed to force herself to meet Jenny's eyes. "And maybe never. You must learn to take him as he is."

Jenny only nodded. She could not speak for disappointment. Outside, she tried to comfort herself. He may never be like other men, but I loved him first because of that, she thought.

As she neared the chapel, she saw Cospatric walking with his head down as though lost in thought. On impulse, she seized the chance. "Cospatric," she said, "I would speak with you. Will you step into the chapel?" She saw him hesitate and realized he thought it dangerous to be seen alone with her now. She struggled to keep her temper. "For pity's sake, just give me a moment of your time." She hoped he might be moved if she begged, and he was.

Inside the chapel, her words rushed out. "I heard those musicians talking to you in the hall. It hardly matters whether you leave now or later, I suppose, but tell me, Cospatric, please, would you take my sister with you if you could?"

Even in the dim light, she saw him pale. "What manner of question is this, my lady? Do you mean to see me hanged?" Jenny could see he was badly shaken. Only in the ballads could a harper gain the love of a noblewoman. Even then such love was often fatal.

"I cannot bear to think of Isabel in that priory. It is loathsome to her. You could marry her and take her away. I think my father might agree."

He relaxed a little, and Jenny realized he had imagined she was suggesting something far worse. She cursed her clumsy tongue.

"Does your sister know you ask me?" He seemed to warm to the thought.

"No. Her modesty would never allow such a thing."

He looked shocked. "Then why would you ask?"

Jenny silently begged Isabel's forgiveness before she went on. "Because I know her heart. She loves you, Cospatric."

Now he looked torn. "But you ask the impossible. Even if we somehow won your father's approval, my life is hard. Your sister would go hungry. She would sleep on the ground and walk abroad in all weather. How can I ask her to share such a life? She is far too fine." He poured his heart into that last sentence.

"But you do love her. Why not let her decide whether she prefers the life you offer to that of the priory? Then I will ask my brother to intercede on your behalf. My father loves Isabel dearly, in spite of everything that has happened. I feel sure he will not refuse her as long as you agree to leave Teviotdale forever."

Cospatric put his hand to his forehead.

Jenny bit her lip. "Cospatric, you must not dither. This must be settled before Halloween. Go now, before anyone finds us here." She dismissed him quickly before he could ask why she felt the need to act with such urgency.

Jenny hoped Cospatric's love would overcome his natural caution. She watched Isabel for some sign that he had spoken. For two days, Isabel was unchanged. On the afternoon of the third day, Jenny lay down for her nap, afraid the harper would never find the courage to speak to her sister. When Jenny awoke, the afternoon sun was low in the sky. In the outer room of the bower, she found Galiene and Isabel working as usual, but Isabel blushed scarlet when she saw Jenny, and fumbled with her shuttle. Isabel never dropped her shuttle.

"Do you know where Eudo is?" Jenny asked Galiene.

"I believe your brother is over at the forge," she said, with a look that told Jenny she knew something was afoot and she was not entirely sure she approved.

Jenny found Eudo at the forge, talking to the smith about a new kind of saddle-girth fastening he had seen at

Lilliesleaf. Jenny paused to take pleasure in the sight of her brother. She would always feel Isabel was close as long as he was near, they were so alike. When he finished, she drew him aside, telling him everything about Cospatric and Isabel.

Eudo was astonished. "And my sister agreed to go with him?"

Until that very moment, the thought that Isabel might refuse had not occurred to Jenny. "I . . . I am not certain."

Eudo laughed. "Jenny, do you imagine every girl's heart is as easily won as your own? We must ask, for I cannot speak to Father without first knowing what Isabel wants."

In spite of the sting of her brother's joke, Jenny smiled, for he had agreed to help her.

Isabel had regained her composure when they found her in the bower. Eudo dismissed Galiene in a way that neither Jenny nor Isabel would have been able to. "Now sister, tell us," he said as soon as the old nurse had left. "Has Cospatric asked you to marry him?"

Isabel met his gaze directly. "He has."

"And will you take him, if our father allows?"

Isabel blushed deeply, but she smiled. "I will, Eudo. I would give my heart to him gladly. He has promised to take me to his land. We will live among folk who will not scorn me." Jenny noticed something new in her sister's manner, a strength beneath her gentleness that had not been there before.

That night, Eudo paid all the musicians to play for the folk in Langknowes, and asked their father to talk in the bower after supper. Jenny insisted that both she and Isabel be present.

Jenny had feared her father's temper, but when Eudo finished talking, he sat in a stunned silence for a long time. All his anger seemed spent. Jenny realized how greatly he had changed.

"What of the Church?" he said finally. "How can I disappoint the Church?"

Jenny had not expected this question so soon, but she had the answer. "Now that my betrothal with Earl William is broken, the Church will want a tocher, and we have only one. Papa, if I cannot find a father for my child, I will go in Isabel's place." Jenny had made this decision after speaking to Cospatric. She was fairly sure she would never see the priory, no matter what happened. She would either save Tam or die in the attempt.

"But I shall be disgraced in the eyes of men," her father said.

"No, Papa," Isabel said gently. "We will go in secret to Galloway. All will know me as the wife of a harper, who sings for her supper beside him. I will be Isabel Avenel no more."

"Isabel, can this be what you want?"

Isabel held her head up and looked directly into her father's eyes, even as the tears spilled down her cheeks. "It is, Papa. I love Cospatric."

Jenny thought her heart would break at the sorrow in her father's eyes. "Then I give you my blessing, child. But go soon, before I have a chance to change my mind." He looked like a very old man. Jenny had won, but she felt no joy.

Eudo sent the other musicians on their way early the next morning so that they could spread no gossip and, after mass, asked Brother Turgis to perform the wedding. As Jenny had expected, the priest sputtered and fumed like a wet candle. "This cannot be. She was promised to the Church."

Jenny was surprised to hear her father speak. "No vows were made. Lady Isabel is still mine to give, and I have made my decision. Let the sin be on my head. If Lady Jeanette does not go in her stead, I will accept whatever penalty the Church places on me."

Even Brother Turgis could see it was useless to argue. He pursed his lips. "I will hear the lady's confession first, then the harper's. The wedding will take place at noon."

Jenny ran to the bower to see what warm, plain clothing she might have to give her sister for this new life. She opened her trunk. Lying on the very top was her scarlet silk dress, shredded to tatters. As Jenny picked it up, it fell to pieces in her hands. It was utterly destroyed.

Chapter Twenty-two

❧

ISABEL AND COSPATRIC WENT the next morning, into a gray October dawn that promised rain. Only Jenny and Eudo saw them off. Their father would not. The harper did his best to look solemn, but his joy could not really be hidden.

Jenny wondered if she would ever see her sister again, and tears came to her eyes. Isabel hugged her. "No tears for me, Jenny. I have won a love I dared not hope for. I only wish the same for you." Too late, Jenny realized she had not had a chance to tell Isabel about her love. Everything had happened so quickly, and since the wedding, her sister had not left Cospatric's side.

On the road outside the bailey, just before they disappeared into the mist, Jenny saw Cospatric put his arm around Isabel and draw her close. She looked safe and protected.

"I hope they will be happy," Jenny said to Eudo.

"I think they will. Cospatric is a good man. He spoke with me yesterday after the wedding. They will go to his master's house where he apprenticed, in Girvan, for the winter. He can teach there. He plans to teach her to play as well." Eudo looked embarrassed. "I gave him money enough to buy a harp for her. That was my wedding present."

Jenny squeezed her brother's arm. "I will sleep easier when the winds blow, knowing Isabel has a roof over her head. Does our father know?"

"Not yet. I will tell him when he seems ready to hear."

"I could give Isabel nothing but warm clothing." Jenny sighed. "Will we ever see her again?"

"When I am lord of this land, Jenny, they will be welcome in my hall."

Later, as Jenny went about her work, she wondered if she would live to see that day. She had said nothing to anyone about the scarlet dress. Tomorrow was Halloween.

The storm that had threatened all day came late in the afternoon, bringing night down early with it. For the first time since the spring, the hall was empty of music. The entire bailey seemed bereft. Jenny woke in the night to the drumming of rain on the bower roof, and she prayed that Isabel and Cospatric had found shelter. She thought of Tam in roofless Carter Hall. This might be his last night on earth. She pictured him under an eave with his thin summer blanket over him, and she wondered if he was lying awake too, listening to the rain and thinking about the next night.

The storm continued all the next day. Cold, heavy sheets of rain slapped Jenny's face when she ventured outside the bower. Wind pried through cracks in the thatch, making leaks in roofs that were usually sound. In the afternoon, as it grew dark, Jenny found herself alone with

Galiene and gave way to despair. "Surely this is not an earthly storm. How can I ride to Miles Cross in such rain?"

"Hush now, child. The wind is falling. I think the storm has blown itself out. We will soon see. Remember, you must not sleep tonight. When you know your father is asleep, slip away. Eudo knows you are leaving. He will not stop you. Alric will have your horse ready. Ride straight to Miles Cross and tether La Rose out of sight, then wait by the side of the road. You must be brave now, if you would win your love. I have done everything I can to help you on your way."

Galiene was right about the storm. By the time they ate supper, a few stars showed through rents in the clouds. By bedtime, the sky was mostly clear, though the wind had come up again.

Jenny lay in bed, rigid with fear, trying not to think ahead. When she could hear her father snoring, she slipped from the covers, fully clothed. She had given her heavy cloak to Isabel, but Galiene's was waiting for Jenny by the bower door. She grabbed the cloak, leaving as quietly as she could.

In the stable, Alric stood by La Rose, who was already saddled. Jenny took the reins, then turned and kissed the boy on the cheek. "You have been faithful to me, Alric. I will never forget that."

"Must you ride tonight, my lady? The souls of the dead slip their graves and go abroad on Halloween." The boy chewed his lip.

Jenny heard her own fear in his voice. "I must," she said. She smiled to reassure Alric, and in doing so calmed herself. He helped her onto her horse.

Some of the wildness of the storm had stayed in La Rose, or perhaps she felt Jenny's fear, for she was skittish. The wind sounded in Jenny's ears as they galloped along, making it hard for her to think. She tried to keep her eyes on the road; it was still muddy, and La Rose felt uncertain under her. She told herself that the things flashing at the edges of her vision were just bits of leaf or grass, blown by the wind. Until they were in the forest. Then, as Jenny slowed La Rose to a safe trot, she realized that unearthly things were all around them. Ghosts floated among the trees in outlandish clothing. La Rose shied and wheeled, trying to escape, but Jenny quickly understood that these spirits were harmless and seemed unable to see her. She comforted her mare and urged her on past the pale, glowing shades of those long dead. Her fate was not with them.

A lifetime seemed to pass before Jenny reached Miles Cross. Off the road, she tied La Rose to a rowan and counted herself lucky, for rowan trees had a magic of their own. No matter what happened to her, at least La Rose would be safe. But the land was low here, with a water-filled ditch between herself and the road. Jenny jumped it and crossed to the other side, where the forest was more level. Then, she could only wait.

Miles Cross was nothing more than a crossroads in the woods, where the road to Rowanwald met the road that led to Berwick, far away on the North Sea. The ghosts that haunted the woods this night were absent here. Jenny wondered if this place could be so dangerous as to frighten the spirits of the dead. Even the wind was gone. Jenny lost her sense of the passing of time, her mind blank with fear.

When she finally heard the faint jingling of bridles, she thought at first she was dreaming. But no. A great crowd appeared, riding toward the crossroads at a stately pace. Jenny shrank back behind a tree. Was she too far from the road to reach Tam? She could not tell.

The fairy queen passed first, looking just as beautiful and cruel as she had that day by the river. She looked neither right nor left but straight ahead, as everyone did, as though they could see their destination. After her came the knights. Jenny saw the black horse, then the brown. Then her heart leaped into her throat as she recognized Snowdrop. She shot out from behind the tree like an arrow from its bow and leaped higher than she knew she could. She grabbed Tam by his waist and let herself go limp, using her weight to pull him down. She felt him throw himself with her as they fell into a heap together, and Snowdrop went on without him. She buried her face in his shoulder and held him tightly.

But suddenly his shoulder was gone. Tam was gone. She felt something wet in her hand. She looked down. It was an esk, a black newt as long as her hand with a crest running the length of its body. It was cold and loathsome, but she forced herself not to scream and shake it from her hand. She looked away to calm herself, but as soon as she did, she felt it change into something heavier, a dry and leathery rope that writhed as she grasped it. She looked to find a black snake with yellow markings; a head shaped like a flat arrowhead; and cruel, copper-colored eyes—a poisonous adder. This time she did scream, but she held it tightly, closing her eyes and waiting for the snake to strike. Instead, she felt it change and grow into something so large she had to stand with her arms around it. She dared to hope it might be Tam until she breathed the rank odor of its fur. Jenny looked up into the face of a bear. He opened his mouth of huge yellow teeth. Jenny closed her eyes again, waiting to be torn to pieces. As soon as she did, she felt the creature change. Jenny suddenly understood that the transformations happened only when she closed her eyes or looked away. Now she was kneeling with her arms around a large animal with rough yellow fur. It growled. She was holding some kind of huge cat. Jenny burst into tears but forced herself to close her eyes. Suddenly, she was holding a red-hot rod of iron.

As her flesh burned, she tried to remember what Tam had told her. If he burst into flames, she should throw him down. But he was glowing, not flaming. Would she lose him now if she let go? She closed her eyes against the pain and suddenly found a flaming coal in the palm of her hand. The procession was past now. Her flesh was seared. She ran to the water-filled ditch by the side of the road, but hesitated. Could she let him go? She almost closed her eyes again but stopped herself and threw the coal instead. It described a long, orange arch of flame in the night, then vanished into the black water with a hiss.

For a long moment, nothing happened. Jenny stood there, clutching her burnt hand at the wrist, thinking she had failed. Then she heard a gasp, and he was there, standing naked up to his ankles in the water but somehow drenched to the bone. She ran and threw the cloak around him, then stood in the water hugging him, caring only that he was safe. She could stay in his arms forever.

He held her tightly. The pain in her hand vanished. She could not tell if he was shivering, laughing, or crying. Perhaps all three. But he became still as an oak at the sound of a woman's voice.

"Ill-faced girl, you have taken the best of my knights and gotten yourself a stately groom. If I had known, Tam Lin, you would betray me, I would have taken out your eyes and put in two of wood."

And then they were truly alone.

"She cannot harm us now, my love." Tam spoke for the first time, stroking her hair. "The thread that held me has snapped. She can never touch us again." A shudder ran through his body.

"We must find shelter," Jenny said. She looked around. Snowdrop was gone with the rest of the procession. La Rose was too small to carry them both, but Tam was too weak to walk, and barefoot besides. Against his protests, she bundled him into the saddle and led La Rose away. She never wanted to see this place again.

"I have clothes at Carter Hall," he said, already chattering with the cold. Galiene's cloak left his legs exposed to the cold night air.

Jenny cursed herself for throwing him into the water. Had she come through all this only to lose him to something as earthly as the weather? Carter Hall was miles away, and her father's home beyond. There was no shelter between. She tried to keep close to him, to give him a little of her warmth, but La Rose could not be led that way. Jenny was beginning to realize just how hopeless the situation was, thinking things could not be worse, when she saw men on the road ahead.

"Oh no," she said. She could only think they were about to be beset by robbers.

"My lord, is that you?" a voice cried.

"John?" Tam said, "John! For the love of God, man, give us aid." He sounded giddy with relief. Jenny realized that these men were his freebooters. The nightmare was over. When the man John came forward, Jenny fainted into his arms.

Chapter Twenty-three

❦

THE MAY AIR FELT ALMOST as soft on Jenny's cheek as the blond down on her son's head, but she bundled him into a warm blanket, just in case the wind still held a touch of winter. Since Halloween, she could not bear the thought that anyone about her might be cold. She had spent the winter weaving thick, fine blankets, finally proving to be a skilled weaver.

She found that Tam's rescue had transformed her in everyone's eyes from a woman disgraced to a heroine, but Jenny thought little of that. The very men who praised her had reviled Isabel. But if her sister had destroyed one knight and she had saved another, Jenny knew they had both faced their fears with courage and honor, and Isabel was her equal in every regard. She only hoped for a chance to tell Isabel as much, and show her little Andrew one day.

The baby cooed when he focused on her face. His eyes were still changing, trying to settle on a color somewhere between her light blue and his father's golden brown. "Andrew Avenel," she crooned, kissing his fingers. "This very day, you become Andrew Lin. But where is your father? He should be here by now. Galiene, we will wait for Tam by the gate."

Galiene clucked. "Bad luck follows if the groom sees his bride before the wedding."

"I am hardly a blushing bride."

"Well, whose fault is that? Your lord father would have seen you married before Christmastide."

"Tam wished to wait until Carter Hall was fit to live in. Now that the roof is thatched, Andrew will be snug there." But Jenny knew that was not the only reason. She thought back to the long hours Tam had argued over the winter, with her father and Brother Turgis, then with Brother Bertrand and the earl of Roxburg himself. Everyone had demanded they marry, then urged, and finally begged. Jenny would have surrendered months ago, but Tam would not be swayed. Jenny was pleased to find such iron at his core. He had waited until he could provide a life for her and their son at Carter Hall. But, more than that, she knew he had wanted to be sure he was fully an earthly knight again. Now, he felt certain he had recovered from all the years of enchantment, and he was ready to bring Jenny home.

At least her father had enjoyed the chance to become friends with the earl of Roxburg over the winter as the two men plotted to see Tam and Jenny wed. They both agreed the couple could never live at Roxburg, in the shadow of the king's court, and the old earl had been generous in providing for the restoration of Carter Hall. He was waiting in the great hall now with her father and Eudo. This wedding would be quiet, without public celebration, as befit a couple who already had a child. But Jenny knew a fine stallion was waiting for Tam in her father's stable, a wedding gift from the earl to replace Snowdrop, who had never appeared again.

She looked across the river. Already, great swaths of bare ground could be seen as lay brothers from Broomfield Abbey swarmed over the land. Jenny was grateful that the Broomfield entitlement ended well before Carter Hall. She could not bear to think those great trees by the river might ever come to harm. But here, the forest of the fairies was falling for pasture. It was the same all over Teviotdale. The Church would surely drive the fairies from the land and tame it forever. Jenny knew this should give her comfort, but she could not welcome the change.

As Jenny strained her eyes against the sun, she saw Tam coming along the road that led out of the forest. He was far away, but she knew his gait as well as she knew the sound of his voice, the touch of his fingers, or the curve of his neck. Every aspect of his being was steeped in her soul.

With him came his men, including the freebooters who had saved them in the woods on Halloween. They were part of his household now, having formally bound themselves to Tam soon after her father gave him Carter Hall. The oldest man, John, once had been a stable boy— the same stable boy who had survived with Tam when everyone else in the Lin household died. All winter, Tam's men had worked with servants sent by the earl of Roxburg to fix Carter Hall. Now, they were busy clearing land for crops. It might be a meager living at first, but Jenny felt sure they could survive the lean years, even without the tocher that had once been Isabel's and was now forfeit to the Church.

She knew Tam saw her now, for he quickened his pace. She hitched little Andrew up on her shoulder and started down the road to meet him.

Glossary

Bondsman—An unpaid servant in a noble household. Bondsmen swore an oath, promising to give all the profit of their labor to a lord. In return the lord gave them food, shelter, and clothing. Bondsmen belonged to the household and could move from one place to another if their lord did.

Fermtouns—Literally farm towns, but in medieval Scotland these were outlying farming settlements belonging to a lord but removed from the main holdings. They were not towns in the modern sense but small farming outposts. A fermtoun consisted of four to eight families of tenants who shared a single team of plow horses or oxen and worked the land together.

Hen—A term of endearment, mainly used with children and young women.

Hospital—The place in an abbey where travelers were given shelter and hospitality. The place where the sick were cared for was called the infirmary.

Ill-faced—Ugly. An insult.

Knowe—In Scots, a hill. Langknowes means Long Hills.

Neyfs—Agricultural workers who literally belonged to the land they lived on, in the same way trees and buildings do. Like bondsmen, neyfs exchanged their labor for food, clothing, and shelter, but if the land changed hands, the neyfs would stay with it.

Rigg—A plowed field.

Tiend—A regular payment of crops or money made by those who owed allegiance to someone more powerful. This is a Scots word. In English, the word is *tribute*. Tenants who worked the land would pay a regular tiend to the lord who had been granted that land by the king. (Legally, all land belonged to the king.) The lords, in turn, would pay their tiend to an overlord who paid the king, or pay directly to the king himself.

Tocher—The goods, land, and money a girl took into marriage with her, provided by her family. A dowry.

Historical Note

The plot of this book was taken from two ballads, "Lady Isabel and the Elf Knight" and "Tam Lin." Ballads are songs that tell a story. "Lady Isabel and the Elf Knight" was sung in different forms in almost every European language. In this book, Isabel's story begins where the ballad ends. "Tam Lin" originated in Scotland and was only sung there, but by 1549 it was already said to be old. I have tried to be as faithful to the plot of "Tam Lin" as possible in *An Earthly Knight*.

Teviotdale, where most of the book takes place, lay in that part of southeastern Scotland now called the Borders. In the twelfth century, King David I invited many Anglo-Norman noblemen from England to settle that area, mostly landless younger sons. These were the French-speaking descendants of the Normans who had conquered England about one hundred years before. King David also encouraged religious orders from continental Europe to establish houses in this and other parts of Scotland. To raise the sheep that provided their prosperity, the abbeys in Teviotdale cleared away great tracts of the forests that had covered the land for centuries. These forests never returned.

The abbeys in this book are fictional places, but

Rowanwald is very much like the Augustinian abbey established in Jedburgh in 1154. Broomfield resembles the abbeys at Melrose and Dryburgh to some degree, though neither had a healing shrine like St. Coninia's well. Coninia was in fact a real person, an early Christian woman whose burial place was discovered in 1890 near Peebles in the Borders. I bestowed sainthood upon her myself. Many of the local saints of the earlier Irish Church did not survive the transition to Roman Catholicism.

The site of the old town of Roxburgh is just outside present-day Kelso, where the Teviot and the Tweed meet. The ruins of Marchmont castle lie just upstream, neglected and all but forgotten. Roxburgh was destroyed so many times during battles with the English that the town was finally abandoned. The stone castle that replaced the twelfth-century wooden hall persisted until 1550.

King Malcolm IV, called the Maiden for his vow of celibacy, ascended the throne of Scotland as a lad of twelve, when his grandfather, King David, died. Earl Henry, Malcolm's father, had died not a year before. Earl William, who was known by his mother's name, de Warenne, was one year younger than his brother Malcolm. When Malcolm died in 1165 at the age of twenty-four, his brother succeeded him to become William the Lion. William was twenty-three when he was crowned. Before he finally married at the age of forty, he fathered at least six children out of wedlock. He ruled Scotland for forty-nine years.

The fictional events in *An Earthly Knight* are set in the year 1162.

ACKNOWLEDGMENTS

The Newfoundland and Labrador Arts Council provided a travel grant for which I am sincerely grateful. The money enabled me to visit the Borders area of Scotland in the summer of 2001 and poke around in the twelfth-century abbey ruins that dot the land. Hugh Chalmers, Carrifran Wildwood Project Officer with the Borders Forest Trust, helped me to imagine what that landscape might have looked like when old-growth forests of ash and oak still covered most of the land. Julie Ross and her staff at the Edinburgh Bird of Prey Centre generously allowed me to spend time in that remarkable aviary, where I learned that raptors are, in fact, very docile birds. Dr. David Caldwell, Depute Keeper of History and Applied Art at the National Museum of Scotland, patiently answered many questions about everyday life in medieval Scotland and directed my reading.

Of all my novels, this one has had the longest gestation by far. My interest in the ballads dates back more than twenty-five years. I discovered these wonderful old song texts while studying with Edith Fowke, my first teacher in folklore. During that time, I also performed French folk songs with Andrea Haddad, who taught me many of the French ballads referred to in this text. Much later, in graduate school, I learned a great deal about the fairies from my dear friend and fellow student, Barbara Rieti. Her book, *Strange Terrain: The Fairy World in Newfoundland*, details the amazing research she did for her doctoral thesis with living bearers of these very old beliefs in our home province. This long, winding path of serendipitous discovery allowed me to gather the fragments that finally became *An Earthly Knight*.

I must also thank my husband and daughter for cheerfully allowing me to spend most of my life with my imaginary friends. Without their support, I would not be a writer.

Janet McNaughton has a Ph.D. in folklore. She wrote *Catch Me Once, Catch Me Twice* and *To Dance at the Palais Royale*, which won the Geoffrey Bilson Award for Historical Fiction, the Ann Connor Brimer Award, and the Violet Downey Book Award, IODE National Chapter. Her third book, *Make or Break Spring*, won the Ann Connor Brimer Award, the Newfoundland and Labrador Book Award, and was shortlisted for the Ruth Schwartz Award and the Governor General's Award, among others. Her most recent book, *The Secret Under My Skin*, won the Ruth Schwartz Award, the Mr. Christie's Book Award, the Ann Connor Brimer Award, and the Newfoundland and Labrador Book Award—the Bruneau Family Children's Literature Award. Janet lives in St. John's, Newfoundland, Canada, with her family.